MEG

*Charlotte Hardy titles available from
Severn House Large Print*

Sarah

MEG

Charlotte Hardy

Severn House Large Print
London & New York

This first large print edition published 2008
in Great Britain and the USA by
SEVERN HOUSE PUBLISHERS of
9-15 High Street, Sutton, Surrey, SM1 1DF.
First world regular print edition published 2007 by
Severn House Publishers, London and New York.

British Library Cataloguing in Publication Data

Hardy, Charlotte
  Meg. - Large print ed.
  1. Women art students - England - Fiction 2. World War,
  1939-1945 - France - Fiction 3. English - France - Provence
  - Fiction 4. Love stories 5. Large type books
  I. Title
  823.9'14[F]

  ISBN-13: 978-0-7278-7697-3

Printed and bound in Great Britain by
MPG Books Ltd, Bodmin, Cornwall.

'We talked about the usual things –
art, sex, death...'

One

North London, 1965

Alice had still not come to terms with it – not with the actual fact of it. It was as if it were happening to someone else, as if it was not *her* mother who had died. It made no sense. For one thing, her mother had been too young. She was healthy, she had no vices. Watching her mother during the last months, watching her fight the disease, watching the efforts of the doctors, she had asked herself why *her*? Why, why, why, why? She remembered the horrible afternoon when during a visit to the hospital the surgeon had bluntly informed her that it was too late to operate. How could he say that, quite like that, so coldly? *I am sorry we can't operate, it's too far advanced. I am afraid your mother is going to die.* And how could she then go and sit by the bedside and hold a pleasant conversation with her mother – who looked perfectly normal, sounded perfectly normal – discussing household arrangements, her father's meals, his laundry and so on, while this thing, this *thing*, was eating her alive? It made no sense.

Alice was still numb. No doubt she would feel it later, they told her. They seemed to know so much about it. But of course in a hospital that's part of their job – laying out bodies, comforting grieving relatives. And that's what Alice was, after all, a 'grieving relative'. Not someone who had grown up with her, who had known her voice, her laugh, her moments of concentration, of distraction, of irritation or confusion, her unhappiness, all her life. Now, this morning, as a woman of twenty-five, she was 'immediate family', walking to the undertakers, dressed demurely in black, to pay her last respects. Her father wouldn't come. 'You're sure you won't come, Dad?' she had said, but he was still in that strange mood, still being difficult. He just sat there in his chair – and that was not like him at all either, at ten in the morning, sitting in the armchair. He only shook his head. She had knelt by him, touched his arm. 'You're sure?' But he wouldn't look at her, said nothing. So at last, unwillingly, she had come alone.

Just as she had expected they were ready for her, obsequious, bowing, speaking in hushed, unctuous tones. 'Just show me please,' she said quietly, 'and leave me alone.'

And then, under some sort of indirect light – a subdued half light, a gloom – there in the middle of this empty room was the coffin, open, and there as she approached, looking strange, unreal, and yet exactly like her real self, lay her mother. It was her mother, and yet it wasn't her at all. It was most strange. Although she had been destroyed by this thing inside her, it left no mark on her face. Her mother lay in the coffin exactly as Alice had known her. And yet, of course, not as she had known her. As she bent to kiss the forehead, it was, as she knew it would be, cold. Cold as a stone. It *was* a stone really, an object now, a thing, not the real woman her mother had been. Alice continued to stare at her, trying to absorb into herself this truth and unable to do it. There was a gap of understanding, unfathomable, unknowable, between what lay before her and the mother she had known, and there was no way of crossing that gap.

There was a chair to one side of the room and Alice sat. She didn't know exactly what she wanted, felt oddly neutral, but she needed to wait, to absorb the strangeness of it. As she sat, however, she realized she was trembling. For all her preparation, it affected her more than she had anticipated.

She sat and waited. There, two feet away, was the cold calm face, relaxed, at peace, and Alice knew this was the most she could extract from the interview. It was a cliché, she knew, but her mother was at peace.

Then, as she was about to leave, she noticed something. In her mother's hand, lying on her breast, there was a small photograph, barely two inches square, face down. For a moment Alice stared at it and almost, tentatively, reached her hand towards it, but then drew it back. No. Leave it. It's hers – Mum's – whatever it is.

Out in the street again she still felt trembly and had to go into a café, to sit and drink a cup of coffee very slowly. Her mind was empty at first, still filled with the strangeness of that room, her mother glowing white amid the gloom. It was almost as an afterthought that she remembered the photograph. Of course it might mean nothing, and yet somehow she knew it was not nothing. It was a last request and therefore very precious to her mother. Very precious. In fact it was the most precious thing, summing up her life, rounding it off.

Her father had said nothing about it but that was not necessarily odd. It must have been some promise between them, Alice thought at first, some sacred agreement, something private to them alone. She as a daughter would not necessarily have been informed.

Yet later, as she made her way home, a nagging thought gradually grew in her mind. There *was* something odd about that photograph. The truth was, as Alice had long been forced to admit, her parents' marriage had not, in their last years at least, been altogether happy. She herself had scarcely lived at home for seven years now – since going to university – and frankly had been glad to get out. She had only moved back into the house temporarily to be with her father in the weeks since her mother had been taken into hospital.

It had not been easy. She and her father had not been close. He was a tall, spare man with a slight stoop – Alice had inherited some of his height – and although not yet fifty, there was something about him that made him seem older. A jaundiced sarcasm in his manner, a critical judgement that was intended – when she tackled him about it – to cut through hypocrisy and what he called 'false judgement' but was to her mind rather a failure of charity. 'They're only doing their best, Dad,' she would argue, to try to jolly him into a more comfortable view of the world. More than once she had felt the force of this harsh side of his nature when favourite projects of her childhood years had been subjected to his critical attention. He was not an easy man to love, it had to be admitted.

His parents fortunately lived not far away and her grandfather made up in humanity what his son lacked. He was quite the opposite of his son, a worldly man, at home with people, a 'hands on' man, adept at all sorts of useful skills. Mending bicycle punctures, for example – or indeed taking the thing entirely to pieces and greasing all the parts that needed greasing – and was happy to teach her how to do it too. Alice's grandmother Nelly, his wife, was a homebody whose kitchen always invited with smells both sweet and savoury. There would be something tasty for tea whenever Alice chose to call – and there was no need to make arrangements. She was free to drop in whenever the fancy took her.

This was in contrast to her mother's parents, who were terrible sticklers for rules and etiquette. There was no question of cycling over to see them on impulse. Such things were arranged weeks in advance, and formal visits were attended with the full ritual of place settings, doilies, serviettes, the best teapot, and a cake from Fullers. No homely smells emanated from that kitchen.

* * *

11

When Alice arrived home she found her father as she had left him. As it was nearly one o'clock she glanced into the living room and asked him gently if he was ready for a bite of lunch. She waited as he sat, staring across the room, the newspaper unread on his lap as if he had not heard her. In the end she crossed, pulled a chair near to his, and tentatively touched his hand.

'You have to eat something,' she whispered.

Still he said nothing.

'Dad...'

'Oh for goodness' sake, leave me alone!' He stood up abruptly and stamped out of the room. She followed him quickly as he pulled a raincoat from a hook and was making for the front door.

'Dad! Come back! You must have some lunch – and we've still got to talk about the arrangements—'

He swung on her. 'What arrangements?'

'Well, the funeral's tomorrow, and people will want to come back, you know, for sandwiches and wine, that sort of thing...'

'I'm having no one back here.'

'What? But surely—'

'Don't you understand? Your mother has died. Do you think I want a lot of strangers crowding in here for a free drink? So they can sit around stuffing themselves with sandwiches and port while they chew over her life – discuss our private affairs?'

'Strangers? *Dad!* Who said anything about strangers? There's the family! It would be grossly discourteous not to have them back. Granny Nelly and Granddad for a start. You know how they felt about Mum. We *must* invite them back!'

He stopped at the threshold, the door knob in his hand, and suddenly appeared defeated. She took the raincoat from his hand and tossed it on to a chair, led him into the kitchen and made him sit down.

'There's no question of strangers,' she repeated quietly. 'Just the family. And leave it to me. I'll ring Granny and we'll do it together. It'll just be something simple. Now sit there and I'll make us some lunch. Then this afternoon why don't you lie down and rest? It might be best – you know, before tomorrow.'

'So long as there are no strangers,' he muttered.

Even so, there were quite a number of strangers at the funeral, people Alice had never seen before as she stood at the door, greeting mourners as they arrived. She had placed a notice in the local newspaper with details of the funeral, but was still taken by surprise; the strangers present outnumbered the people she knew. It later occurred to her that Granny Pat, her mother's mother, had taken the thing in hand and written to old acquaintances. Heaven knew what sort of affair it would have been if it had been left to her father. He was sitting at the front staring at the coffin. Whether he had slept the previous night Alice had no idea. He looked tired and drawn when she met him in the morning and she practically had to stand over him and help him to dress. Now he sat round-shouldered in the front pew while behind him at the door Alice greeted all these strangers he had been dreading. She was careful to mention the reception afterwards only to those who she could be sure would not upset him.

Her younger brother Nick had arrived late the previous evening, but was here now standing at the other side of the door.

Then one woman appeared before Alice, a sort of larger-than-life woman, perhaps of her mother's age, a bit blowsy, heavily made-up, and dressed in a rather stylish black ensemble. Alice didn't take in all the details instantly, but saw that the effect was striking and memorable, and would cause a few heads to turn anywhere, but especially in a small English church on a grey morning at a funeral. The woman stopped right in the doorway and stared for a long second at Alice before coming forward. 'You must be Alice?' she said in the sort of voice made husky by long years of cigarette smoking.

'That is correct.' Alice was a little taken aback as the woman held her for another long second at arms' length, looking her over with an intense scrutiny.

'Yes,' she breathed. 'I see her in you.'

She glanced behind her where other mourners were arriving. 'We'll have a little chat afterwards.' She smiled, laid a hand on Alice's arm, and found herself a pew near the back.

Alice was fully occupied greeting the other mourners as they continued to fill the little church. Then when things were ready she rejoined her father and reached to squeeze his hand as

14

they both sat staring at the coffin a few feet away. Her father withdrew his hand after a moment.

Staring at the coffin she noticed it was standing on two wooden trestles, worn-looking and old. Immediately she wondered how many other coffins had stood on those trestles. And why did she think that irrelevant, useless thought? Because she was afraid to look at the coffin itself? Afraid to contemplate the reality of what they were gathered here to do this morning – to place her mother under six feet of earth, to put her in the bottom of a pit and then shovel in soil on top of her? That was what they were going to do – and in a very short time. In an ancient ceremony, hallowed by long tradition, they were going to bury her mother. Stick her in the ground. And inside herself, despite all the schooling she had put herself through, despite every ounce of self-control she possessed, a protest rushed up through her like a tidal wave. *No! No!* she wanted to scream. *No!* She wanted to rush forward and throw herself on her mother's body. *No, they shan't put you in the cold earth!* And despite everything, as this image came to her the tears gushed to her eyes and she clasped her hands before her face and wept helplessly.

Nick placed his hand on her shoulder and murmured something. Her father was rigid beside her, his eyes fixed on the coffin.

'Thanks,' she hiccuped at last and glanced up at Nick. 'I don't know – it just came over me...'

By the time the ceremony was over Alice had

15

managed to digest her feelings, felt she had regained control, and was in a reasonable frame of mind to greet the other mourners afterwards and chat to one here, and one there as they told her anecdotes from the past. Her father was near her, and her attention constantly strayed to him as he stood, his hands behind his back, staring rigidly before him as he was greeted, barely condescending to reply to their warm expressions of friendship and sympathy. Her grandfather was her favourite and he was soon beside her, putting his arms about her shoulders, giving her a little squeeze.

Then the strange foreign woman reappeared, and took Alice's arm in a familiar way, leading her to one side.

'You don't know me, my dear. No matter. You will.'

This was a strange greeting, and became even stranger a moment later.

'I was your mother's oldest friend. Her very oldest.' And she looked deep into Alice's eyes. Alice almost had to step a pace back at this extraordinary remark.

'I'm sorry...'

'You don't know who I am.' The woman shook her head sadly as she continued to stare at Alice. Then she seemed distracted, looking her over again. 'Extraordinary, the resemblance.'

Alice was completely bewildered. 'May I ask who—'

'Oh of course.' The woman smiled. 'I was Heather Grey when your mum and I were friends. Since then I've become Madame

16

Lagrange, a strange mutation, and on the whole a happy one, I'm glad to say. Paris suits me better than London. Alice...' She became serious. 'I came of course to see your mother off. I was terribly sad to hear of her death. Terribly. But there is something else...'

At this moment Alice was conscious of her father behind her.

'You were not invited,' he said coldly. Alice spun round.

'You were not invited,' he repeated forcibly, 'and you are not welcome.'

'Edward—'

'I am not Edward to you. I must ask you to leave. This minute.'

'Dad...' Alice touched his arm. He shook her off. He was rigid with rage, his face contorted. 'I knew this would happen! I made it clear – specifically made it clear – that you or any of you were not to be invited! Specifically you!'

Alice turned in alarm to Madame Lagrange but she did not appear to be unduly alarmed at this explosion.

'Have no fear, Edward,' she said lightly, 'I won't cause any embarrassment.' She held up her hands in mock surrender. 'I'm going!'

But then as Edward stood stiff, almost trembling with rage, she touched Alice on the sleeve, smiled at her and murmured, 'Not a good time to talk – I'll write. Goodbye. I'm so glad to have seen you at last.'

17

Two

After the guests had gone, Alice and Nick went for a walk. He now lived in Bristol so they saw less of each other than they had before. He too had been glad to escape the unhappy atmosphere at home.

'Did you see what happened at the church?' she asked as they strolled down the suburban street that evening, hands in pockets. 'That strange woman who came up to me?' He hadn't. 'I suppose it's natural to meet strangers at a funeral,' she went on thoughtfully. 'People from Mum's life, people she had lost contact with. Inevitable, when you think about it.'

'Who was she?'

'She said she was Mum's oldest friend. Yet, if that were the case, I can't work out why Mum had never spoken about her. I mean, if she had known her at art school, she would have mentioned her – or written. I've never seen her receive any letters from Paris, have you?'

'Who, Mum?'

'Yes. This woman lives there – married a Frenchman presumably.'

'What did she say?'

'Almost nothing. Dad came steaming up and shouted at her, more or less threw her out. It was very embarrassing. I mean, I know Dad's been acting strangely, but that's understandable seeing what's happened. Even so, he took me by surprise.' She paused, thoughtfully. 'She said she was going to write.' Another pause. 'There's something else. I went to see Mum's body yesterday at the undertaker's.'

'Rather you than me.'

'Nick! It was all right, nothing frightening or anything. You know, sort of peaceful. But there was one strange thing. There was a photograph in her hand.'

'A photograph?'

'Trouble is it was face down so I couldn't see what it was of. I didn't like to touch it,' she added.

'So you think...'

'I don't know what to think. Dad must have placed it there – or at least given the order because he didn't go to the undertaker.'

'Didn't he?'

She shook her head.

'Mm.' Nick was silent for a moment too, and then went on, 'Odd, isn't it, to think of Mum now, back there in the church yard? We're moving on but we've sort of left her behind. She's back there in the ground, and she's still holding that photograph. Now, at this minute. I wish you'd had a look at it,' he added.

'It wouldn't have been right. If she had wanted me to know what it was, she would have told me.'

'Anyway,' Nick drew a breath, 'probably just an old snap of them together, honeymoon maybe, or a wedding photo.'

She changed the subject. 'When are you going back to Bristol?'

'Tonight. I only got the one day off. What about you?'

'Well,' she drew a breath, 'I'll have to stay a bit longer. Dad's in no fit shape. I'll talk to Granny Nelly. She might come and stay for a bit. God knows whether my job'll be there when I get back. And my flowers will all have died.'

When they got back to the house, they found their father had opened a bottle of wine. It stood half empty on the table and he sat with a newspaper and a glass of wine in his hand. Nick made a brief awkward farewell and disappeared. Alice was left facing her father.

They surveyed one another for a moment, then her father said, apropos of nothing, 'One useful thing my father taught me was to appreciate wine. Fine wine,' he repeated, holding up his glass. She detected the alcohol in his speech. 'Yes. It's a skill that never goes out of date. Unlike printing,' he added.

'What do you mean?' she asked uncertainly, sitting opposite him.

'I've been having a word with the old man,' he went on, suddenly eloquent. 'Changes will have to be made. The stone is dead. Dead as a stone,' he repeated with a slight drunken slur. Alice knew that 'the Stone' was a term used in the printing trade. Her father owned the printing business he had inherited from his father and from which the old man had largely retired.

Even so, on this day, there was something un-kind in that cold-blooded phrase. Alice waited. 'Yes,' he repeated, 'I have been thinking and I have decided to make a trip to America. There's a lot to learn, and I don't intend to be left behind. Left behind in the Middle Ages,' he added.

'I think that's a good idea,' she began tenta-tively. 'To keep busy, I mean.'

'Yes.' He took another long draught of wine and refilled the glass. 'Now this is a Montrachet '47. A particularly good year for Burgundies – as my father could tell you better than I.' He held up the bottle, studied the label drunkenly, then showed it to her. 'This, incidentally, is by way of being a family heirloom, handed down from father to son. And what better occasion to open a bottle, eh?' He glanced lightly at Alice with a raised eyebrow.

There was nothing she could say. If her dad wanted to get drunk on the day of his wife's funeral, maybe that was the best way. Best for him, at least.

'I shall make a trip to America to study the latest technology,' he went on. 'This is the Age of Technology, the "white heat of technol-ogy" and we must keep up with the Americans. Don't want to be left behind. And now that I'm free—'

'Free?' she asked quickly.

He sat back and looked straight at her. 'Yes, free. Free at last.' He raised his glass. 'Here's to freedom.'

'Dad...' She swallowed and forced herself on. 'Mum's died,' she croaked in a half whisper.

'And you talk of being free?' She got up quickly and ran out into the kitchen, tears smarting in her eyes, and for a moment could see nothing, hear nothing. It was beyond her, incomprehensible.

The following morning while her father was still asleep, the empty wine bottle beside his bed, she went to her grandmother and talked over the situation. She herself had to get back to work. In the meantime, during the few days since her mother had died, Alice had gone through her things and tidied up what she could. Her father had been of no use, of course, but she had expected that.

'He's not fit to be left alone, Nelly.'

Nelly was thoughtful. 'It might be best to bring him here. I can keep a closer eye on him, and make sure he eats.'

Alice soon returned to her own flat and work. It was only some weeks later that she received a phone call from her other grandmother, Pat, to say that a letter had arrived directed to her.

'It's from Paris.'

'That must be the lady I met at the funeral. Er ... Madame Lagrange.'

'Heather, yes.'

'Gran, was it you who invited her?'

'That's right, dear. I found her details in an old address book.'

'How did you know her?'

'Oh goodness,' the older woman laughed, 'I knew her before the war.'

'When Mum was at art school?'

22

'Yes. In those days Heather was a harum-scarum, red-headed, untidy girl full of fun. Still is, as far as I could make out.'

'Did you speak to her at the funeral?'

'Yes.'

'Dad wasn't very polite,' Alice said hesitantly.

'No ... well...' Pat dried up. 'Of course he was under great strain. It hit him very hard.'

'Yes.'

'Anyway, I'll forward the letter.'

My dear Alice,

I have left it a few weeks before writing as I imagined you would be very busy, have a lot to think of, arrangements and re-arrangements to make, and so forth. I hope by now at least you will have had a chance to draw breath and get back to your own affairs. As for the *contretemps* at the funeral, I confess I rather expected that reaction from your father, so don't blame him too harshly if he seemed less than courteous. It was a very trying time for him. I certainly don't bear him a grudge about it, I assure you.

However, it did prevent us from having a little talk, and there are things I want to tell you, better said face to face. And also something I have to give you. Sounds mysterious, doesn't it? It's also partly for a selfish reason – I want to get to know you better.

So, my dear, what I want you to do is to come over to visit. You will find I live in reasonable quarters in a very nice part of Paris – near Les Invalides, with a view of the Eiffel Tower! – and I can promise you a comfortable stay. So don't say no, but get some time off work, and let me know as soon as possible that you'll come.

With fondest regards,

Heather Lagrange

Madame Lagrange met her at the Gare du Nord a few weeks later. It was a chilly April day, and Alice was in an overcoat and scarf. She recognized her mother's 'oldest friend' immediately. She stood out in the crowd – indeed she would stand out in any crowd – as Alice came up the long platform carrying a small overnight case. Alice had visited Paris a couple of times before and knew her way about in a basic sort of way. Heather Lagrange was waiting at the barrier in a splendid overcoat, very long in an extraordinary thick wool weave, almost a hand-woven fabric it seemed, in a kaleidoscope of unexpected colours – pink, mauve, eau-de-nil – and a large hat in dark indigo with a feather. A brilliant silk scarf was thrown loosely about her shoulders. She was altogether larger than life and took Alice over immediately, directing her towards the taxi rank.

'We don't own a car, my dear. No point in Paris. As you will see, we live in a very, *very*, convenient spot. You can walk practically anywhere.'

Then as the taxi set out into the busy streets of Paris and Alice inevitably was distracted by the

24

sights and sounds about her, Heather asked, 'Did you manage to get time off from work? I do hope you won't have to rush back immediately. You have no idea how I have looked forward to this moment.'

Alice didn't like to ask why she had never got into contact before. Perhaps that would come. For the moment she contented herself with answering Heather's questions. 'No, I have a few days,' she smiled.

'And what do you do, my dear? In the day time, as it were?'

'I am a solicitor.'

'*Really?* You look far too young.'

'Thank you!' Alice laughed. 'Actually not all solicitors are dusty old fogies.'

'So it seems. And what sent you into the law?'

Alice was silent for a moment but shrugged at last. 'They say every generation rebels against its parents. Since my mother loved art, it made sense for me to do something as dry as possible.'

Heather gave her a strange look but said nothing. They roared through crowded streets, vibrating over cobbles past magnificent palaces – she recognized the Louvre – then were crossing the river and she caught a glimpse of the Eiffel Tower. Driving through a more sedate residential neighbourhood now, it seemed to encapsulate all the sights and sounds she recognized from other visits, the memory everyone has of Paris, the high Edwardian facades of apartment blocks with their wrought-iron balconies and steep sloping mansard roofs, the plane trees just beginning to come into leaf, those strange poster towers, a lady walking a miniature dog, a man on a bicycle, and the shops – the patisserie, the *boulangerie*...

'How wonderful to have an excuse to come to Paris!' she couldn't help exclaiming, feeling a tingle of excitement.

'One never needs an *excuse*, my dear,' murmured her companion.

The taxi now pulled up beside one of the apartment buildings and in a moment Heather had produced a large bunch of keys and let them into a dim cavernous hall that smelled of old damp stone, where she exchanged a muttered greeting with an old woman who materialized from a tiny cubby hole beneath the stairs and handed her some letters. They didn't use the stairs but rather an antiquated lift, which clicked and whirred and descended with arthritic slowness from above and whose old gates, when it finally arrived, they wrenched open with a metallic clang.

At the fourth floor, a dusty nondescript landing, Heather produced her large bunch of keys once again, inserted one into a high, battered and peeling door, and suddenly, from this most unprepossessing beginning, Alice found herself in a spacious and sunny flat which, as she went to the window, she saw did indeed enjoy a view of the Eiffel Tower. The apartment was all of a piece with its owner: large, opulent, but with a wonderfully relaxed and slightly Bohemian feel to it. Every wall was hung with paintings, clearly done either by the lady herself or her friends. Large old pieces of furniture were strewn with

26

exotic and colourful coverings and cushions.

Heather threw her coat over the back of a wide sofa. 'I'll make some tea – you'll be ready for it. And Jean-Luc will be in soon.'

In a small kitchen she busied herself with a kettle, a teapot and other bits and pieces, talking all the while.

'I haven't told you much about myself so far. Well, it's soon told. Jean-Luc and I make a living of sorts from the brush, in case you hadn't already guessed. We both teach part-time and in between pursue our *métiers*. Mine pays better than his – which is a source of complaint and causes debates on the nature of art, etc, etc. I do still-lives, mainly to order – another source of dispute – while he ploughs a more uncompromising furrow. Geometric abstracts at the moment. He's forever experimenting and draws behind him a small band of disciples. Good for him. I am afraid he regards me as hopelessly commercial. But, frankly—' she turned with a world weary smile – 'I long ago left those sort of expressions behind me. Commercial, non-commercial, who cares? I paint what I like and luckily for me some other people like them too and are ready to buy them off me. A slice of cake?'

'Thank you.' Alice followed Heather back into the sitting room, where she set down the tray, throwing some newspapers and magazines on the floor, and shifting some coats and books from the sofa to make room. They sat down.

'Madame Lagrange—'

'By the way, dear, that's enough of that.

27

Heather, please.'

'Oh, sorry, Heather.' She hesitated as Heather poured tea. It was served clear, golden, in paper-thin porcelain cups.

'Lemon all right for you?'

Alice nodded, and began again. 'You said in your letter you had something to say...'

Heather sat back and lit a cigarette. 'Something to show you – to give you, to be precise. But I also wanted to talk to you and to ask how you're coping. Have you managed to – shall we say – get back on to an even keel? It was damned unfair your mother dying so young. But then Meg never had much luck.'

Alice put down her cup, incredulous. 'I beg your pardon?'

'No, I'm being tactless. I mean perhaps things were difficult for her. More difficult than she deserved.'

'You must explain,' Alice said quietly.

Heather studied her carefully for a moment. 'You're wondering why you've never heard of me before, aren't you? I'm afraid your father laid down rather strict conditions when they married and one was that your mum should have no dealings with her old friends. His idea was that he and Meg should start afresh. He had no time for art students of any stripe.'

Alice felt hot, confused by this unexpected revelation. 'But for heaven's sake, *why*?'

Heather shrugged. 'Perhaps one day you'll be able to ask him yourself. It ought to come from him.' She paused thoughtfully. 'It was an odd marriage. I often wonder...'

'What?'

'I wonder whether she wouldn't have been better off on her own, despite everything.'

'What *everything*? I don't understand at all.'

'Well, as I said, she was forced to give up all her old friends. It was a wrench, for her as well as for us. I tried to keep up a bit of a correspondence through her mother, but it was awkward.'

They heard the door open, and a moment later they were joined by a little man with a thick moustache in an old tweed jacket and corduroys, holding a briefcase.

'*Allo? Elle est arrivée?*'

'*Oui.*' Heather turned to Alice. 'My husband speaks not one word of English, Alice. I'm sure you'll cope.' She winked.

'I'll certainly try,' Alice smiled. But she was still extremely upset by the extraordinary things Heather had just said. Fortunately all that was set aside for the moment as husband and wife exchanged mundane remarks on the day's business.

That evening they went out to a brasserie on the corner for dinner and, sitting on a banquette against the wall, she studied the other diners in the hundred reflections of bevelled mirrors etched with old advertisements for exotic liqueurs on the wall opposite, listened to the lively hum of chat about her, noting the silent traffic passing beyond the window in the darkening street outside, and finally concentrated on the long discussion over the menu between husband and wife opposite her and the sober

29

decisions which Jean-Luc finally arrived at. 'I'll leave it in your hands,' she said simply.

'We recommend the fish soup, Alice,' Heather said. Then, reminded of something, she went on thoughtfully, 'Your mum and I had fish soup the first night we arrived in St Tropez. It's just come back to me.'

'The South of France?'

'Mm. That was one of the things I wanted to talk to you about.'

'You went together?'

'Just before the war. Meg was mad keen on Cézanne and was determined to go to Provence. So I went with her.'

Alice was thoughtful. 'It must have been wonderful.'

'Oh, it was – and nothing like as crowded as today. We had it to ourselves, practically.'

'She never said anything about it to me.'

'No – as I said, it was the agreement.'

Later that evening, when they were back in the apartment, Jean-Luc disappeared to another room which they used as a studio and Heather and Alice sat sipping brandy.

Suddenly Heather stood up. 'Now, my dear, prepare yourself. No, don't move. Stay just where you are. I want you to look at this picture.' She crossed to where one painting hung among many others on the wall and pointed to it. She waited while Alice studied the picture. It was an oil painting, perhaps two feet square, an impressionist picture of a nude. The model was seated upright in a large cane chair, her whole body exposed to the viewer, but with her head turned to one side as she seemed to gaze thoughtfully out of a window at a view through trees to the sea. Alice studied the picture and there was a long silence while Heather waited.

At length she enquired, 'What do you think of it?'

'Did you paint it?' Alice asked tentatively.

Heather chuckled. 'No – but by golly, I wish I had. Go on,' she continued, 'doesn't anything strike you about it?'

Alice turned again to the picture. 'It's very pleasant,' she said at last.

'Would you like it?'

Alice looked up in bewilderment. 'What do you mean?'

'I mean, my dear, that it is yours. Your property. Your mother asked me to keep it for you.'

Alice was suddenly very hot and her head felt stuffed. She stood up abruptly, pressing her hand to her forehead. 'I'm sorry, this is all too sudden for me.' She walked about in the room for a moment then returned to where Heather was still standing by the picture. Heather said nothing, but watched her.

At last, as the two women stood facing each other, Heather said softly, 'Sit down, Alice. There's something else.'

'What?'

'Sit down.' Alice sat again, and Heather went on, 'Now look at the picture again. Isn't there anything about it that strikes you?'

'You must tell me! I can't stand this! What is

this picture and why did my mother give it to you?'

'Calm down, and answer my question. You'll see it may answer your own question.'

'What question?' Alice asked helplessly.

'As I said, isn't there anything about the picture that strikes you?'

'*What?*' Alice was desperate. 'What should strike me?'

'Anything about the model?' Heather said carefully.

Alice thought her head would explode. There was something very strange happening here. 'You mean...'

Heather nodded. 'It's your mum,' she said prosaically.

Three

There was a silence that seemed to go on and on. Alice stared at the picture, turned briefly to Heather who was watching her carefully, then turned to the picture again. She got up and went closer. The model was a girl of nineteen, or twenty perhaps, with auburn hair clustered prettily about her face. She wasn't exactly beautiful, but she had the attractiveness of youth. Her body was slim, taut, with high breasts. Her arms rested on the arms of the chair and she seemed completely at ease.

'Yes, it is Mum, I see it now,' Alice said at last. 'She was beautiful.'

'She didn't think so,' Heather said with a chuckle. Alice turned to her as Heather went on, 'You know yourself, we all find something wrong with our appearance. It's the price you pay for being a woman.'

Alice relaxed and went even closer to the picture. At last she said, 'You said Mum gave it to you to keep for me?'

'Mm.' Heather returned to the sofa and as she lit a cigarette Alice caught the characteristic smell of Algerian tobacco. 'Your father wouldn't have it in the house, she told me. Perhaps he found it embarrassing. After all, what *would* a man do with a nude painting of his wife? Hang it on the sitting-room wall – a talking point for visitors?'

'I really don't understand. If I were he and loved my wife, I would never give it away. It's lovely.'

'It certainly is.' They both turned again to the painting. 'It's also very valuable, I ought to tell you.' Heather looked at Alice. 'It's by Bonnard.'

There was a pause. 'Bonnard?' Alice began tentatively. 'Er – *the* Bonnard?'

Heather nodded. 'There's only one. I dare say you've seen his work in the Tate – or in the Jeu de Paume?'

Once again Alice was thrown into confusion. 'Bonnard painted my mother?'

'Mm. As I told you, we went to St Tropez – where we had the fish soup – and while we were there we met Bonnard and he painted Meg.' It sounded very simple.

'I never knew Mum and Dad went to the South of France. Dad always said he hated France.'

'Your father didn't go. It was just Meg and me.'

'This was before my parents met?'

'To tell the truth, I'm not exactly sure. They may have known each other. It was before they married, of course.'

'So – when was this?'

Heather lifted the picture off the wall, and turned it over. Scrawled in charcoal on the back of the canvas were the words *Les Cigalettes 1939*.

'What does that mean? *Les Cigalettes*?'

'The Little Crickets. It was the name of a house, a big house where we stayed. Bonnard was staying there too.' She changed the subject awkwardly. 'I didn't bring the picture with me when I came over; there would have been a lot of duty to pay. You'll have to decide what you want to do with it. Take it home or sell it here.'

'I shall take it home,' Alice said instantly.

It was a long time before Alice got to sleep that night. Listening to the rumble of late-night traffic in the street below, she lay awake staring at the strip of light across the ceiling from a gap in the shutters. Why had her mother never mentioned this trip to her? Why never tell her she knew Pierre Bonnard? That she had posed for him, been painted by him? Surely it was something to boast of? And why was her father so hostile – both to the picture and to Heather? Her parents' marriage had latterly been difficult but surely they must have been in love when they married – and any newly-married husband would surely have been entranced by such a painting – especially by such a famous painter. *If I had been Dad*, she thought, *that picture would have had pride of place in my house.*

There was something more. It was a happy picture – that was its dominant characteristic – and it was a generous picture. The model – her very own mum – was happy, and wanted to show herself off, to share her happiness with the world. That was an enormous reassurance to Alice, because the mother she had known more recently had not been happy. By the morning she had made up her mind and at breakfast she informed Heather she intended to go to St Tropez and see *Les Cigalettes* for herself.

'When?'

'Today. You won't mind, will you? I must take this opportunity while I'm in France and I have to be back in London in a couple of days. I'll leave the picture here for the moment.'

'But you're taking it back to England?'

'Of course. I'll phone now, if I may, to check the train times?'

Heather smiled. 'I'll do it for you, but let's finish our coffee first. You'd probably be best to take the night train.'

'It's abominably rude, Heather, to rush off so soon after arriving, but everything you've told me has thrown me into such a commotion. I shan't be able to relax until I have seen *Les*

35

Cigalettes myself. It took me hours to get to sleep last night.'

Alice was at the Gare de Lyon that evening at seven o'clock, found her train and her *couchette*. Despite the extraordinary revelations she had to think about, and all the distractions sleeping in a train involves, she and the other occupants of the compartment folded down their beds at around ten, climbed in, and Alice enjoyed a reasonable night's sleep. Early in the morning the other occupants of the compartment were stirring before she awoke to the distant sound of a gong as the attendant went through the train announcing breakfast. She soon took her place in the restaurant car as a white-jacketed waiter poured her coffee and placed a basket of brioches in front of her. Outside, the Provençal countryside slid past, blasted by an intense light. This came as a real shock after the dull cloudy sky of Paris; she could have been in another continent. The sheer pleasure of this unexpected trip cheered her and she was content for the moment simply to enjoy the novelty of the experience.

At St Raphael she left the train and eventually a bus took her round the rim of a wide bay to St Tropez. To her left the sea glinted and glittered in an intense blue and everywhere yachts billowed full-sail and motorboats left white trails. Pine trees fringed the shore and white villas were dotted everywhere. The road seemed filled with large open-topped cars in which elegant people in sunglasses leaned back, chatting with one hand idly on the wheel. It was all very relaxed and corresponded to everything she had read about St Tropez, the home of France's rich and famous. Here one expected to see film stars and millionaires' yachts and all the time Alice was thinking, *Mum was here – and never said anything about it.* The weather already felt like mid-summer, and she had taken off her raincoat and jacket.

The approach to the town was unpromising – a wilderness of billboards, garish neon signs, junk yards, car repair workshops, and cheap bars and cafes. However St Tropez itself, when she finally arrived, was – or had been – a charming little fishing port, a few narrow streets clustered between the harbour and the castle. It was crowded with holidaymakers even in April and it was clear that the season was well underway. It was late morning when she made her way into the town and soon found a small hotel in a side street. She didn't really feel justified in spending more on one of the smart hotels on the waterfront and even this one was not cheap. She would only stay for the night. Once she had found *Les Cigalettes* and satisfied her curiosity, she would have to get back to London. And then there would be questions to be answered.

As she explored the narrow streets – the *ruelles* – she passed shops full of smart cosmopolitan clothes, jewellery, handbags and hats. There were chic restaurants too, where waiters were busy setting out tables for lunch. The quayside was lined with huge yachts where beautiful people lounged on deck, drinking and chatting.

And where was *Les Cigalettes*? The hotel

concierge had never heard of it. He recommended she try the tourist office, where sure enough the assistant produced a little map of St Tropez and circled the place. It turned out to be on the edge of the town and as Alice made her way up the sloping road she found herself surrounded by recent developments, well-watered lawns, little bungalows with white walls, and neatly arranged hedges of box and broom. It was all very proper, well-maintained, and smart – very bourgeois and typically French.

She arrived at a gate, open between pink wash posts and giving on to a private road, immaculately maintained between lawns and clumps of flowers and shrubs. A smartly painted notice at one side read *Les Cigalettes* and she shortly found herself before a large luxury apartment block. As she looked it over Alice realized instantly that it could not be more than five years old. She turned to look at the notice again. This was *Les Cigalettes* and there could not be two of them. It was early afternoon by now and there was a deathly hush everywhere, save only for the rasping of crickets. There was no one to be seen, no one to ask. Clearly it was siesta time.

Thinking hard she made her way back down into the town. Here too things were quiet; the tourist office was closed, so she returned to her hotel to await the reopening of the town. In her room she fell briefly asleep, her mind full of questions.

When she did return to the tourist office later that afternoon, the young assistant could be of no help. There was no other *Les Cigalettes*, he assured her, thumbing through the telephone directory. He summoned his colleague and together they looked through a number of catalogues and reference books, much used, which they extracted from beneath the counter, but in the end they drew a complete blank, and she left the office once again. As she wandered disconsolately through the town she asked herself whether there might have been another apartment block on the site twenty-five years earlier. Even so, that did not make sense. Heather had referred to a house. It was very frustrating and as she finally found a restaurant and took her seat – for she had not eaten since her breakfast on the train that morning – she was undecided what to do. It was too late to take the night train back to Paris. In the end, fortified by dinner she decided to stay and probe a little deeper – though how she was to do that she had no idea.

The following morning, feeling more refreshed and hopeful, Alice was walking through the town, on the lookout for ideas, when she passed the public library and on impulse she went in. It had only just opened, and she and the librarian were the only two people in the building.

'Excusez-moi, m'sieur, est-ce-que vous connaissez par chance la maison Les Cigalettes?'

He pushed his spectacles up on to the top of his head, rested his knuckles on the counter, and shook his head sadly. *'N'existe plus,'* he said curtly.

'Mais –' she was hopeful – *'vous la connaissez? Elle existait une fois?'*

'*Bien sûr.*'

Then to her relief he broke into English. 'It was a lovely house,' he went on, 'but they have demolished it and put up that barrack instead. *Vandales! Barbares!*'

'And did you know the people who lived there?'

'It belonged to a lovely old lady, *une Irlandaise – mais, hélas, elle est morte.*'

'Oh. I'm sorry. Did you say Irish?'

'Oui, Madame Leary. She lived there for many years. She was very wealthy, very generous; she had many famous people as her guests.'

'Pierre Bonnard, perhaps?'

He shook his head uncertainly. 'Per'aps.' Then he looked at her. 'Why are you asking?'

'I believe my mother was a guest there once, and that she was painted there by Pierre Bonnard, and I wanted to see the place – the place where she had been happy.'

'Your mother?'

Alice nodded.

After thinking a moment he said, 'The library closes at one o'clock. Come back then. I will take you to the cemetery and we shall see Madame Leary's grave.'

She spent the rest of the morning going through the local newspaper for 1939, in search of any information about Madame Leary, *Les Cigalettes* or Bonnard. It was a tiny sheet, barely four pages, crudely printed, with unfamiliar advertisements, and was otherwise filled with stories concerning the imminent war, notices of mobilization, details of air-raid precautions, or else local gossip and scandal. There were very few photographs and none of *Les Cigalettes*. She drew a complete blank.

At one o'clock as he promised the librarian took his beret from a peg, locked up the library and together they walked through the town to the cemetery which lay a little beyond the town. The sun was merciless, the sky cloudless, and the intense blue of the sea stretched away to the horizon. The cemetery bore no resemblance to any she had ever seen before. Instead of the sort of gravestones she knew from English grave-yards, this one was a miniature village of tiny houses, or temples perhaps, with stone doors, and many were the property of families rather than individuals: inscriptions on the doors said things like 'Famille Du Bois' or 'Famille César', with a list of names beneath.

This puzzled Alice. 'Is there a grave beneath this tomb?' she asked, pointing to one.

'*Mais non*. When a person dies, the door is broken open, and the remains are deposited inside.'

'But is there room? How many can it hold?'

He smiled. 'It is a little macabre perhaps. When the body is placed inside, the tomb is sealed with a stone door. It is then left beneath our Mediterranean sky – it is warm, you notice, even in April? You may imagine what becomes of the *défunt* after even one year. As if you were to place a chicken in the oven and leave it to cook for a year.' He raised his eyebrows as this image intruded into her imagination. 'So, by the time they come to open it up for the next

41

occupant, there is not much left of the last one. A few bones only. Ah...' He was distracted. They had come upon a grave, not a little house like the others but a large plain flat slab where she read: 'Abby O'Leary, *née* Mayo, Irland 1862; *morte* St Tropez 1953.' And in English, *She did not forget her own.*

'Ninety-one. She lived to a good age. What did they mean, do you suppose, by that inscription?'

He shook his head but at last said, 'As I told you, she was very generous, and liked to fill her house with guests, artists, painters, and so on —'

'Painters? So she might have had someone like Bonnard?'

He shrugged. 'It's possible.'

That evening Alice took the night train back to Paris. Lying in her *couchette*, listening to the rhythmic rattle of the wheels and the clanking as the train passed over points, watching the lights that occasionally flashed on the ceiling and then were gone again, and waiting for sleep to come, Alice was filled with conflicting thoughts. In a way the trip had been a failure. She had not seen the house and had found out almost nothing about Madame Leary or Pierre Bonnard. Furthermore, the librarian had been at pains to emphasize that the town had gone to the dogs, commercialized, overcrowded, overbuilt. It bore little resemblance to the sleepy little fishing port it had been before the war. *'Avant la guerre! Hélas!'* he would sigh as they strolled back into the town.

Lying in her *couchette* she struggled to

42

imagine the St Tropez of *'avant la guerre'* which her mother had known, where she had been happy, where she had taken off her clothes for the famous Bonnard.

Back in Paris she took her farewell of Heather.

'We must keep in touch,' Heather said. 'You must come again and stay longer next time.'

In the meantime Alice had made up her mind what to do with the picture.

'I am certainly taking it with me.'

However the problem was that if it were impounded by the customs officials at Dover the duty might be so great that she would have to sell the picture in order to pay it.

'In which case,' Heather said, 'you should either sell it here, or leave it with me – then you would have an extra reason for coming to visit!'

But Alice had decided on another, high-risk strategy. 'I am determined to keep it, and I want it in England. I shall smuggle it in.'

'How?'

'Well,' Alice said thoughtfully, 'I admit I don't know much about art, and that is what I shall tell the customs man. I shall say I picked it up in the *Marché des Puces*. If he asks for proof of purchase, I shall shrug my shoulders and say, "In the flea market?" The picture is signed but it's not at all clear. If you're not looking for a famous name, you probably won't find it.'

There was one other matter that the revelation of the painting had pushed into the back of Alice's mind. Before she finally bade farewell to Heather, amidst the noise and bustle of the Gare du Nord, she mentioned the photograph she had seen in her mother's hand. It was a long shot but she thought Heather might have some clue as to its significance.

'Have you any idea what it might have been?'

Heather was very struck by this question, stared for a long moment into Alice's eyes, and only after what seemed a mental struggle dragged her eyes from Alice's. There was a long silence in which she seemed to be groping for the right words and she was looking anywhere but at Alice now.

Finally, and rather unconvincingly, she shook her head, raised her eyebrows and stared into the middle distance. 'A photograph?' she murmured and shook her head again dubiously.

'Heather?'

'Yes, dear?'

'What is it? You seem uncertain.'

Again Heather shook her head, apparently dismissing the subject. 'Your mother never said anything?'

'No.'

'Your father?'

'I presume it was he who gave the photo to the undertakers. I mean, who else? And I suppose it may have been a wedding photograph – or a honeymoon snap?'

Heather sounded relieved at this solution. 'Very likely. Very likely.'

And with that Alice took her leave and found her place on the Calais train. She didn't give too much thought to what Heather had said or not said. Her behaviour was a little odd, but it had seemed unlikely she would have anything to contribute. It had been a long shot, after all.

In Dover she carried the picture openly beneath her arm, wrapped in newspaper and tied up with string. As she unwrapped it she told the customs official she had paid two hundred francs for it and added, 'I think I was probably overcharged.'

The customs official looked it over and said he was inclined to agree. He chalked a large cross on her overnight case and Alice boarded the London train.

Back in her own flat she unwrapped the picture again and spent some time searching for the right place to hang it. When she did settle it to her satisfaction, she was able to make a cup of coffee and settle back on the sofa to study it again. There was something deeply satisfying about that picture. The unhappy mother whom Alice had last seen lying cold and white in her coffin lived again, here, as she was at the sunniest time of her life, when she was young and happy.

Four

Alice went back to work, and every evening as she returned to the flat, the picture awaited her. She loved that picture – it had automatically become her most prized possession – and could still not quite grasp that this most tangible link with her mother was here right in her living room and with her every day. It had been a stroke of good fortune such as she could never have imagined.

But it also raised a problem, because sooner or later her father must see it. The question was, how would he react when he saw it? She had a clear idea of how it would be. Should she merely hide it when he came? Pretend it did not exist?

Alice rebelled against this idea. She believed that it was her father who had made her mother unhappy. Her father who – through his caustic manner, his indifference – had turned the happy young woman in the picture into the miserable mother Alice had known in her last years. Something in Alice was determined that her father should confront this picture – should be made to acknowledge what he had done.

The only thing she could think of was to invite him to dinner and to leave the picture on the wall. Let him see it. She had made no secret of her trip to Paris so, since Heather had told her that her father knew of the picture, he might have guessed she would have it. The event might very well blow up in her face but she could see no other way for it.

She telephoned him at work. 'I went to Paris, Dad – I told you.' Silence. She pushed on. 'Just stayed a couple of nights with Heather. She sent her regards.'

'Alice,' he began ponderously, 'what is the point of this? You know exactly what I think of Heather Grey – or whatever she now calls herself.'

'Yes, I know, I know, Dad,' Alice hurried on, 'but still she was a friend of Mum's, and we talked about her and their times together—'

'What did she say?' he interrupted quickly.

Alice stopped. Actually, when she came to think of it, she had not said very much. 'Just their time at art school before the war and the trip to the South of France.'

'And?'

'What do you mean?'

'Is that all you talked about?'

Alice was bewildered. 'More or less. Anyway, I just rang to ask whether you'd like to come over for dinner one night this week?'

'I've been staying with my parents for the moment. Until I can get myself sorted out. I'll probably sell the house. In any case, I'm flying to America next week.'

'Oh yes – you mentioned the White Heat of Technology. Well, look I'm sure they'll spare

47

you for one night. Do come – Friday be all right?'

He finally agreed.

By the time Friday came, by the time she had rushed to the shops, gathered the ingredients, rushed back to the flat, put things into the oven, set out some flowers, showered, washed her hair, and changed into a dress, she was exhausted. And still she had no idea how she was going to introduce the picture, and most importantly how she was going to handle her father when he saw it. She had taken it down from the wall and kept it in her bedroom for the moment. It would not be a good idea for him to see it the moment he arrived. He might very well storm out again and all her culinary efforts would be wasted. This way he would be fortified with wine and casserole before she produced it. Wine – that reminded her: she must try to stop him drinking too much.

When he did arrive, he looked tired, stooped, and seemed distracted.

'I've had a terrible week,' he began. 'Trying to get everything in order before I go.'

'When are you off?'

'Monday. A couple of orders came in on Wednesday, big ones, important, things I would normally deal with myself. Consequently I've had to leave a sheaf of instructions. I've also been telegramming the States all week confirming dates and times for meetings.'

'You never told me what it is you're going to see.'

They had by this time gone into the living room, where she offered him a drink. He took a whisky and soda and threw himself on the sofa. He looked about him as if noticing it for the first time. 'I must say, Alice, you've made this room very nice – very comfy.' He took a sip and seemed to relax. 'It's the print. I've been looking through a lot of journals lately, and there are huge changes taking place. It's being transformed. And we're still using machinery that's sixty or seventy years old. It's perfectly good, serviceable, but I can see things are going to change, and I don't want to be left behind.'

Alice disappeared into the kitchen and checked the casserole. When she reappeared with a bottle he got up. 'I brought one myself – a contribution.' He returned a moment later. 'I'll just decant this. Have you a decanter?'

Alice could produce nothing more than a milk jug. He seemed to cheer up. 'Well, it'll do,' he said and laboriously decanted the bottle into the jug.

'Another heirloom?' she asked lightly.

He handed her the bottle. 'Chateau Margaux '53, *Premier Grand Cru Classé*.'

'I'm honoured. Hope I'll be able to do it justice.'

'You're my daughter, aren't you?'

She smiled, and reached for his hand.

Throughout dinner her father became more and more affable. She hoped this wasn't solely due to the casserole and the claret. At the same time, however, as she saw him relaxing she could feel herself getting more and more tense as

49

the time approached when she would produce the picture. It had occurred to her, rather late in the day, that there might be a very prosaic reason why her father wouldn't want to see it – or to see her seeing it. After all, he and her mother had been married, had been intimate, and there was, now she thought about it, something very intimate about the picture.

Nevertheless she did produce it. Some instinct in her told her that she owed it to her mother to show the picture to her father – to remind him of the happy young woman her mother had once been, and of the unhappy older woman he had made her.

Eventually, after she had made coffee, and her father was hinting it was time to be moving, she got up quickly and went into the bedroom.

'There's something – something Heather gave me. I brought it back...'

She returned with the picture and stood it on a chair. Her father stared at it while she waited, trembling now, for his reaction. There was a very long wait indeed, as his gaze seemed to bore through the picture – that simple image of happiness – and his face seemed to harden before her eyes.

'I told your mother I never wanted to see that picture again,' he muttered in a low voice. 'It's all that interfering woman's fault – I told her she wasn't welcome. And I told you – I *told* you – I wanted nothing to do with any of them ever again! I don't want to see it!' He got up, pushing his chair back harshly.

'But Dad,' she began, helplessly, 'it's a lovely

50

picture. Can't you see that? It's not embarrassing! I'm not embarrassed. It was such a long time ago! Why shouldn't we remember Mum as she was once?'

He did not hear her, and was already in the tiny hallway, reaching for his coat.

'Thank you for dinner, Alice,' he said as he reached for the door. 'I'll be in touch when I get back from America.'

She caught his arm. 'Dad! What is it? Why can't you be happy for Mum now she's ... she's gone? Let's remember her in happier times.'

She heard his feet rattling on the staircase. There was clearly no point in chasing him and she returned to the living room where the picture still stood on the chair and remained for some time gazing at it. Her father's reaction had been – on the surface – so irrational that she was completely at a loss to account for it. Was it simply grief for his dead wife? Or was there something more? This was not something they could discuss again, that was certain, and Alice despaired of ever knowing what it was that had made him – and her mother – so unhappy.

As a matter of fact the explanation was placed in her hands only a few days later. Alice was executrix for her mother's will and had to undertake a number of simple procedures: the closing of her bank account, the cancelling of one or two standing orders and settling of accounts at a couple of shops. Her mother had also owned a few shares. It was all very straightforward. But when, one morning, a week after the dinner, she

51

received a letter from the bank she was puzzled: she had already closed the account. This letter stated very briefly that her mother had deposited a parcel in the vault. Would Alice call in one day and collect it? They apologized for not informing her sooner.

That lunchtime she stood at the counter and the bank clerk, having seen the letter, disappeared and after what seemed an age returned with a package wrapped in brown paper and tied with string. There was something old-looking about it – the knots in the string were embalmed in red sealing wax, which she hadn't seen since she was a child – and Alice was astonished when the clerk gave her a document to sign and she saw that the package had been deposited in 1944.

She stared in incomprehension for some seconds. 'Has this parcel been here since 1944?'

'Never been touched. We would have a record if it had.'

Looking again at the document she saw her mother's signature across a penny stamp bearing the king's head and the date.

She carried the package back to her office and all that afternoon it lay on her desk as she went through other business. She got out her mother's will. There was no mention in it of any package deposited in the bank. Moreover, the parcel had no inscription on it. A label had been affixed by a bank clerk with her mother's name, Mrs Margaret Tremayne, and that was all.

That evening at home the parcel lay on the table and now a problem presented itself to Alice. Who had the right to open this parcel?

Should it not be opened in the presence of the whole family? Perhaps it contained valuables? This was complicated by the fact that her father was in America and her brother in Bristol. Should she wait? But then, she thought, she was executrix of the will and responsible for disposing of her mother's effects, even those she had apparently forgotten about.

The parcel lay on the table and Alice stared at it. Somewhere in her a decision had been made without her direct conscious involvement. She must know what was in it. Tonight. This need involve no disloyalty to her family; she was after all a legatee of her mother as well as executrix. And there was another factor: did the parcel contain something else like the painting – something her father might not wish to know about?

The string was soon cut, the brown paper – stiff, brittle, old – was unwrapped, and disclosed a sheaf of handwritten paper in her mother's handwriting. She placed it on the table, staring at it. To whom was this addressed? And what was it – a letter, a novel, a memoir, or just random thoughts? And whose was it – or was this an heirloom descending through the family? She picked it up, flicked the pages through her fingers: pages and pages of it. She recognized her mother's handwriting but this was a younger woman's hand, larger, and seemed written with lightning speed, straggling across the page, dashed off.

Alice glanced at the clock, got up, went into the kitchen to make a cup of coffee, came back, settled herself on the sofa and began to read.

Five

Edward won't let me talk about it. Day after day I carry it about in me but there's no one I can tell it to. Edward was very kind – is very kind – and I owe him everything, only I must tell this, say it, write it down, scratch it on a wall, or I shall go mad. There is a world around me and every day I go through it, smile and do my duty, and I have my children – God knows I should be on my knees thanking Him for what I have – but inside, I have a wound which never heals. I know this is being selfish, I know I have much to be grateful for, I know how much I owe Edward, I know all that, but it's – well, that's all in the head and it's my heart, dead inside me, that weighs me down. I think Edward knows – in himself he knows this – though we have never discussed it, not after the first time when we made the agreement. The agreement is a just one, I know, a generous one and I swear to God I make every effort to fulfill my side. It's just the not being able to talk about it.

He's been away over a year now and I get letters from him, posted in North Africa and now Sicily, that arrive months late. Perhaps if he were here it would be easier. But he isn't and who knows when I'll see him again. So, now the children are asleep, I shall make a start, and hope that by writing it all out – even though no one will ever read it – I shall be able to shake off my burden, or at least ease the weight.

It was in the summer of 1938 that we met. Extraordinary to think I was eighteen and had only just taken my Higher Leaving Certificate at Mill Hill Grammar, had only just said farewell to school uniforms, hymn singing, hockey sticks. Was it really so few years ago that I was that self, had such energy for life, was so full of a thoughtless confidence and optimism? I have been looking at an old photograph of myself in tennis whites and at that age I seem to be all legs. Was I really that young girl, with her curly hair, confident cheerful smile, her legs?

It was at the tennis club that I met Edward. Actually I had had my eye on him for some time. He was the best-looking man there and one of the two or three best players. In the changing room during the summer evenings he was the foremost subject of discussion and several of the other girls had tried their luck with him. There was one girl, Beryl, who he was with for a time and every evening when we saw the two of them driving off in his open-top sports car my heart swelled with frustration and envy. Then Beryl stopped riding in the sports car and for a few days he was driving home alone. Once again my hopes rose. So of course, did those of several others; I listened in silence as they discussed him in the changing room.

'He's got money, you know.'

'So it would appear, judging by the car.'

'How old is he?'

'Twenty-three?'

'Bit young for you, darling.'

'I'll ignore that cheap jibe.'

'His father owns a printing works.'

'Have you met his father, by the way? He's very handsome – even more than his son.'

'But then, you've always gone for the older man, haven't you, Joanie?'

'Thank you, dear. Even so, I wouldn't mind a fling with him, though I say it myself.'

'Who, the father?'

'Mm. His wife seems rather a faded bloom. I expect he'd be willing.'

'God, you're so hard. Is that all you think about?'

'Isn't that all any of us think about? It's not my fault if I'm more honest.'

'Blunt, even. Anyway, we were discussing the son. He needs taking care of. I simply can't bear to watch him driving away by himself every night. He looks so lonely.'

'Anyway, what went wrong, Beryl? We thought you had it all sewn up.'

A silence for a moment as the girl pulled her dress over her head. We had all turned to hear her reply. Finally as she was shuffling the dress down over her hips, she muttered without looking up, 'All he wanted to talk about was art. I got bored.'

'Oh, poor thing. You'd better work your magic on him, Betty. Only do your homework first. Get down to the National Gallery as fast as you can.'

'A girl can but try her best. It's only fair.'

'Charitable, even. You've such a kind heart.'

'I have, haven't I?'

I listened to this and much more like it in silence. But my determination was hardening by the minute; no one, not Betty nor Joan nor any of the others, were going to ride in that car. That place was reserved for me. The mention of art had merely sealed it. If he wanted to discuss art, so much the better. But it might take a bit of thinking out.

As a matter of fact my opportunity came a few evenings later. We were playing mixed doubles. I was a good player, ambitious too. People sometimes said taking part was more important than winning. I never understood that – I wanted to win, I played to win. When I was on that tennis court nothing else mattered. I saw nothing else, only my opponent readying herself – or in this case, himself – for the serve. I was all nervous energy, light, responsive, instinctive, and I went after that ball as swift as thought. I knew too that people were watching; they must see only the best. I could not bear to lose in front of spectators and when I did lose it took every ounce of self-control I possessed to walk to the net and shake the victor by the hand with a cheery 'well done'.

As I said, that evening we found ourselves in a foursome, mixed doubles. Edward was a good player, I had already noticed; he played with style and looked very handsome in his tennis whites. My partner, a stolid middle-aged chap, seemed hopelessly past it and I returned three quarters of the shots. I flew about that tennis court.

Well, we lost, but after the game as the evening dimmed and some of the others were packing up, I plucked up courage, strolled to the net and quietly suggested one last game, just the two of us. I nodded over my shoulder towards the other members on their way home, calling to each other in the cool, clear air.

'Now that we aren't weighed down by the oldsters we can play some *real* tennis. What do you say?' I grinned conspiratorially. It was a challenge and to my relief he responded instantly.

'I dare say I could fit in another game,' he replied casually, glancing at his watch. 'If you're not too tired.'

'Just getting warmed up.'

He took his place at the line, bounced the ball a couple of times, then, just as he was beginning to serve, called across, 'Don't worry, I won't make them too difficult. Just a friendly knock-up, eh?'

I knew he was teasing and called back, 'I only play to win. Sorry. I hope you won't be embarrassed losing to a woman?'

He bounced the ball a couple more times, then looked up again. 'Enough of this frivolous badinage.'

He slammed a serve to me and I returned it with a thumping back-hander which he missed. As he went after the ball I called, 'Oh, sorry. Too fast for you?'

'Not bad, not bad at all,' he said as he returned to the line. 'For a girl,' he added gallantly. 'I was just testing you.'

'Thanks, I appreciate that. Now we can really start to play.'

'All right.' He drew a long breath as he readied himself to serve. 'Only don't say I didn't warn you.'

He served again, and again I was ready for him. This time though he was ready for me too, returned the shot, and the ball went back and forth several times in a powerful rally. He was smiling, alert, on his toes, and I was too. There was an unspoken bond between us just then, a kind of conversation in which, although nothing was said, we understood each other instinctively as the ball slammed back and forth across the net.

When he eventually lost the point and was going after the ball he called cheerily, 'You definitely show promise. A little more work on the back-hand and I think we could turn you into quite a tolerable player.'

'You're absolutely right. My coach has been nagging me about it for ages. If you like I could give you his phone number. He might be able to help you with your serve.'

'There's nothing wrong with my serve.'

I wondered for a moment whether his sense of humour wasn't wearing thin.

I won the first game and it was my turn to serve. The others had all gone home by now and we were alone on the court and it was beginning to get dark. The sun had set, the big elms were silhouetted against the evening sky, bats swooped between them, and insects, great cockchafers, cruised by in leisurely style. A faint mist was rising across the park.

'Not too dark for you?' Edward called in a concerned tone. 'Can you still see the line?'

'I can if you can.'

He was fighting back, and I had long since grasped that he was as ambitious as I. He played up against the net and I couldn't get past him, though I played as hard as I had ever played. He had provoked me and in the gathering gloom I could just make out that teasing smile on his lips. The world had emptied, there were just the two of us, concentrated on each other, battling it out as the light faded. By the time we were finally forced to quit he was in the lead. Oddly, I didn't mind losing to him after all.

The club house was deserted by this time and I disappeared into the women's changing room. Things had been going well, but still not well enough for me. I suspected that Edward might need that extra nudge and as I was changing I was thinking hard. Then, in a kind of all-or-nothing desperation, I stood on a bench with a towel in my hand and took out the light bulb. The room was plunged into darkness.

'Oh drat!' I called. I opened the door a little. 'Edward! I say! Would you believe it, the light's gone in here and I can't find a thing!'

He was standing right outside the door.

'Oh thanks!' I gasped with a huge smile. 'I'm floundering about here in the dark and can't find my other shoe. Could you give me a hand?'

I was ostensibly in the process of putting on my blouse which was still only half buttoned up and hanging outside my skirt. Noticing this, he murmured, 'Why not?'

So of course within a second we had blundered into each other's arms and were kissing furiously in the darkness. Even so I affected to be surprised. 'Oh, Edward, I had no idea...'

The things girls do. It seems extraordinary that I could remember that evening word for word. It is quite uncanny how everything floods back once I concentrate.

I was determined to go to art school. I don't think my parents were particularly bothered – they probably regarded it in the light of a finishing school and thought I would be married in a year or two anyway. If I hadn't gone to St Martin's, however, I might never have gone to France the following summer, everything would have been different and I would not be writing this now.

That autumn I started at St Martin's, which is in Charing Cross Road; I wanted to be in town near the galleries and museums, near the theatres and shops. I wanted to be in the thick of it. This meant that I found myself going into town every morning on the Northern Line with Father – all thirteen stations of it – which gave him plenty of time to do the *Telegraph* crossword. In those days he was manager at Marshall and Snelgrove.

I enrolled in Fine Art. I'd been drawing and painting for years. Since the children were born I haven't had a moment for drawing, and after everything that's happened the desire has vanished. It's all gone, somehow seems irrelevant, yet in those days I drew incessantly. I drew everything – our house, our cat, my parents. I drew my school at different times of the day, like Monet with Rouen cathedral, early morning, bright afternoon, long evening shadows. My school under snow; when the cherry blossom was out; when the trees were bare.

But my god was Cézanne. I dreamed of landscapes of red earth, pine trees, olives, bare mountains, stony little villages. I knew Provence long before I ever went there.

Going to art school was a revelation too because first of all I was mixing with people who were interested when I talked about things that excited me. Also because there were people who were older than me, men and women who had done things in the world, had jobs and travelled and who had an air about them – knowing, experienced. They were people who did not live at home with their parents, people who lived together without being married and had rooms in Soho or Charlotte Street.

They dressed the part too. What was the point of being an art student if you didn't look like one? Sombrero hats, cloaks, gaudy scarves, shirts of many colours. One group were known as the Victorians and dressed like a group of undertakers. One chap affected a gold-topped cane, wore a wing collar and waistcoat with a fob watch in it and led a whippet on a lead.

It was frustrating that every afternoon I had to leave all this and take the tube back to Mill Hill and I determined to have a place of my own before too long. However, Father was strict. There had to be some good reason to keep me in town after six. And not unnaturally, because I was still only eighteen, a large part of me still mentally inhabited Mill Hill. I still went to the tennis club, still went out with Edward. I still helped my mother with the washing-up and ironing. For a long time the two sides of my life didn't conflict.

Teaching at St Martin's was old-fashioned by modern standards and I, like a lot of other students, chafed under the strict regime. We drew; we painted. All day, every day. In those days we still used to draw from plaster casts of antique sculpture. Training the eye was what it was about. 'Don't think – look!' Mr Robinson used to say. For hours at a time we sat and drew – the Apollo Belvedere, the Cnidian Venus, drunken Hercules, from every angle, getting to know the naked body. We had life classes too, usually dumpy middle-aged ladies who would come into the studio with bags of shopping, hats and umbrellas; they would sit naked for us then slip on a dressing gown while they drank a cup of tea and chatted in a companionable way during a break.

Our heads were full of more interesting things than the Apollo Belvedere, however, with its cold, chaste perfection. Picasso and Braque were supreme, and students experimented with collages of newspaper, restaurant bills, bus tickets, theatre posters, photographs torn from fashion magazines. Or we painted portraits in imitation of Picasso's latest work. Surrealism was very big at that time too, and many canvases depicted haunted streets, uncanny beneath a cold moon-

light, or figures frozen in impenetrable significance on a sea-shore; or else we worked at cubist
abstracts, cones and cubes arranged in arresting
juxtaposition; some experimented with surreal
abstract, and their cones and cubes acquired a
weird dream-like significance.

There were some students who even at art
school I saw were going to be successful. It was
quite simply because they were wholly dedicated to their work. When the doors opened in the
morning they were waiting; when the doors were
closed at night, they were the last to leave. There
was one I remember who now hangs in the Tate.
I can see Victor Ridmore now, in baggy flannels
and tweed jacket, smoking his rolled-up cigarettes. He didn't appear to have any money and
was forever scrounging from other students to
buy canvas, which he stretched himself. He used
to go down to the river, always the river, the mud
flats – grey days, misty days, evenings along the
river bank – and there would be these mournful
empty scenes, slightly surreal: the river at low
tide, the mud, the stillness, a barge lying and
perhaps one figure simply perceived alone.

There was also Augustus John in his cape and
beret, a terrible old man leering and flirting with
the girls, and genuinely believing he was irresis-
tible. We found him repulsive; his teeth were
yellowing or missing, and his breath smelled of
his pipe, a cavernous stench. And though he did
have an awesome reputation, being young, we
couldn't take him seriously. His style was utterly
dated – academic, the most damning judgement
we could pass.

Six

The following Sunday in the early afternoon Edward called for me. I had been waiting for him for some time, fidgeting with a book, when at last – late – I heard the fruity sound of his sports car. I threw the book down and would have dashed straight out but my father restrained me. He was eager to meet Edward, it was clear.

'It's not manners to rush out, Margaret. Wait till he knocks.'

My parents are full of these tiny rules.

A moment later there was a knock at the door, and Edward was there in a sports jacket and open-necked shirt. He looked just as handsome as he had the previous Wednesday.

'I think the parents want to inspect you,' I whispered as I ushered him into the parlour. They made a pretence of being surprised, my father put down the Sunday paper, my mother put down her knitting, and introductions were made.

During the few minutes they chatted, my father let Edward know that his father and he knew each other slightly at the golf club.

'Don't play golf myself,' Edward said cheerfully. 'I'd be bound to miss – or to drive the ball into some impenetrable scrub!'

'Don't underestimate the golf club,' my father admonished him. 'You never know who you might meet. I've made valuable contacts at the club over the years.'

As we were getting into the car I saw in the back an enormous kite.

'*Edward!*' I was astonished as I examined it. 'My God, it's *beautiful*!'

It must have been six feet long and was clearly hand made, and with considerable care.

'What is it made of?'

'Paper,' he said, as if it were obvious.

It was painted with designs in black and gold with a Chinese dragon motif. 'It's a work of art. You must have spent hours on it.'

'I did.' He hopped over the side of the car. 'Come on.'

We drove to Hampstead Heath and parked the car near Kenwood House at the northern end. I helped Edward lift out the delicate and ungainly structure. A breeze caught at the kite as I carried it. As I held it, I found something inexplicable about this thing on which so much care had been lavished, yet which seemed so fragile.

We found ourselves at the top of the heath on a gusty day, a blue sky with little high clouds scudding far above us. Sunday afternoon strollers were dotted over the long green slopes beneath us and in the distance, half lost in a grey summer haze, London spread itself far, far away. The dome of St Paul's rose clearly. We stood for a while taking in the view.

'Lay it on the ground or you'll be blown away.'

'Wouldn't that be wonderful!' I couldn't help exclaiming. 'Imagine being carried by a kite over London. One day you should build a really monstrous kite, Edward, big enough to carry me.'

He was busy with his wheel of string and unravelling the long tail of streamers.

'Now listen, Meg. What I want you to do is to take up the kite, and when I give the word, run down the hill and, when you can feel the wind lifting her, let her go.'

I did as he ordered and in a second, after barely two paces, the wind had sucked it out of my hands and as I gazed after it, shading my eyes, it was already a hundred feet above me.

I made my way up the slope again and stood by him as the wheel whizzed round in his hands. The kite rose farther and farther till it seemed just a small dot swaying far above in the immensity of the bright afternoon sky.

'Here – you hold.' He passed the wheel to me. Immediately I could feel the force of the wind in my hands. 'Hold tight or it'll catch you by surprise.'

I had to brace myself to take the force of the pull. Far, far above me the kite rose and swooped, the tail weaving and dancing beneath it, and all the time I took the strain on the line. I thought *if I let go, it would just go off into the blue, high over London, floating away.* There was something wonderfully romantic about this.

Edward corrected me. 'If the line broke,' he said, 'the kite would simply fall to earth. It's only you holding the line which keeps it up.'

67

This seemed a contradiction but, as it happened, a moment later the line did break and the kite came down, falling over and over on itself, twisting and turning as we raced down the grassy slope until it struck the ground at a terrific speed. As we reached it I could see that the main strut was broken in two, and the kite lay buckled over on itself. As we knelt I was beside myself to see the beautiful thing mangled and broken.

Edward took it more calmly. 'It's always happening,' he said as he attempted to straighten it out. 'Don't worry. I'll mend it.'

'It's always happening?' I echoed.

'String's not strong enough, I suppose.' He was busy over the kite. Several people had gathered and were watching him as he worked, I noticed. It was not surprising; the thing was a work of art.

There was something strange here. 'But if the string's not strong enough why not use stronger string?'

He knelt up, looked at me with a bright but perplexed smile.

'That's what makes it so precious, don't you see? So beautiful, so fragile. It's ephemeral, like fireworks.' He shrugged. 'If I made it stronger, well – I can't explain.'

'Has it done this before?'

'All the time.'

'But, Edward...' I didn't know what to say, and for a moment we just stared at each other.

'You don't understand, do you?' He took up the broken kite. 'Well that's it for today.' As we got to our feet he glanced up. 'I say, shall we look round Kenwood House?' And then, 'Yes, do let's. There's someone I'd like you to meet.'

Behind us, at the top of the green slope, serene in the afternoon sunshine, stood Kenwood House, with its backdrop of trees, the perfect eighteenth-century country house. I had never been inside and so accepted his abrupt change of plan at once.

With the broken kite under his arm, Edward led me through the house (which is an art gallery) and did not pause until we were standing before a large painting.

'This is my favourite picture, my favourite in all the world. Meg, I should like you to meet Mary, Countess Howe. Your ladyship, this is Miss Meg Stephens. Curtsy to the countess, Meg.'

He turned to me with a teasing smile. Taken by surprise I stood for some time staring up at this large picture, which is painted lifesize and depicts an elegant lady in a summery pink eighteenth-century costume and straw hat. She has bright dark eyes and a small, confident smile on her lips. This is a woman completely at ease in her world, relaxed, gracious, and stepping forward to meet us.

I didn't know what to make of it. Since Edward thought highly of it, there must be something there but for the life of me I could not see it. Of course, in the simplest sense, it was a pleasant picture. But it offered no challenge; it was not dangerous in any way. It was completely conventional, inoffensive in the way a design of flowers on the lid of a box of chocolates is. In short, it contradicted everything I had learned about art until that moment.

Edward saw me hesitate. He leaned in a little, concentrating on me, and spoke quietly. 'Don't you like her? What's the matter?'

'Well...' I forced myself to answer. 'It's very nice, I suppose...'

'*Very nice?* Meg, it's beautiful!' He laughed, then checked himself. 'All right, you don't have to answer. I expect they teach you about the Impressionists and moderns – surrealism and all that. My dear – with respect – Sunday painters! Look at Cézanne, son of a rich banker! Of course he could afford to paint how he liked and to experiment. He didn't need to earn his living. But Gainsborough was serious. This was his livelihood. If Lady Howe didn't like her portrait his children would go to bed hungry.'

All this time I had been staring at the woman above me. In spite of what he said, I still saw an utterly conventional academic portrait. This was not what art was – not to me.

'Maybe Cézanne didn't need to earn his living. But surely that's the point! In his time academic painting had become empty. It was just an exercise in virtuosity – painting to please a wealthy patron. How could Gainsborough develop anything new when he was tied to his patrons? Cézanne *was* trying to do something new. That was important, surely? He changed the whole course of European painting. Gainsborough didn't change anything.'

There was a silence, and at last Edward drew a

long sigh. He looked perplexed. 'It's a beautiful picture,' he said at last, shaking his head, 'and you can't see it.'

'I can see it,' I replied. 'I agree it's beautiful. But that's all. I'm sure her ladyship was pleased with it and Gainsborough's children got their dinner.'

After this we wandered through the gallery looking at other paintings and ended in the tearoom. All the same, I could sense a breach had opened between us and wasn't sure how to heal it. I was also dimly aware that there was more to the question than I had realized; aware that Edward had a point, though what it was I couldn't see, just as I couldn't see what he meant about the kite. Looking back, I see now how priggish and conceited I must have sounded.

Edward didn't allow us to linger over art, however. As I poured the tea, he told me about his horse, which he rode to hounds, somewhere out in Hertfordshire. He said I ought to draw a picture of him on his horse since I was an artist. I shied at this; I had never drawn horses and would suffer untold agonies if put to the test. But I liked the idea of him on a horse. He told me he was in the Yeomanry and in the summer would go out on 'Field Days'. They spent two weeks under canvas somewhere on the Chilterns and would fight it out in mock battles over the wild open hilltops. This was all new to me. I knew nothing about the Yeomanry, scarcely even that they existed.

'Oh yes,' he said and leaned in. 'It's a cunning ploy, Meg – getting in on the ground floor.'

'What do you mean?'

'Well, look, the way things are going now, I mean, there's going to be war, isn't there?'

'Are you sure?'

'It's obvious. Unavoidable. Look at the way Hitler's been putting on the pressure – first the Rhineland, then the Saar plebiscite, then Austria, and now Czechoslovakia. He's a maniac, anyone can see it. The trouble is, people don't want to. Unpleasant memories of the last show, you see. But that isn't going to stop the next one. It's coming, as sure as sure.'

'And is that why you're in the Yeomanry?'

'Quite right. Once the show hots up everybody's going to be clamouring to get in. But the insiders will get all the plum jobs. See? So I plan to be on the inside. I don't want to end up in the catering corps or signals, Meg. I want to see action! And the moment the whistle goes, it'll be the Yeomanry who will be first off the mark.' He leaned back, smiling at his own cunning. 'That's the plan.'

This was all new to me. Of course I had watched the way Hitler had been moving, the build up of military power, and I knew too the agonizing arguments about how we should react. 'No more war!' was the cry for a long time. The first war had been the war to end all wars; it was indescribably painful for people to confront the rise of fascism. My parents, for example, as my uncle – my father's brother – had been killed in the first war. My father did not believe in the war. 'Hitler will cave in at the last minute, you'll see,' he would say, folding his *Telegraph* neatly as he settled to the crossword. 'He's a coward at heart. All bullies are cowards. He may be able to walk over the Czechs, but he'll have another think coming if he tries it on with us. The Germans got a thrashing in the last show. They'll be a bit more careful next time.'

My father deeply wanted to believe this and I think many other people did too. But Edward that afternoon knew better. He had the confidence of his youth and was scornful of the timidity of old men. He was not blinded by words and had read the signs rightly; besides, everybody else in the regiment thought the same. They had no illusions and when the time for action came, they would be ready.

I found all this intriguing and when Edward invited me to go out when they next had their field day, as a 'civilian observer', I was very happy to accept.

There was another reason why Edward was so keen to join the army, which I found out later.

That evening, after Edward had brought me home, my father enlightened me a little on his background. He knew Edward's father from the golf club, as he had already hinted.

'Self-made man, Tremayne,' he told me over dinner. 'Not exactly a gentleman; pulled himself up by his bootstraps. No background to speak of, no connections. Just started in the print, he told me, and little by little made himself what he is today. Shrewd feller. Back in thirty-two, when people were being flung out of work on all sides, he said to me, "Y'know what, ol' man? There'll always be a demand for printing, even if it's only to print out redundancy notices." There's nothing he doesn't know about the business – and he's not ashamed to get his fingers inky either. That's how you tell a man – when he knows every branch of the business inside out. He told me there's no task in the print shop he couldn't do himself if he came to it. Done very well for himself, too. Bit rough at the edges, perhaps, but good luck to him.' He gave me a long look. ''Course, Edward is taking over the business after him. I expect he's told you. Lucky feller. He'll be well set up. No shortage of money there. They have two servants, you know?' He glanced at my mother.

He said no more. He didn't need to. My mother smiled at me.

Seven

Reading through what I have written I realize I have not yet mentioned Heather Grey. I met her during my first year at St Martin's and she quickly became my best friend. Heather's parents were abroad and she had been at boarding school before coming to London. This gave her a freedom I envied. I have here a photo, taken when we were in St Tropez, shading her face from the sun beneath a wide straw hat. I can see now that she wasn't particularly beautiful, but you never thought of that; she was just very lively, very popular.

We met during my second term. I had seen her often already; she seemed always to be in a crowd of men, and all the most interesting men too, so I had been very envious of her. Living at home meant that I hadn't got to know the others very much at all, and I had already formed the impression that life for them didn't start until classes were over. They would drift off in groups talking among themselves as I made my lonely way to the tube.

I got to know Heather through another student, Andy, who'd smiled at me once or twice then got chatting at tea. So, that evening in March, for once I didn't go home, because Andy stopped by me and stood looking at the canvas. It was a still life.

'It's good,' he said.

I was so grateful for any approval that I couldn't help smiling up at him.

'I like Cézanne too,' he added.

'You can see the influence?' I asked carefully.

He nodded, then looked round and waved vaguely. 'We're just going round to the Coach and Horses. Are you coming?'

Suddenly everything was easy; I was in my painting smock, my fingers covered in paint, or I would have hugged him. I don't know why I had taken so long to break the ice; but suddenly it was broken, and with no effort at all. The pub was packed with students, most of whom I recognized, and Andy stood me a glass of beer.

We talked about Cézanne but soon the conversation was taken over by someone I had never seen before, a tall, willowy man with a black cape thrown back over his shoulders, a large floppy bow tie, thick horn-rimmed spectacles, and grasping a huge Sherlock Holmes pipe. He had an educated accent and a stutter.

'We have to m-make a stand!' he was saying.

'Are you proposing to beat him up personally?' someone asked.

'I shall make my p-presence felt.' There was laughter.

'Who's he?' I whispered to Andy.

'Ivor,' he whispered.

'Is he a student?'

'No.'

'What does he do?'

'No idea.'

'I think we should all go,' someone else said.

'Hear hear.' Several people joined in.

'Besides, I want to see Ivor stand up for his principles for once,' said a girl who turned out to be Heather. This was the first time I'd seen her close to.

'So you shall – if you have the st-stomach for it.' The willowy man turned on her. 'If we don't sp-speak out against fascism, who will?'

There was another laugh, but several men called, 'Hear hear!'

'All right, we'll meet at Whitechapel tube on Saturday at two.'

It turned out that Oswald Mosley was due to make a speech in the East End and they were proposing to go down and heckle him.

'Are you game?' Heather turned abruptly to me.

'Yes,' I said without thinking.

It was chilly so I put on a warm coat and beret. I told the parents I was going into town to meet a friend, and found quite a number of students at the underground station when I arrived. Andy was not there but Ivor was conspicuous in a cloak and a wide sombrero hat with his horn-rimmed specs and pipe. There were several other girls there too, including Heather. We moved together along Whitechapel High Street. It was a cold, bright Saturday afternoon and the market stalls ranged along the curb were beginning to pack up for the day. There were remnants of vegetables in the wet gutters, broken boxes and puddles of black water from recent rains. People hurried past us, a pub door swung open and I felt a sudden breath of stale beer and cigarette smoke. I had never been to Whitechapel before.

The Black Shirts had actually been banned a couple of years earlier so Mosley's men were no longer permitted to wear uniforms; this reduced his impact, I imagine. When we arrived, we heard music broadcast from a tinny and distorting speaker, and a large number of unhealthy-looking men were trying to appear imposing and ready for trouble, arms folded ostentatiously across their chests. Some were holding placards with legends like 'Britain Awake!' and 'Face up to the Jewish Threat!' with an evil caricature of a Jewish face, or 'Jewish Bolshevism – The Hidden Menace' with a sinister figure stealing from

77

the shadows.

Quite a large crowd was gathered. Then, after some whispered conversations between two or three men, one of them mounted the rostrum, which bore a thunderbolt motif and the legend 'British Union of Fascists', and began to speak. His job was to introduce Mosley, who I now noticed standing just behind him. He was of middle height, stocky, with a square face and small moustache. But there was something about his eyes, which became much more obvious when he got up to speak: a fixed stare, of manic intensity. I can only call it madness, and I wondered immediately who could possibly take him seriously. No one except the strutting mediocrities gathered round him.

Ivor did not take long to make his presence felt. 'You are a d-disgrace!' he called in his high, Oxford tones when Mosley was no more than five minutes into his speech. 'A disgrace to a civilized c-country!'

Heads turned and Mosley thrust out his arm. 'There!' he thundered. 'Hear that? The result of generations of inbreeding! That's exactly what I am saying! It's men like him, degenerates, that are dragging this country under!'

'You are t-talking nonsense!'

One or two of the others joined in, to back up Ivor. 'Get down! You should be ashamed of yourself!' Then I even heard myself calling, 'Down with Fascism!'

This was what Mosley had been waiting for. Several of his men pushed their way quickly through the crowd towards us, with very ugly looks. We glanced at each other; there was a crowd all round us so we couldn't move very easily. But the bully boys were thrusting people aside, looking businesslike, and concentrating on us. By now the crowd were shouting and beginning to push and jostle and Mosley was still shouting too, so the air was filled with a confused noise and no-one was quite sure what was happening. Two of these louts had grasped Ivor and were shaking him and one landed a fist in his face. But as he did so, one of us – Mike – had grabbed him by the neck from behind and was trying to bear him to the ground. People were pushing and shoving about us and it was very frightening. But I was so angry that they should have attacked Ivor, who was the least physical person I had ever met, that before I knew what I was doing I seized the other man by the hair – the one who was shaking Ivor – and tried to pull him away. As I did so, he released Ivor and swung his arm round with huge and unexpected violence and caught me across the cheek. It caused an explosion of pain on my face. I screamed out and staggered away and, as the crowd pushed and lurched about us, I found someone had me by the shoulders and was trying to get me out of the crowd. Soon there was someone else helping too and we pushed our way free.

It didn't last long; the police were already in the thick of it and breaking up the fighting. I stood on the pavement among some vegetable barrows, feeling very shaken, very quivery, and about to burst into tears. 'Has anybody got a mirror?' I remember asking, over and over. Then this girl, Heather, was in front of me.

'My God, you clocked it,' was all she said, and pulled a mirror from her shoulder bag.

Looking in it I saw there was a gash over my cheekbone. Heather took out a pocket handkerchief and began dabbing at it.

The other students were gathering about us. Ivor had lost his specs, and his cape, bedraggled with mud, was gathered over one arm. 'The b-brutes, they've broken my specs,' he protested as he rearranged his clothes. 'I c-can't see a b-blessed thing.'

Heather was still busy dabbing at my cheek as they gathered around us. 'What an absolute bloody unmitigated swine!' she shouted. 'Scum!'

I was vaguely aware now that things had broken up, that people were about us, talking excitedly.

'Meg's caught it. The swine! Fascist bastard swine!' She dabbed again. 'We'd better get you home and clean it up properly. It's stopped bleeding for the moment.'

I was still feeling very shaky and allowed myself to be led off among the others. We made our way down into the tube and eventually found ourselves back in Soho, not far from the college, in a narrow alley called Meard Street, off Dean Street. It was old and rickety, and very cheap. The flat was on the second floor and our steps echoed on the uncarpeted stairs as we clattered up to her two rooms.

Heather got me into a bathroom on the half floor at the back of the house, washed my face and put a sticking plaster over the cut. 'Should heal up all right, though a bruise is coming up too. He must have been wearing a ring, which has cut the skin,' she said as she worked. 'I must say it was bloody brave of you, Meg,' she went on laconically. 'I saw you grab that man's hair.'

I had recovered my nerve somewhat by now and we were joined by the others. Someone lit the fire (Heather kept coal in a cellar under the pavement), bottles of wine appeared, and someone else was cooking a spaghetti bolognaise. I was drinking red wine and with that and the after-effects of our fight, I became almost hysterical, but we were all laughing as we talked through our adventure of the afternoon. There must have been eight or nine of us sitting about the room. Heather had some rickety pieces of furniture – a battered sofa, an armchair, a deal table with several kitchen chairs. Her pictures were all over the walls: collages, after the manner of Braque. These were things I noticed later because I came back to her flat many times after this. But that evening the spaghetti was passed round, the glasses were refilled, and we talked. We talked and talked, until I suddenly realized I would have to leave if I were to get home before eleven o'clock.

Sitting in the quiet, sleepy tube, I was still riding on the elation of our experience, still fired by that intoxicating mixture of adrenalin and cheap Italian wine.

My parents were waiting. Seeing them, it came to me that I had been out since half past twelve. The second they saw me, my mother sprang forward.

'Margaret! What have you done?'

They dragged me into the sitting room.

'We were worried sick! Where on earth have you been? And whatever have you done to yourself? Have you been attacked?'

'Sort of,' I murmured and smiled, suddenly sleepy.

'We very nearly went to the police,' my father said.

'Why? I was all right.'

'You don't look it. What *have* you been up to?'

My mother was anxiously examining my face. I realized I would have to explain. But then, being at home, I understood how it was going to seem to them. There was no explanation I could give that would make sense. My father was very angry.

'You have been extremely foolish,' was all he said.

After our mix up with Sir Oswald Mosley, I was always in and out of Heather's flat. After the empty suburban streets of Mill Hill it was bliss to dive into Soho and wrap it round oneself like a blanket. How lovely to call in at the French Patisserie at eleven in the morning, buy a couple of *pains au chocolat* and go back with Heather, make coffee, and talk. We didn't have much money, which was why I used to bring sandwiches for my lunch.

One day early in the summer term, a couple of months after our encounter with Sir Oswald Mosley, at the end of the morning's class as the others were all leaving, Heather noticed me settling down to read a book. My face had healed up by now though there was that very faint scar, quite small, where the skin had been cut against the bone.

'Aren't you coming for lunch?'

'No,' I called, without looking up, 'you go on.'

She came across and stood examining me. 'I always thought of you as having plenty of money,' she said in her laconic way. 'Nice, well-brought-up middle-class girl.'

'Not so much, it seems.'

'Well, bring them round to the flat anyway, and I'll make some coffee. I'm not much of a one for lunch.'

Sitting in her front room, looking down into Meard Street, now mercifully quiet, I opened my lunch.

'Mummy make the sandwiches?' Heather inquired ironically as she was making the coffee.

'I'm saving up,' I said simply. 'I need every penny I can get.'

'Saving – what for?'

'To go to the South of France.'

'Really?'

'There's going to be a war soon. Everybody can see it. I may not get another chance. We don't know what's going to happen, do we?'

'Where are you going to stay?'

'I expect I'll find somewhere when I get there.'

'Phew.' Heather put down the kettle on the blackened old gas cooker, and stared out of the grimy back window. 'What a whiz idea.'

'Heather, I shall burst if I don't go to Provence! I simply must get there! Supposing war breaks out. I may never go! I may be middle-aged before the war's over – I may be dead! We haven't the faintest idea how things are going to turn out.'

'Are you going alone?'

'If necessary.'

'What does Daddy say?'

I paused. 'I haven't told him – yet. It doesn't matter anyway. It's my own money.'

She carried the coffee into her little sitting room. By day, its ragged scruffiness was revealed in a glaring light. The fire was cold, a saucer stood on the mantelpiece filled with cigarette ends. Cups with the remains of cold coffee stood on the dirty carpet beside the chairs. A bit of faded curtain had been drawn back from the window, which was open this morning in a rare day of warmth, a hint of approaching spring. We could hear the footsteps on the pavement below and voices sometimes. Occasionally there was a whiff of rotting fish.

'It's Mrs Starr; she lives in the basement. She puts out bits of cooked fish for her cats, and we get every cat within a mile radius round here for a free meal.'

Indeed, every time I arrived at the door, these animals were sitting on the step, or circling each other warily and occasionally erupting into a screeching match that would quickly be over, as one or the other fled down the street.

I'd stay more and more often in the evenings, too. My parents disliked this. There had been a

84

growing tension between us since the day of the Mosley rally, which had come as a nasty shock to them. It was not what they had had in mind when I had proposed going to art school. They could sense I wanted more freedom too and were intent on resisting me. They knew that I could not afford to move out. My father knew too that he had the power to remove me from the college. We both understood.

It was during one of our suppers together that Heather suggested I move in with her.

'Heather, it would be my idea of heaven, but my parents would never stand it.'

Heather told me a bit more about herself. Her father worked for a tea company and he and her mother lived in Ceylon. Heather had gone out to live with them after boarding school, but after two years she persuaded them to let her come back to England and enrol at the college.

Then one morning in a painting class Heather asked if she could join me in my trip to the South of France. I jumped at the idea, we discussed it animatedly for the rest of the morning, and by the time I went home that evening I was ready to put the plan to my parents.

They were flat against it.

'An unescorted young girl all that way from home? My God, anything might happen!'

'I won't be alone, Father! Heather's coming.'

'She's even more scatter-brained than you! And a sight too free and easy. You'd be bound to get into some scrape – or worse. I won't hear of it!'

'That's absurd. I'm nearly twenty.'

'Exactly. And until you're twenty-one, you'll do as you're told.'

My father's opposition only strengthened my determination to go. But it would need a bit of thinking out.

Eight

I was invited to dinner with Edward's parents.

I had made myself a long evening dress for this occasion, crouching over the sewing machine in the front room, my mother assisting. In fact, after I had finished, she could not resist taking it to pieces again and adjusting it in one or two places. As I was getting ready, I studied the little scar on my cheek in the bathroom mirror. With powder it nearly disappeared. I put on lipstick.

As far as my parents were concerned, Edward was the only thing in my favour at that moment. So long as I was still going out with him, they felt reassured.

And Edward in dinner jacket and bow tie looked very attractive; I must say he wore evening dress very naturally and comfortably. Father offered him a glass of sherry before we set off; Edward lit a cigarette and offered me one too. My father had never seen me smoke but Edward was looking relaxed and elegant, and I, in a long dress and make-up, felt old enough to please myself. Father said nothing – he couldn't in front of Edward – though I knew I'd hear about it afterwards.

On the way to his house Edward at last mentioned my scar. I had never spoken of it and he had never noticed until this evening.

I told him about Sir Oswald Mosley. He was very impressed.

'My God, you didn't! Really? Meg, you got into a fight? By Jove, what a story to tell your grandchildren!' He burst out laughing. Then he changed his tune. 'By the way, I shouldn't mention it to the parents.'

'Why?'

'Well...' He was suddenly embarrassed. 'To tell the truth, Meg, something I'm not too proud of, I'll be honest.'

'What?'

'My father...' He coughed. 'To tell the truth – well, the truth is – he thinks rather highly of Mosley.'

There was a silence. At last I said, quietly, 'Tell me you're joking.'

'Wish I were.' He stared gloomily ahead.

There was another long silence. At last I breathed, 'Strewth. I can't imagine it. Do you have rows with him about it?'

'Not exactly. He rants about the Communists and the Bolsheviks and all that rot. I just keep quiet.' There was another silence. 'So it'd be probably be best to steer clear of all that. I mean – if he asks you about the scar...' His voice trailed off.

I really didn't know what to make of this. There were a hundred questions buzzing in my brain. At last I said, tentatively, 'Have you thought of leaving home?'

'All the time.'

Another pause until I forced the conversation on. 'Well, why don't you?'

'To tell the truth, Meg, it would be difficult.' He paused. 'You see, with me working at the firm, my father pays my wages. And – well, he doesn't pay very much, since I live at home, and when I mention it he says the money all goes back into the firm, times are hard just now, and it's all going to be mine one day and what would I do with it anyway...' He paused, drew a breath and went on, trying to sound more cheerful. 'To tell the truth, it does have its advantages.'

'What does?'

'Living at home.'

'Such as?'

'Well – you know – Mum does the cooking, I have my own room. What would I want with a flat anyway? Deuced bore having to go shopping and cooking and washing my own clothes – see what I mean?'

Nothing more was said. I was still trying to take all this in. In spite of everything he had said I did find it extremely odd that a man of twenty-three was still living at home – especially in view of what he had just told me about his father.

We turned into the drive of a large, comfortable house set well back from the road behind laurels and with a gravelled drive. As we stood on the doorstep he turned and whispered, 'Don't forget about the scar.'

I understood, though privately I wasn't sure I

would able to keep quiet if it were mentioned. A moment later the door was opened by a maid in black with a white doily in her hair. Then I was introduced to Mr Tremayne. I had been prepared for the worst, but as a matter of fact I found him attractive. He was a heavy, solid man with an imposing, forthright manner. If he was not exactly a gentleman, as my father had said, that certainly didn't bother me. He was dressed like Edward in a dinner jacket, bow tie and wing collar but, as he took my hand, his own felt strong and fleshy – a man not afraid of hard work, I could tell, though greedy perhaps and fond of pleasure. In love with life, to put it bluntly, and very different from his aesthete son. He held my hand a long minute as he looked deep into my eyes and seemed to be sizing me up, inspecting me carefully; under other circumstances I realized he would not have hesitated to flirt with me. His wife had disappeared to the kitchen whence I could hear preparations. We were standing in a spacious drawing room, a comfortable room decorated with taste and, glancing round it, I could see why Edward might be reluctant to move into bachelor quarters.

Mrs Tremayne reappeared as her husband handed round glasses of sherry. 'Eddy was telling me you are planning a trip to the South of France?' she said pleasantly.

'That's right. A painting trip. I'm very anxious to go soon – in case the situation gets any worse.' I was aware of Edward smiling wickedly. 'I'm particularly fond of Cézanne and want to see the places he painted.'

'Sunday painter!' Edward murmured and flicked a glance to his mother; I could see there was a very close relationship between them.

'Edward doesn't believe in the Impressionists,' I explained with a smile. 'He doesn't believe in anyone after Gainsborough.'

'Oh, I've nothing against them,' he explained airily. 'It's just that I don't take them seriously. As I have already explained.'

As we talked my gaze was gradually fastening on a group of framed pictures on the wall and a little later I remarked on them to Mrs Tremayne.

'Eddy and I bought them together at auction. They're Heath Robinson.' We both moved to take a closer look. They were delicate drawings – from the turn of the century, I imagined – fairy scenes. I didn't know what to say. 'They're very pretty.'

'Do you like them? I'm so glad. Eddy has exquisite taste.'

'Oh, he chose them?'

'Of course. Let me show you some others he found. Come.'

She led me into the hall where other prints hung framed.

'He chose those too. Dulac.'

I studied them.

'Has he told you about his books?'

I shook my head.

'Eddy has a collection of illustrated books. He is quite a connoisseur. It's an interest he shares with his father, though Bob is more interested in them from the technical side, as you can imagine.'

Edward, who had been hovering behind us, turned to a glass-fronted bookcase, unlocked it and took out a huge leather-bound volume.

'Wagner's *Ring*, illustrated by Arthur Rackham. Just the first volume, you understand: *The Rhinegold*. First edition, Morocco binding.'

Holding it, he opened it reverently to an engraving protected by a sheet of tissue paper. 'Look at that,' he said. It was a picture of three naked mermaids diving through the water. 'The Rhine maidens,' he breathed. 'Superb.'

His father took the book casually out of Edward's hands. He turned it over in his hands, looking at the spine, examining the end papers, running his hands over the leather surface, treating the book very much as a precious object. Finally he shook his head. 'They don't make 'em like this any more. Look at the marbled end papers. Feel that paper, Meg – take it.' He placed the heavy book in my hands. 'Real rag paper. That'll last a thousand years and be as white as the day it was made. And the binding – hand-bound – see the way the book just falls open? That's an art.' He shook his head. 'Trouble is, no money in 'em. Books like that have been priced out of existence.' He passed the book to Edward who replaced it reverently in the cabinet.

Soon afterwards dinner was announced and we went into the dining room. The cutlery was set out on a polished mahogany table and the light from the candles in silver candle sticks glinted in the three different wine glasses at each place setting. A vase of flowers stood in the centre of the table. Here for the first time I caught a strong whiff of *arrivisme*; Mr Tremayne was out to impress. He also liked his wine. That was all right by me: so did I. However, I was becoming more and more aware of Edward's somewhat subdued manner in his father's presence and it provoked a mood of rebellion in me. He might tyrannize his son but he wasn't going to tyrannize *me*. I could tell he hadn't decided yet what to make of me, and was biding his time.

'You're at art school, Eddy tells me,' he said as the maid ladled out the soup. I was seated on his right-hand side, opposite Edward. Mrs Tremayne sat to my right.

'Yes, at St Martin's.'

'Ah yes.' He attacked the soup, then carried on talking. 'Never was at college myself. Went straight into the print, served my apprenticeship. Seven years in the university of life. By the time I was twenty-one I knew pretty much all there was to know about printing. Solid grounding, never goes out of date. I was set up for life. No substitute for getting your hands on the tools, you know. And you can't start too soon. What branch?'

I was taken by surprise for a moment. 'Oh, fine art.'

He grunted. 'And no doubt they fill you with a lot of useless fiddle-faddle notions, eh? Picasso, all that?'

'We do study Picasso, yes,' I replied politely, 'but most of the time we learn to paint.'

He shook his head wisely. 'Well, it'll do you no harm, I dare say. You'll soon have other

92

things on your mind, eh?' He smiled roguishly.

'The war? That's true,' I said quietly.

'Oh no, not the war.'

'I don't understand.'

'You will, you will, soon enough.' He laughed expansively, greatly amused by his own wit. I glanced across at Edward, who was looking uncomfortable, and suddenly felt sorry for him. It was time to change the subject.

'Edward was telling me about the Yeomanry and the field day in June,' I said brightly. 'I'm looking forward very much to it.'

Mr Tremayne's face clouded instantly. 'Oh yes.' He coughed brusquely.

I detected the tone of disapproval but pushed on. 'Edward was telling me how it would help him to get into the regular army once the war breaks out.'

'The war hasn't broken out yet,' said his father savagely, 'and, if you want my opinion, it isn't going to.'

I was taken aback by his vehemence. 'But surely—'

'It's all a lot of gossip and he should know better than to spread rumours. It's all damn nonsense!'

We had finished our soup and the maid came to clear away the plates. Mrs Tremayne took the opportunity to change the subject. 'Eddy was telling me about your own painting,' she began.

I murmured something suitably demure. On one visit to our house I had shown him some drawings and paintings I had done and which he had criticized with intelligence and considerable perception, I thought.

A piece of beef now made its appearance and, as the head of the household carved it with a huge carving knife, Edward poured claret from a decanter that had been standing on a sideboard. His father was distracted from his carving.

'Take your time with that, Eddy, and watch for the lees, for God's sake. How many times have I had to tell you!' Edward almost froze with concentration as he continued to pour. His father glanced at me. 'It's a Montrachet '27. I'd be surprised if you've tasted a wine like that before – or will again in a hurry.'

He carved with this huge knife a few inches from my nose as I sipped the wine. It tasted slightly sour.

For a moment there was silence as vegetables were served by the maid. Mr Tremayne sipped his wine. He looked up suspiciously, then sniffed it. 'Hmm, damn me – the cork's got at it!' he muttered. He sipped again, frowning, then stood up suddenly, throwing down his napkin. 'Damn wine's corked!' he roared. 'Confound it! That's another one! Here, give me your glass!'

I handed him the glass and he poured the wine back into the decanter. The others did the same. Then Mr Tremayne stormed out of the room, and I just heard him shouting, 'I'll have a word to say to that fool of a wine merchant!'

There was an awkward silence until a moment later he returned with another bottle, stooped to open it at the sideboard, and returned to the table in a black mood. 'It won't have had time to breathe, confound it. Well, no matter...' He poured wine into our glasses from the bottle and sat down again at the table.

After this little eruption we began again on our roast beef. However, it was clear that the war was on his mind, because after he had attacked his meat for a moment and taken a mouthful or two of the wine, he began again.

'There's no need for a war. None. We can do business with the Germans any day of the week. What's the point of it? They don't want it, neither do we. It's simply a question of trust. Any fool can see it. What we need, what Chamberlain should have done last November, is to agree a common front against the Russians. There's where the danger lies. But – ' he sighed – 'the man's a fool.'

'Who, Hitler?' I couldn't help asking.

He turned on me as if he'd been shot. '*No!* Chamberlain of course!' He set down his knife and fork. 'You see, Meg,' he began learnedly, 'Hitler is a man who has been greatly misunderstood in this country. Greatly. That man has single-handedly saved his country. Pulled her up by the bootstraps, set her on her own feet again. The German people have good reason to love their Führer.' He watched me carefully to see whether I agreed with him. This was obviously some kind of test. 'That man,' he went on heavily, 'has done more for the German people than any other in history.' He nodded sagely. 'The only pity is that there are so few in this country who appreciate him.'

'Other than Sir Oswald Mosley, you mean?' I said lightly. I could see Edward watching me carefully, but I felt driven on.

'That's right.' He pounced on me. The other two were watching in frozen concentration, all pretence of eating flown. I took a sip of wine.

'I heard him speak once,' I continued. I felt sorry for Edward, but I couldn't allow this to pass.

'Lucky girl. That was an experience, I bet.'

'As a matter of fact, I thought he was mad.'

There was a long silence. At last he repeated, uncertainly, 'Mad?'

'Yes,' I said quietly, looking at my wine glass. My heart was hammering in my chest, but I was certainly not going to give in on this one.

'*Mad?*' he repeated, his voice rising a note. 'Edward – did you know about this?'

Edward, suddenly caught in the crossfire, coughed. 'Well, we did discuss it once, yes...'

'You did discuss it?' his father went on in frank disbelief. He turned back to me. 'Do you realize, young lady, that the entire future of Europe may depend on our making a treaty with Herr Hitler? This is not the time for flippancy. It is not a laughing matter!' He drew a breath and leaned back. 'This, I suppose, is the sort of thing you discuss at art school, is it? A lot of communists, eh? Conchies, nancy boys, perverts? Eh?'

'Bob...' Mrs Tremayne pleaded weakly from my right.

There was another tense moment as I looked down at my plate and I was aware of Edward watching me. At last, unsure of my voice, I said quietly, 'I'm not sure about the nancy boys and the perverts but there are a few communists,

96

yes.'

He thumped his big hand on the table so that the silver rattled. 'I don't believe it! And in my own house.'

'Bob...'

There was now a very long silence as we all stared at our plates.

'Eddy...' The father turned magisterially to his son. 'What exactly did you mean by this?'

'Please don't blame your son, Mr Tremayne,' I interrupted quickly. 'He is not responsible for my opinions.'

'I damn well hope he isn't. Of all the confounded—'

'Perhaps it would be easiest if I went home now,' I said, standing.

'Yes.' He was staring into space, his face rigid. 'I rather think it would.'

'Dad!' Edward pushed his chair back from the table with a rattle.

'I think you had better take your friend home, Eddy.'

'Oh, *Bob*!' Mrs Tremayne cried, and burst into tears.

'Please don't worry, Mrs Tremayne.' I was feeling slightly dizzy but my head was cool. 'I am sorry to have caused this unpleasantness. It's all right, Edward, I can easily...'

Edward had already risen and came round to me as I made for the door. His father remained at the table staring at his plate.

'What are you talking about?' he hissed. 'Of course I'll take you home. I'm so very, very...'

He didn't finish his sentence as he helped me

on with my jacket. His mother was behind him and took me by the hands, her face flushed with tears. 'What must you think?' She was incoherent. 'Oh my dear, I am so glad to have met you. And I do, do apologize for ... I could kill him! Eddy, take care of Meg. I do so hope we can meet again. It's been a pleasure. Oh! I could kill him!' she repeated.

In the car we were silent at first. I did not know what to say and I thought Edward must be furious with me. He had, after all, asked me specifically not to bring Oswald Mosley into the conversation and must be wishing he had never set eyes on me. At the same time I was still reeling from my confrontation with his father.

'Phew,' I murmured after some time. 'I don't know how you stand it.'

Abruptly he swerved to the side of the road and brought the car to a standstill.

He sat staring forward as I watched and waited. At last he suddenly slammed his hand down on the steering wheel. 'Now you know why I want to get into the army!' he cried, and in those words, desperate, terrible, he seemed to compress all the frustrated anger of the evening. Instantly I felt a great wave of tenderness towards him. I reached a hand to his arm. He turned to me in the semi-darkness and I could just make out his face.

'You can't imagine what it's like. Well...' He drew a long breath. 'I suppose you can now.'

'Poor Edward,' I murmured. 'Why do you stick it?'

He drew another gargantuan breath. 'Oh – because of Mum partly.'

I felt so sorry for him just then, and as his head seemed to droop towards me, we found ourselves, quite naturally, subsiding into a kiss. It was a long, languorous kiss, full of tenderness; a healing and comforting kiss, and I could feel his body relaxing, the tension floating away.

'Thanks,' he murmured, staring into my eyes as we parted. 'I don't know...'

'What?'

'I don't know what I'd do without you,' he said very simply. And then, when we were outside my house, he said, 'Meg, you will still come to the field day, won't you?'

Of course I said I would. He took my hand and held it a long time. I was acutely aware of the strength of his feelings as, at last, he raised my hand to his lips and kissed it gently, almost reverently.

'Thanks,' he whispered.

Nine

That evening threw a shadow over relations between Edward and me. Whatever we did, whether a trip to the theatre or an art gallery, his father now seemed to hover over us. He coloured our conversations. Whatever Edward said, I was conscious of what his father might

99

say, and how – or whether – Edward would have said it in his father's presence.

He was embarrassed by it too, I was aware, and this inhibited me from raising the subject. Edward was a sensitive soul, and I didn't want to hurt his feelings. I might be outspoken in his father's presence because I had seen instantly that he could take it. Edward was different. The result was that he now seemed slightly to over-act; a note of false jollity crept into his behaviour more and more. Even so, though we studiously avoided mentioning his father or the dinner, on one occasion, inevitably, it did come up. We were wandering through the National Gallery. Edward was, as I had long since discovered, an intelligent and knowledgeable critic and I learned a lot from him. On this occasion we were standing before the Rembrandts.

'Why don't you simply chuck the firm?'

It came out without my really thinking. I could see however that I had said the wrong thing. His face clouded and his tall, thin body seemed to sag. He stared down for a long time. He looked so miserable that I was about to apologize and try to cover over my faux pas. Then, without looking up, he said, 'My father expects me to take over the firm. That's the whole point. It's what he's been building towards all his life. I don't think I could walk away from it.'

'Do you enjoy the work?'

He shrugged. 'Moderately. It's a job. It's steady. It's reliable. There's quite a lot of money in it – you've seen for yourself we do pretty well.' He drew a breath. 'Anyway, I've never done anything else.'

'No.'

Finally he brightened. 'In any case it looks as if the decision will be made for me.'

'The army?'

'Mm.'

We changed the subject. But as Edward talked about Rembrandt the conversation ran through my mind. I felt deeply sorry for Edward. For any other young man, the answer would be simply to put as much distance between himself and his father as he could; in his case the firm chained them together. Or seemed to. I couldn't help wondering whether another young man, less sensitive, more wilful, might have seized hold of his own life and fashioned it in the image of his own choosing, instead of having it made for him. Edward's interest in art, his collection of prints and drawings, his prize volumes, were all consolation prizes for a fundamental failure of will. Deep down, though I didn't spell it out to myself then, I was disappointed in him.

It has to be said, Heather did throw wild parties. I know that young people in every generation believe their parties are the best ever and that poor old fogies twice their age never knew how to enjoy themselves. I know all that. Still, I remain convinced that we alone had the secret.

It was summer by this time, which is the best time to have parties – they tended to spill out on to the pavement or we might climb out on to the bit of roof outside Heather's kitchen window. You can wear fewer and thinner clothes, too. The party was in fancy dress, which as any ex-art student can tell you is a wonderful excuse, and that night I was in a flapper dress with layer upon layer of long black fringes, which I had bought in Petticoat Lane when Heather and I had gone foraging for old clothes one Sunday. Others were similarly dressed but Heather, having instructed everyone to come as gypsies or pirates or cowboys, took it into her head to be the pinnacle of elegance in an ankle-length gown with no back to it, in a soft fabric which clung to her and emphasized the contours of her body, especially as she appeared to wear nothing underneath.

Another man who eschewed fancy dress was Ivor – or 'the bishop' as we had started calling him since we discovered his father was one. Ivor had an allowance from his father and lived in a room not far from Heather's. Fancy dress was not for him for the simple reason – pointed out by Victor Ridmore – that he wore permanent fancy dress anyway.

Victor was someone else I had got to know at Heather's. He was a student at the college whom I had noticed soon after I arrived. He did not wear fancy dress either; no one could imagine Victor in fancy dress, partly because he was too poor, and partly because he was so serious about his work. Unlike most students, he did not regard being a student as an excuse to have a good time. Victor had enrolled at the college to paint; it was all he ever did and everyone recognized that he was going to succeed as a painter. There was a strange relationship between him and Ivor. Not sexual (neither of them seemed to have much interest in women – or men, either, I might add) but in their different ways they were dedicated, lived solitary, single lives, and seemed to put all their life into their work.

It was well known too that Ivor subsidized Victor; he was quite open and relaxed about this.

'Pr-property is theft,' he said as he lit his cavernous Sherlock Holmes pipe.

'Are you accusing your right reverend father of being a thief, Ivor?' someone said. 'That's sacrilege.'

'Indirectly, yes.'

'But you're happy to go on living off him?'

'For the time b-being, I have no alternative. After the revolution, of course property will be r-redistributed. In the meantime I do wh-what I can.'

I turned to Victor. 'And you don't mind living off Ivor, do you, Victor?'

'No I don't,' he said in his blunt way. Up to this moment he hadn't said anything and had been steadily drinking. No one had an answer for this but, after a pause, he went on, 'I don't mind who I live off. It doesn't matter where the money comes from. I don't care about that; I would live off him all my life if necessary. All that matters is the work. That's why I'm different from you layabouts. I mean, what are you? Dilettantes. Look at you, Meg. Imitation Cézannes. You've never seen an olive tree in your life. You copy – just like you copy life. You've never felt that heat on your neck, never got that red earth under your fingernails.' He paused and took a mouthful of wine, then went on, steady, unstoppable. 'But it's more than that. You've never experienced a great emotion. Until you do, you'll continue to do shallow derivative work: genteel, amateur lady-painter stuff.'

Before I could think up an answer sufficiently robust, attention was distracted by Ivor leaning out of the window.

We had been clustered by the front window, enjoying the warm soft summer night air. Below us in the narrow street several prostitutes were standing, one leaning against the railings, another further up on the corner keeping an eye open for the police.

Ivor had had a few drinks. 'Ladies!'

We took hold of him to stop him falling, as he waved his pipe.

'Ladies! It is sh-shameful, degrading to human dignity that you should have to s-sell yourselves to satisfy the brute lusts of the b-b-bourgeoisie! Rise up! Throw off the chains of your oppressors! Refuse to lie down beneath capitalist expl-pl-ploitation!'

'Ivor!' We were bursting with giggles as we tried to pull him in again.

The speech had attracted their attention however and two or three shouted back.

'Hark at 'im – *don't lie down*?' And they screamed in raucous laughter, 'Get yer 'air cut! Tosser!'

But though the party continued until the small hours, Victor's words had stuck in my mind; I had been stung. He didn't know that the thing I hungered after was precisely to feel the sun on

104

the back of my neck, precisely to get that red earth beneath my fingernails. That was what I wanted above all. Also I felt with peculiar intensity his reference to the lack of a great emotion. I was sure everybody in the room looked at me pityingly as he said it – a pathetic virgin, hopelessly ignorant of *real life*. Hadn't he understood that it was what I was seeking above all? To seek extremity in any form, to dare, to fly, to climb mountains, sail the oceans, feel spray on my face, the heaving of the deck beneath my feet? To encounter the strange, the unusual, to grasp the vast complexity of life, to look into canyons, to scale mountains – oh I needed to *breathe*!

But how could I explain that to Victor in the middle of the party, with people around in drunken giggles over Ivor's antics? In any case, at the moment it didn't look as if I were ever going to make it to France.

Later, however, as I was about to drag myself away to share a lift to Mill Hill – it must have been half past three – Heather found me.

'I say, Meg, I meant to tell you I've got a plan.'
'Yes?'
'For France. I've been speaking to brother Jack, who just *happens* to be in London, and just *happens* to be going to Paris in June.'

I didn't understand.

'Don't you see? We can tell your father my brother is escorting us! Problem solved.'

'You said he's going to Paris.'

'Don't be so literal! We go to Paris together, then Jack can pop off to do whatever he wants to do and we carry on to the jolly old Côte d'Azur.'

I kissed her. 'Heather, you are without doubt an angel.'

Heather, who had met my parents once or twice, was invited for tea and the plan was explained. My father grudgingly agreed to it, especially when Heather told him that her brother was in the diplomatic service. He was – or rather had been, she told me afterwards – a part-time consul in Ceylon for a couple of years while he worked for his father.

In the middle of June Edward went on manoeuvres – or 'in camp' as he put it – with his regiment. I went with his mother as 'civilian observers'.

Edward had arranged for a car to carry us up on to the Chilterns. His father was not coming. Mrs Tremayne was already in the car and as I got in there was a moment's silence before she turned to me.

'Meg, I am so glad you are coming today. Eddy has been looking forward to it so much, and I know he would have been disappointed after – you know...'

'I hope neither you nor Edward were caused too much embarrassment after I had left,' I said quietly. 'Edward had warned me what to expect.'

'Oh no—'

'I felt so guilty afterwards that I had ruined the dinner.'

'Not at all. It was not you, I assure you. My husband can be intolerable sometimes.'

There was silence between us. She took my hand and gave it a squeeze. 'We won't talk any more about it,' she said with a smile.

Luckily it was a gorgeous summer day, clear sky and hot sun, and we could wear light clothes. Somewhere I could hear a skylark, and we stood, high up on the grassy slope looking away across mile upon mile of fields golden with ripening barley and wheat, broken by clusters of woodland and could just make out somewhere far off the grey outline of London. Over it, as the vista spread away into the distance, a faint summer haze gradually thickened. A light breeze moved the gorse bushes near us, splashed with yellow in summer.

The regiment was under canvas – bell tents arranged in precise order, white shapes against the vivid green of the downland turf – and three or four marquees, which I soon found out were the officers' mess and regimental HQ. Soldiers were everywhere, orders were being shouted, officers were on horseback, and then after we had waited some time, and been shepherded to a viewing point together with a crowd of other visitors by a polite subaltern, Edward appeared on his horse. My heart skipped a beat. The horse was a gleaming chestnut with a white spot on her forehead and Edward looked very high up. He was dressed immaculately in khaki, with polished brown boots and belt. Clearly everything had been made ready for the event of the year. He seemed a knight of old and looked so gorgeous I could have eaten him, and I could see he was having the same effect on his mother too. Best of all, or perhaps because he was aware of this, he adopted a modest and relaxed air, saluted us, and explained the programme for the day.

Northland were fighting Southland, he said. He waved into the distance across the undulating downs, the clusters of gorse bright with gold, the combes and clumps of trees in the hollows. Then he was called away and with a glint of spur and a jingle of bridle, he cantered off to where a pow-wow of officers was clustered on horseback and soon after they set off together and disappeared over a brow of the downs.

We waited. I suppose I vaguely expected something like one of those old battle paintings, or perhaps something from the films – Errol Flynn in the charge of the light brigade – massed ranks, the thunder of cannon, men falling bravely from their saddles.

In the meantime Ellen was telling me how much Eddy had been looking forward to this, how he had prepared for it. The pressing of his uniform, the polishing of his belt and boots – though while in camp he had a batman, she assured me. Ellen and I waited for the battle to begin.

Eventually the subaltern who was in charge of us, and who had been looking anxiously at his watch for the last five minutes, announced that battle was about to be joined. C and D Squadron, representing Northland, were stationed away to our left in a clump of trees; A and B Squadron, representing Southland, would be coming from our right and would endeavour to effect a surprise attack.

Another glance at his watch. 'And now here they come!'

A frantic bugle voluntary was repeated over and over, hoarse cries and shouts and several dozen men came running in a ragged line across the turf in the direction of the woods. Several officers on horseback were with them. At the same time there was a crackling, popping noise and puffs of white smoke appeared here and there. Meanwhile several men were now appearing from the woods, rifles were levelled, the air was thick with this crackling, popping sound, bugle rallies, and confused shouts – orders, curses, oaths too, I'm afraid. A horseman galloped nearby. The fight retreated into the woods, though we could hear the confused sounds emanating in random bursts. It seemed very confused.

Then things went quiet. People were asking the subaltern what was happening now and to his embarrassment he did not seem to know.

Once we heard a whistle, and briefly some men reappeared in the distance on the opposite side of the combe among the trees, ran a little way, and then disappeared again. Later two men were seen galloping across the green turf in the distance. We waited and talked, and talked and waited. Ellen could talk only of Edward, which I understood, but as the day dragged on it became repetitive. His school days, his cough (which had now cleared up), his car (which she wished he wouldn't drive so fast). I realize now that

Ellen, beneath this patter, was sizing me up as a potential daughter-in-law.

A man appeared from the woods leading a horse and as he passed us, cursing under his breath, I caught the words, 'Bloody girth strap broke.'

Lunch came. The men reappeared, the officers on their horses, and we were shepherded into the mess tent for sandwiches and white wine. We were desperate to sit down by this time. Edward was nowhere to be seen.

During the afternoon there was another exercise and the men all put on gas masks and capes which gave the event a surreal air.

Around four a cup of tea was brought to us by an orderly, and as we were drinking it we heard shouts, men were running and, over the brow of the down, a cluster of soldiers were hurrying towards us carrying something, and another leading a horse. *At last*, I thought with relief, *something's actually happened.* As they came nearer I could see they were carrying a man. Someone had been wounded! But then as we went forward, another officer came up. He looked very serious. 'I'm afraid there's been an accident.'

Ellen started forward. 'Where is he?' She clutched his arm.

'If you'd come this way...'

The two of us hurried with him into a marquee tent, set aside for first aid. A number of soldiers were fussing about a camp bed, and we found Edward lying on his back. As we were approaching he cried out in pain and his mother darted forward. 'Eddy!'

The officer restrained her. 'The doctor's examining him, Mrs Tremayne,' he said quietly. 'He came off his horse and hurt his leg.'

I took Ellen's arm, to try and soothe her, and a few moments later the doctor got to his feet.

'Bring up the ambulance.'

Ellen broke free from us.

'Doctor, what's happened?'

He noticed her and turned towards us. 'Lieutenant Tremayne took a fall and I'm afraid he's broken his leg. We're getting him into hospital right away.'

'Will he be all right?'

He frowned. 'Too early to say. We'll do our best.'

She broke through the men surrounding the camp bed and knelt quickly by her son. I was behind her.

'Eddy darling, are you in pain?'

He turned his head as he saw her; he was frowning. 'Mum, you shouldn't be here.' He winced.

'Eddy darling, don't worry, they're bringing the ambulance.'

Edward now noticed me standing behind Ellen. 'Seem to have broken a leg, old thing.' He winced again, then smiled. 'Pity. It was my favourite leg, too.'

Ten

Looking back over what I have just written I remember now that it was at this time of year that Edward was in camp, and had his accident.

They carried him to an army hospital in west London, and the following day I went to visit him. He was on a bed with his leg in plaster and hoisted on a canvas sling. He looked very brave and very pathetic and quite charming and he drew from me all my motherly instincts (which, until that instant, I did not know I possessed). At first he made flippant remarks, determined to show that he was keeping up a brave face. I understood that, and sometimes wished he wouldn't. But I could soon see how frustrated he must feel.

'It's coming soon, Meg,' he said on one occasion.

'What's coming, Edward?'

'Well – you know – there's got to be a show-down soon, you can just feel it. Every single time the government's been nice to Hitler, he's just upped the ante. He takes what he wants. They're old, that's their trouble. Don't want to face reality.'

He paused, then frowned.

'What is it?' I asked.

'Oh nothing – just the blasted leg – it itches you know and I can't scratch; drives me mad sometimes.' Then it came out. 'The thing is – suppose the balloon goes up, and I'm still stuck in this blasted bed? That's what I can't stop thinking about.'

But after the bouts of ill-temper, the damning and blasting that erupted throughout our conversation, as I was leaving he suddenly became quite touching. He took my hand and seemed to concentrate on me for the first time. 'Look here, Meg my dear, sorry I'm being so cranky and all that – but you know, I really appreciate you coming to see me. Look forward to it, you know. And the other fellows here – they all ask about you. They think me a really lucky fellow to have such a pretty girl to hold my hand and mop the fevered brow. Will you come again soon?'

I told him I would.

And then on another occasion – because I went to see him several times before going to France – he came out with what was really on his mind. By this time he was allowed out of bed, and was sitting in a chair in pyjamas and dressing gown, still with his leg in plaster, and a walking stick over the arm of the chair. It was sometime in June, a beautiful summer day, the window open, trees all in heavy leaf.

As I came into the ward he struggled to his feet, and after a few words of greeting, gestured to the open French windows.

'Let's take a walk outside.'

He was able to hobble now on his stick, and we made our way slowly along the paths, between neatly cut lawns and flower beds, now thick with colour. Something was clearly on his mind as he turned to look at me.

'You know, Meg,' he began, 'lying there, I've had a lot of time to think. As you can imagine – not much else to do. So, anyway, I've been thinking, and of course I've thought about you – and me. I've said countless times, it can't be much longer before something has to give. Well, it's official now: I heard this morning that the regiment is to be put on a war footing. This means, as soon as I'm fit again, that I'll be giving up the firm and I'm likely to be posted away from London. Full active service. Do you see? In a year's time I could be anywhere. So...' He drew a breath, and turned again along the path. 'So I've been thinking. Got to make a few decisions, and all that. And there's one decision I've made. I mean about us. The thing is – ' he turned to me – 'I love you and I want us to be married. Would you – will you – marry me?'

I was taken aback. Edward was looking at me deeply in the eyes and it was a look full of feeling, full of uncertainty, and full of need. And he seemed so brave. Really, I was on the point of saying yes. I was embarrassed and touched, full of confused feelings. There was a very long silence as we looked at each other and a host of thoughts rushed through my mind. On my way there that afternoon I had been full of plans for our trip to France, which was arranged for the following week.

'I mean,' he went on, 'once we're engaged with the enemy anything could happen.' He was

114

embarrassed, and spoke haltingly. 'You know, I'm not very good at saying these things. But I'm going to be posted away as soon as I'm fit and I have no idea when we might see each other again. That's why it's so important.' He paused. 'There's another thing. This may sound selfish, I don't know, but if anything were to happen to me I'd like to know that I had left someone behind me – wife and child and all that. I'd know that I was fighting for something personal to me. As I said, if anything happened to me it wouldn't be that I was just snuffed out and there was nothing left of me ... Sorry, I'm not expressing this very well, but if I thought there was you and our – you know, our baby – to carry on after-wards, it would make it all worthwhile.' He looked away. There was a pause as we were lost in thought and then he went on in a brief, tight-lipped sort of way, 'Well, that's the sort of thing I've been thinking about.' Then he looked at me again.

I must say, I was very moved. He had reached into himself and found a depth of seriousness I had never seen before. But it had come as such a surprise that I simply couldn't give him an answer right away. It was such a huge leap. I was nineteen, I was in the middle of an art course; most of my waking hours were taken up with painting and drawing. It was all we talked of from dawn till dusk. To be presented with this image of the war widow with a baby in her arms – well, it came as a big shock.

I asked him to give me a little time to think about it. All the way home on the bus and the tube his words went round and round in my mind. Then, as I caught a glimpse of the barrage balloons over Hyde Park, I could see how right he was. It wasn't simply him and me; the whole country was caught up in this mood of uncertainty, of anxious waiting, of making plans, and coming to decisions.

I said nothing to my parents, of course. I knew that if I had, they would have given me no peace until I consented. Marriage to Edward was the most perfect choice they could imagine for me. Finally, as I lay in bed that night, I asked myself at last the central question: was I in love with Edward? Could I look at him – had I looked at him that afternoon – and say to myself *I want this man's child*? Could I actually imagine myself holding his child in my arms?

These were huge, life-shaping questions. But even as I answered them in the negative, I was seized by feelings of guilt. What Edward had said that afternoon – and it must have cost him an effort to force the words out – when he had told me he wanted to know there was a wife and child at home when he went forth to risk his life; when he told me that he didn't mind, if necessary, giving his life for his country, but that he would like to know that his sacrifice had been a personal one and not just for something as big and vague as King and country. He would want to know he had laid down his life in defence of his family and that there would be someone to remember him, a child to carry on his name and his memory.

Who was I to stand in the way of something as

big and noble as this? I felt ashamed.

Even when I woke the following morning I was still racked with doubts. I needed time to think it out and when I went to see him a few days later I explained the situation to him as best I could. I had thought long and hard about what he had said, and I told him how touched I was, and honoured too. After all, no one else had asked me to marry them. But I didn't feel able to give him an answer at that moment. Heather and I had made all our plans to go to France. We were leaving in a few days and would be away for the summer, for two months at least. When I returned I hoped to be able to give him an answer.

It was an awkward few minutes. We stared into each other's eyes and, as we did so, I knew in my deepest being what the answer would be. He didn't see that; he brightened after a moment and accepted what I said. In fact he was generous about it, now that I remember; he said it was probably the last chance we would get to go abroad, perhaps for a long time, and we were very wise to grab the chance while we could. He would have liked to come with us, but gestured to his bad leg.

'And anyway,' he went on in this light-hearted vein, 'soon as I am on my feet again, I shall be off to training camp. Some godforsaken corner of Salisbury Plain, no doubt, or a mountain top in the Highlands.'

As I stood up to go, I looked down at him. 'I'll write,' I said. It occurred to me that in setting down my thoughts on paper I might be able to clarify them.

Then I leant over him to kiss him. As we kissed, his lips felt so warm and I could sense the emotion he felt, as if his whole body trembled with it; that combination of his helplessness and the strength of his feelings was so overwhelming that I yearned for one moment to submit myself to him, to be swallowed up in his emotion. Something bigger and stronger than I.

I didn't see Edward again until after we returned from France and war had broken out.

The following Monday morning I met Heather at Victoria station. My father came with me and helped to carry my things. As well as a suitcase I had my painting equipment, a collapsible easel, a large portfolio, and boxes of paints and brushes. It was an unwieldy collection. He was still very unsure about us going at all, in view of the situation.

'Write as soon as you find a place so we know where to find you. And if the situation looks at all uncertain I want you to promise to come straight home.'

'Don't worry, Dad.'

Heather was there with 'Brother Jack' as she called him. Actually his name was John, he was about thirty, but acted much younger. He was pretty good-looking too, and perhaps if I had not had other things on my mind I might have taken the trouble to cultivate his acquaintance. Anyway, he was the real reason my father had come with me; he wanted to make sure I was going to be in safe hands. Little did he know. Sure enough, Jack put on his respectable act, we all shook hands, and the three of us made our way to the train. I was tingling with excitement as we boarded the ten o'clock boat train for Dover. It was quite an effort to get all our bits and pieces stowed safely.

Jack said he was meeting a friend in Paris and they were going to motor down to Spain. He gave us an address in Spain where we could contact him, made us promise to let him know where we were, gave us his blessing, and disappeared. We were on a through train to the Italian border and beyond. According to the timetable that Heather had, the train first stopped at the Gare du Nord, and then went round to the Gare de Lyon before departing at half past seven.

The station was filled with soldiers and, as we waited to depart the train was soon full of them, their heads shaved, with heavy kitbags, pushing up and down the corridor.

That evening, crammed in among them in a third-class compartment on wooden seats, we picnicked, drank our wine, and I told Heather about Edward and his proposal. She had never met him, though I had told her about his family and the evening of the dinner party long before.

'Well...' She became thoughtful. 'When you marry a chap, you marry his family, in a manner of speaking.'

'Actually it might be just the opposite,' I said. 'I think, in a way, he wants me to rescue him from his father. If we were married, obviously he would be able to move out of the house. The mere fact of his asking me to marry him was an act of defiance – rebellion even.'

'Are you sure you wouldn't end up as a buffer between them?'

I hadn't quite thought of it in that way.

''Course, if you love him enough, that doesn't matter.' She was looking at me and for a moment I couldn't meet her eye. At last she said, 'I see.'

Nothing more was said. Nothing more needed to be said.

Eventually, when it must have been midnight, we arranged ourselves for sleep as best we could, huddling on the bench with rolled-up pullovers under our heads.

Eleven

Never shall I forget that early morning, after the train had left Marseilles and was making its way through the mountains towards Frejus. The sky was aflame, brilliant, simply glowing with light, and everywhere about us were the dry red mountains I had always imagined, their slopes dotted with the dark green of pines and olives. How I stared at those pines, those olive trees. I would glimpse white-walled villages too, with their orange tiled roofs, and rocky terraces of ancient stones heaved up out of the red earth, and here and there dotted over the fields women, head to foot in black, would be bent over their work.

120

The people on the train had changed too. Many of those with whom we had shared the compartment during the night had disappeared at Marseilles. The soldiers were gone and we were now joined by another race: sunburnt men with walrus moustaches, wearing wide flat berets and heavy boots, with all kinds of parcels wrapped in newspaper and string, and smoking the harsh black Algerian tobacco which I was to get to know well. The compartment was heavy with its pungent smell and my eyes smarted. They spoke a language I only half recognized. I always thought I had a basic grasp of French, but although this had a French ring to it, I couldn't actually make out what they were saying.

We left the train at last at St Raphael. Heather had been making enquiries and according to her the place to go was St Tropez. I had never heard of it but a friend had assured her it was the right place for us. I didn't mind; in a way, that first glimpse of the red mountains had already half satisfied my long-held wish. I had seen the Provençal landscape, and whatever else we did, I was happy to leave Heather to decide. So we unloaded our things at St Raphael and it was a relief to be out of that hot smoky compartment with its wooden seats and to feel the sea breeze on our skin. It was quiet and there were only a few other people on the platform including a couple looking very English – he in tweeds and plus fours and smoking a pipe – whom I had noticed boarding the train at Paris.

We waited an hour for the local train, which ran on a single track along the coast. Once again we heaved our stuff on board, and soon the train came into sight of the sea. For the next hour we ran along the rocky coast, skirting a wide curved bay, where the pines fringed the sand, and little orange-tiled cottages were dotted among the trees on the hillside.

At last, in the early afternoon, we arrived at St Tropez.

The station was deserted and, as other passengers dispersed, a silence descended broken only by the gentle hissing of the steam and the rasping of crickets, furious and unrelenting. There was a dusty sandy soil on the platform and the sun was overpowering.

'Well, let's find the town.'

Taking up our stuff once again, we made our way through silent narrow streets, past shops with their blinds down, through a deserted market square and came finally to the harbour. The water was mirror-still and ranged along the quayside were fishing boats, their red sails furled, a crowd of tall masts nodding lazily together. The quay was lined with houses, three and four storeys high, in broken and fading stucco, a dirty pink or yellow, and blinds hung over the shop and café doors. Everything was shut and there was not a soul in sight. We stopped eventually outside a café and sat down to look about. It was the most beautiful place I had ever seen.

'Heather, you are a genius. I never want to leave.'

'I'm hungry,' was all she said. We hadn't eaten since the croissants we had hurriedly bought at

Avignon station four hours earlier.

'Hold on,' I said, remembering the last of our iron rations: two hard-boiled eggs and some squashed bananas we had brought from home. We sat eating silently and staring round in awe at the place we had come to. The next thing I remember we were both sprawled across the table, fast asleep, until we were being nudged by a plump man in a long apron and big moustache asking us in French if we wanted anything.

It was now getting towards evening, the sun had lost a little of its intensity, and the harbour had begun to wake up; we were very dusty, very dirty, and very thirsty. We pulled ourselves together and asked for orange squash.

'We'd better ask him if he knows any lodgings,' Heather said. 'Apart from anything else, I'm in desperate need of a wash.'

'Excusez-moi, M'sieur,' I began when he returned with our drinks. *'Est-ce-que vous savez d'une chambre à louer, par chance?'* This was almost my first attempt at a complete sentence in French.

He jerked his chin up faintly, at the same time flapping his hand downward. *'Attendez.'*

The upshot was that there was a room directly overhead which was to let. We climbed a narrow wooden staircase two floors up, and found ourselves looking directly over the harbour. The room contained two beds, a simple wash stand, whitewashed walls, but with a painted ceiling: cherubs and vines, in faded colours. There was a toilet on the floor below. We took the room for two months at a rent of 120 francs a month and gave the *patronne* the first month's rent on the spot. As she left the room, Heather whispered, 'Do you realize that's a pound a *month*!'

We brought up jugs of water from the kitchen, then took it in turns to take our clothes off and wash. It felt a hundred years since we had been clean. I washed out my underwear, then we lay down and slept again.

When we woke it was dark.

'What time is it?' I asked blearily.

'Nine or so,' came the voice from the other bed. 'You hungry?'

'Ravenous.'

'*Moi aussi*. And there is the most divine smell emanating from downstairs. Let's go.'

The restaurant was now crowded, but we were shown to a table, and were handed a small handwritten and grease-stained menu.

'Can you make sense of it?'

We shook our heads. But Heather, who was the more enterprising of the two of us, got up, took the waiter by the elbow and went out into the kitchen at the back.

Soon afterwards she returned. 'It's fish, fish or fish. I've ordered fish – for both of us.'

The first dish was soup. Fish soup. It may be that we were both very hungry – and, in a way, extra hungry after our sleep, and perhaps extra hungry too with the excitement of being here on our first evening – but I have never tasted anything as delicious, before or since, as that soup. I can recall it vividly. It was a golden brown colour, a thick consistency, oddly not especially fishy in flavour, but rich and peppery, and quite indescribable. It was served with small pieces of toast, grated cheese, and pieces of raw garlic. I wasn't sure how we were supposed to eat these – together or one after the other. It didn't matter in any case. We just ate and ate. We also had a large carafe of white wine. I don't know whether it was any good; all I remember is that we drank all of it.

The soup was followed by fried fish and chips. I had never eaten fish and chips like it. I think it was probably because they were cooked in olive oil, which I'd never tasted before.

As the first pangs of hunger were assuaged and we had emptied the carafe, we began to look about us and to take note of our surroundings, which we had barely noticed up till then.

The restaurant was full now, noisy and bustling, with the waiter, Albert, and Mme Constance hurrying between the tables.

Then I heard voices speaking in English, and saw a large group at a table on the other side – there must have been eight or more of them – all in very lively debate. After a while we detected an American accent and another man speaking English but with a middle European accent. Then someone broke in, in French, and the conversation became unclear.

Heather had her back to them but I could watch them and it gradually dawned on me that they must be strangers here like ourselves. They seemed very lively. A girl, in flashing red lipstick with a gypsy scarf round her head, had a very Bohemian air about her, and there was an

Arab, very tall, slender, and graceful who, however, did not speak and seemed concentrated on the man beside him. He was shorter and very slim and, unlike the others, dressed immaculately in a suit, stiff collar and tie, with a little moustache, gold-rimmed pince-nez and holding a gold-topped cane. They had finished eating and were now drinking wine and smoking. The Arab said something to this young man. I could see he was upset, leaning in, almost beseeching, and the other looked at him in a careless way and slapped him on the wrist. I couldn't hear what was said, but a moment later the tall Arab rose suddenly with a stricken expression and fled from the restaurant.

The others turned on the one who had been responsible for this little explosion but he took the cigarette holder from his mouth and waved it airily as if to dismiss the subject. The restaurant was too crowded and noisy to be able to make out what was said but I continued to stare across at them, perhaps in hope of some further drama, when my attention was distracted by Heather.

She drew a long breath, and as I glanced back to her, she was staring down at the table with a distracted expression.

'Is anything the matter?'

'I'm not sure,' she replied after a moment. And then, 'Isn't it hot in here? I can't breathe.' She stood unsteadily. 'I'm going outside.' She lurched against a man sitting with his back to us. He turned round to find out who had nearly pushed his face into his dinner but I caught Heather before she went any further and, holding her arm, steered her out on to the quay.

'Oh that's good,' she gasped, looking up. 'Oh, I needed—' And without saying any more she hurried forward to the quayside, knelt, hung her head over the side and threw up.

I knelt beside her, waiting till I could be of any help. Heather was still balancing on the edge of the stone coping, looking down into the darkness of the water below us. As I waited for her to recover, reassured that nothing more serious was the matter, I couldn't help looking round us. The sky was inky black, filled with stars, and just visible were the outlines of the fishing boats. Further along the quay other restaurants were open, people were sitting out; chatter could be heard, and somewhere an accordion. The air was warm and seemed to caress the skin. I had never seen anything so beautiful and a line of Keats came unexpectedly into my mind from school days.

'"Oh for a beaker full of the warm south, full of the true, the blushful Hippocrene..."'

'For God's sake,' Heather gasped. 'I'm dying here, and all you can do is quote poetry!'

Then we heard a man's voice from behind us.

'Are you all right? Is there anything I can do to help?'

I looked up and could make out his face in the half darkness. His voice had a European accent, I wasn't sure which.

'Oh, thanks. I think perhaps...'

He knelt beside Heather. 'Has she brought up all she is likely to?'

Heather, who was still hanging over the edge,

nodded.

'Then perhaps we should get her to bed, don't you think?'

'Very likely,' I said. 'We've had a long day.'

'Really? You've just got here?'

'Arrived today.'

'Where are you staying?'

I pointed up to our window.

Together we eased Heather on to her feet and, supporting her, got her into the door at the side of the restaurant that led upstairs and somehow conveyed her two floors up the narrow staircase. She was half asleep, half drunk, and very dopey.

When we were inside the room, we laid her out on her bed. She was already fast asleep.

The man, whom I could now see better, straightened up and regarded me with an amused smile. 'And you? Are you going to pass out too?'

'No. Strangely, I feel fine.'

'Well, I suggest we leave her in peace.'

We turned out the light and made our way back down to the quayside. I turned to him. 'Thank you for your help.'

'A pleasure.'

There was an awkward moment as we looked at each other. He glanced into the restaurant.

'Look, I don't really want to go back in there, do you? Why don't we just take a stroll along the quay? A breath of fresh air?'

I couldn't think of any reason to refuse. I certainly had had enough of the restaurant for that evening; it had been hot and out here the air was deliciously refreshing. We walked side by side for some minutes without speaking, until conversation sprang up, slowly at first, exploring, nondescript, vague.

'I noticed you earlier with your friend,' he said. 'In there.' He nodded back.

'You were there?'

'With friends.'

'I did see a group of people. Were you among them? I'm sorry, I didn't notice you.'

'Oh!' He burst out laughing. 'Well! I noticed you, but you didn't notice me! What an admission!'

I couldn't help laughing too. 'I'm sorry. But,' I went on, 'perhaps you can explain something. There was a tall man, slender and rather beautiful – an Arab, I think he was; he seemed to be having a row with another man, and then suddenly ran out. He looked almost in tears.'

'He was in tears. Poor Karim.' He walked on for a moment, his hands in his pockets.

I waited. 'Did you understand what was going on?'

'Oh yes.' He paused, and again we were walking in silence until I wished I hadn't raised the subject. It was obviously rather delicate.

After a while, he looked back at me. He had thick, glossy blond hair, I noticed, and a wide high forehead. It was a strong face. 'How long do you intend to remain here?'

'Two months or so.'

'Well now. If I tell you, I must rely on you not to go chattering about it. Do you understand?'

'Don't tell me if you'd rather not.'

There was another pause as he gave me a sideways, quizzical look, then went on, 'The tall slender Arab is Karim, he's Algerian and a dancer – a very good one too. The man with whom he was having an argument is Alcide. He's French, and he lives just outside the town, up there – ' he gestured vaguely – 'at *Les Cigalettes*. It's a large villa, very elegant and he's the grandson of Madame Leary, who owns it. She is a very old lady, very kind, very generous, very rich too, and likes to encourage artistic people, poets and painters and so on. Well, Alcide saw Karim dancing at a cabaret in Paris, and invited him to stay. Alcide is, you know – ' he gestured vaguely – 'interested in men. Poor Karim is very sweet, very innocent, and tender-hearted.' He paused. 'I'm afraid Alcide has not been behaving very nicely to Karim. I told him so, as a matter of fact. Madame Leary is a lovely old lady. It's a pity she has to put up with Alcide, that's all.'

This was all most odd to me and I was busy trying to take it in. At last I said, 'But why does Karim stay, if Alcide treats him like that?'

He looked at me and I could just make out his eyes in the darkness. 'Ah, why?' he said softly. 'Why do people do what they do, eh? Why do any of us do the things we do?'

I didn't know the answer to this, and we continued to look into each other's eyes for a long moment. 'I suppose in the end we hope to explain to ourselves why we do things.'

He turned away, and we continued to walk. 'A good answer,' he said at last. 'And you have never done anything and afterwards didn't know why you did it?'

'I don't think so,' I answered hesitantly.

We walked on again in silence.

'Then tell me,' he began again. 'What is the most dramatic, emotional thing you have ever done?'

'Goodness! You'll have to let me think.'

'Think! We've got plenty of time. You're not too tired, I hope?'

'No, as a matter of fact I had a sleep before dinner and I feel fine now.'

We had by this time walked right to the end of the harbour where there was a breakwater. We found a ledge and, sitting, we could look back along the quay at the lights in the restaurants and bars and the reflections across the water with the fishing boats silhouetted against them. He offered me a cigarette, a French one which almost tore the back off my throat. When I had finally got my breath back, I said, 'I suppose the most dramatic thing I ever did was to hit a man at a Fascist rally.'

'*Really?* You went to a Fascist rally?'

'To protest, you know. They attacked a friend of mine, and I went to protect him.'

'What happened?'

'I got hit back. Rather harder.'

There was a pause, then he murmured thoughtfully, 'A woman of character.' He turned to me. 'What is your name? If you don't mind telling me?'

'Meg.'

He held out his hand. 'Werner.' It was a strong hand, large and capable, dry and comforting. I liked that hand immediately. 'You are English, I take it.'

I nodded. 'From London.'

'Ah yes. I like London very much. If you are tired of London you must be tired of life, isn't that so?'

'So they say,' I laughed. 'Fortunately I am not yet tired of London.' Then I turned to him. 'How did you know that?' I couldn't help asking. 'You're not English.'

'No, I am not English. To tell the truth I forget where I heard it.'

He said no more, and I didn't like to pursue the subject. My Mill Hill education still inhibited me from asking leading questions. Besides, there was something, at least that first evening, something slightly forbidding about him. I can't explain it. I stood up.

'I think perhaps I ought to get back – to see how my friend is.'

'By all means. Though if you want my opinion she is fast asleep at this moment.'

We set off back along the quayside, and when we got to my door, I turned to him. 'Thank you for your help.'

'My pleasure. And who knows, we may meet again.'

Twelve

Heather was still fast asleep when I reached our room. I pulled a thin blanket over her, undressed and went to bed myself. I was asleep instantly.

The following morning I threw back the shutters – old shutters, I can see them now, the faded green paint peeling, with an ancient iron clasp holding them together. Looking out across the harbour, I was filled with joy. The air was inexpressibly light, the sea beyond the harbour glittered and sparkled, and below us the quay was busy, the old houses bathed in light even at that relatively early hour. Men were at work on the boats, nets were being hauled about, I could hear shouts, and further out I saw a few large cruising yachts.

Sounds rose from the restaurant below, and Albert was setting out tables and chairs on the quay ready for the day.

I looked back. Heather was awake too, among the dishevelled blankets of her bed. 'How do you feel?' I asked.

'Fine.' Turning over, she ran her fingers through her hair. 'Why shouldn't I?'

'Oh – I was just thinking of last night.'

'Why, what happened?'

I laughed. 'Obviously no lasting ill-effects,

133

then. Come on, I can smell coffee, and I'm starving!'

I ran down for a jug of hot water, washed and pulled a comb through my hair. Fortunately my hair is naturally curly, so I've always been spared the nightly preparations my friends go through with curlers. I've never spent much time on my appearance in any case – certainly not compared with Heather, who liked to linger over dressing – so I was ready long before her and went down to find a table on the quayside outside the restaurant and order breakfast. When she finally appeared she was in a flowery blouse, tied up beneath her bust, very wide trousers, a broad sun hat, bright red lipstick, and dark glasses. Clearly dressed for the Côte d'Azur, if not for painting. The doors of the restaurant were thrown open this morning. The restaurant, by the way, was called *Chez Constance*, and we had found out by now that Madame Constance was *La Patronne*. It was she who sat at the till, her husband Frédéric was the cook, and Albert the waiter was a cousin.

He placed in front of us large glazed pottery bowls painted with bright southern colours, very decorative, and a jug of milky coffee. On the table were bread, butter and a pot of apricot jam.

I don't think I've ever eaten quite such a delicious breakfast before or since. All our tiredness of the previous day had gone; we felt bright and alert, and ready to start on our painting. As we sat, elbows on the table, clasping our bowls of coffee – which by the way had a strange flavour which I afterwards identified as chicory

– Heather looked at me over the rim of her bowl.

'Who was that man?'

'Hmm?'

'It's all coming back to me. I seem to remember a man appearing last night from somewhere.'

'He helped me to get you up to our room. Which was just as well, as you were in no fit state.'

She glanced about her. 'I say, look at those!' She was looking out to sea at the luxury yachts. *'Quel* swank!'

I was glad she had changed the subject; I did not want to undergo a cross-examination about Werner. As we studied the yachts a motor launch pulled away from one of them and made for the quay. We watched it.

'If one were to play one's cards right, who knows whom one might meet!' I said dreamily.

'One might just be whisked away to sea and never be seen again.'

'I can just see him,' I said, warming to the subject. 'A devilishly charming Frenchman—'

'A sort of Charles Boyer—'

'A marquis—'

'A millionaire—'

'With a chateau outside Paris—'

'A flat in the *seizième*—'

'A collection of Cézannes—'

'A very large car—'

'Several large cars—'

'Race horses...'

We both stared out to sea, glassy-eyed, for a moment.

'Interested in theatre,' I went on after a moment, dreamily.

'Films.'

'Good food.'

'And devastating in bed.'

There was a pause as we both contemplated this vision, then I jumped up. 'Come on! Let's get started!'

'What?'

'Painting, you chump! We must not lose an instant more. It's too utterly *bijou*! We could just spend two months right here!' I looked at her for a moment, open mouthed as an idea crossed my mind. 'Heather!' I breathed. 'Suppose Cézanne had painted here! To think – he might have set up his easel on this very spot!'

I was dazed at the thought. Heather looked up at me with a quizzical expression. 'I don't remember...'

Three quarters of an hour later we had our things arranged about us. Our easels were set up on the quayside, bags and boxes of paints and brushes ranged about us as we decided just what exactly to paint. I sketched various views with a stick of charcoal.

'It's the colour.'

'The light.'

'It just cries out to be painted. The strongest, brightest colours in the palette. Raw colour!'

I was in a blouse and shorts, and had put on a cook's apron. I thought it would be cooler than the smock I wore at art school. Heather disdained any such protection and remained in her

136

brilliant flowery blouse and red trousers.

As we expected we began to attract various passers-by who stopped out of curiosity but, when they saw how little we had done by then, soon moved on.

But later that morning, after I had started to put paint on the canvas – these were small canvases by the way, twelve or eighteen inches square and convenient to carry – and had become completely engrossed in what I was doing, oblivious of everything, even Heather, we were interrupted by a man.

I was unwilling to be distracted so, when he got into conversation with Heather, I did not take part, trying to concentrate on the dusty old red sails of the fishing boats and the shapes they made where some were half raised; the line of the roofs, their orange tiles and white chimneys; the shutters open with here and there a mass of bedding hanging out, the awnings hanging over the shop fronts, sun umbrellas over the tables outside a restaurant...

Still the conversation continued behind me and after a while I turned to see who the intruder was.

'This is Meg,' Heather said.

He was a tall man in a white shirt and one of those wide French berets and I saw immediately that his blue dungarees and the old espadrilles he was wearing were spattered with paint.

'You're a painter?'

'Clayton.' He held out his hand, also spattered with paint. 'Sorry it's not very clean.' He was American.

'Likewise.'

'Look, you're busy. Don't let me interrupt you.'

'Oh that's no problem,' Heather said quickly. 'I was about ready for a coffee, anyway. What about you, Meg?'

I glanced back at my picture. I was deep in the throes of creation. 'You two go ahead. I'll just do a bit more on this.'

'I'll bring you one.' She turned to Clayton. 'We're staying here.' She pointed upwards. 'Handy for work.'

I heard him laugh as they went across and sat at the table.

Later, after he had left and we sat down for an omelette, Heather leaned across to me in a confidential way.

'*Very* choice. American, paints abstracts. He was a bit sarky about our daubs, but in the nicest possible way.'

'Where does he work? Judging by his fingernails he's been painting this morning.'

'He's staying just outside the town – there's a villa up the hill. *And* he's invited us to view his work.' She narrowed her eyes knowingly.

'Sure you want me along?'

'Of course! Tonight at six. For drinks.'

'Oh well, *pourquoi pas*?'

On the strength of this it seemed appropriate to order a large carafe of white wine with our omelettes and an hour later we made our way a little unsteadily upstairs and threw ourselves on our beds.

'What a very *civilized* idea the siesta is,' Heather said drowsily, 'and how quickly one adapts.' A minute later we were both fast asleep.

It was five when I woke with a raging thirst and I emptied a bottle of mineral water. Soon afterwards Heather woke, and we spent an hour preparing ourselves. I put on a dress, but Heather went one better with a backless halter top. She has good dress sense and an edge of flamboyance, a hint of provocation that singles her out.

As we were making our way up the road, I asked her, 'What's the name of this place?'

'*Les Cigarettes.*'

'Are you sure?'

'Well, it's something like that.'

And then it came to me. 'You don't mean *Les Cigalettes*?'

'Yes!' She looked at me. 'How do you know?'

I was confused. 'Oh – I'm not sure. I must have heard it somewhere.'

The afternoon had lost its heat but it was still blissfully warm. The air was heavy with the scents of pine and thyme, and our ears filled with the sound of the crickets. Bushes of oleander and broom were scattered across the rocky hillside. The dusty track wound up the hill beneath the pines where sometimes between the trees we glimpsed the still brilliant sea.

Then, turning the corner we came upon old stuccoed pillars and ancient iron gates that looked as if they hadn't been closed in years. The name *Les Cigalettes* was just discernible in faded and chipped paint on the pillars but there

139

was no sign of a house.

We followed the track and eventually a villa did come into view. There were signs of a garden and, coming closer, we saw a paved terrace in the middle of which a fountain was playing. Steps led up towards the house; there was a veranda along the front over which wisteria simply foamed down. There is no other word for it. I had never seen wisteria in such abundance.

Around the paved area were stepped terraces crammed with flowers and shrubs, lavender and thyme as well as giant cacti and agave. A series of huge terracotta pots stood at intervals out of which brilliant flowers overflowed, scarlet, blue, lemon yellow. We stopped to take all this in. The house above, in a faded saffron wash, had striped awnings hanging low over the windows.

We could hear voices and the sound of a piano.

Then, from amongst the profusion of shrubs and plants, a figure arose who we had not seen before: an old woman, eccentrically dressed in a confusion of different items – a long skirt, very old, very faded, a scarf tied round her hair, with a battered straw hat perched on top. She was wearing thick gardening gloves, and dusty boots.

'*Excusez-moi, madame,*' I stuttered. '*Nous cherchons Monsieur...*' I turned to whisper to Heather. 'What's his surname?'

She shrugged and shook her head.

'*C'est le peintre,*' I coughed. '*M'sieur* Clayton...'

She nodded prosaically. '*A la derrière – là-bas.*' She gestured, and turned to her work again.

A path led up the hillside between bushes, and eventually at the back of the house we came to a cluster of buildings jumbled together, some looking run down and disused. However, one had its doors wide open and we could hear music, a French popular song with accordion accompaniment.

I looked in. It was a high, barn-like shed, with a dusty window at the far end. There were various pieces of furniture against the walls, a large chest, and a table covered in painterly jumble, bottles, boxes, jars of brushes, tubes of paint, a kettle and cups. On the walls hung some very large pictures – the wildest, most night-marish riot of imagery, hideous faces, animals twisted in pain, but often half obscured by random brush strokes in bizarre colours, figures from classical sculpture but transformed in a surreal way.

On the dusty floor lay a very large canvas, perhaps eight feet square, and there was Clayton, a paint tin in hand, dipping a brush and spattering paint across it. He saw us and stopped. We stood in the doorway. With all that paint flying about we didn't intend to come too close.

The music came to an end at that moment and I noticed a wind-up gramophone on a table. I crossed to lift the needle from the groove.

'Turn it over, will you?' said Clayton. 'There's a *toon* on the other side I like.'

We stared down at the work. 'It won't make any sense from that side,' he said after a moment. 'You have to come round here.'

We edged round this huge canvas. Even from

the other side it still seemed a confused riot. 'It's called *Bacchanale*. It ain't finished yet,' he added inconsequentially.

'Clayton, it's stunning,' Heather breathed. 'There's so much energy; so much violence.'

'That's what I want,' he echoed her enthusiastically. 'Here, we're, you know, at the heart of it. You feel the ancient mystic forces of nature, the sun, the sea, the rocks, the heat. It's where things began – the Mediterranean, the birth of civilization. It's what I came to find: the birthplace. That's what I want to capture – the blood, the violence of birth.'

'I know exactly what you mean!' Heather echoed.

I was still staring at the canvas. I too wanted to share their enthusiasm but something in me could not, though I did not know at the time what that something was. Everything he said ought to have chimed with what I yearned for – to get to the heart of things, to grapple with the raw materials of life. Clayton's pictures did not do that – not for me. To be frank, the canvas just seemed a mess of paint, disorganized, raw, discordant, the colours screaming against each other. I could not explain it to myself but I knew this was not what I was searching for.

'You guys go in. I'm just going to clean up.' Clayton put down his tin of paint on the table, and reached for a large paint rag.

We looked at each other. 'Go in where?'

He gestured. 'Just follow the path – you'll see the door.'

We stood hesitantly outside the doors, looking

down towards the house. Heather pointed. 'Just go in?'

'Yeah'. He was busy cleaning his hands. 'I'll come right down.'

Thirteen

'Don't you think we'd better wait?' Heather whispered to me, when we were out of earshot. We were staring at the back of the house.

I shrugged. 'He said just to go in.'

'What if they're all speaking French? It's all very well for you, Meg, but my French is awful.'

'Oh, come on. If they're all like Clayton, it can't be that bad.'

We could see a door standing open, and made for it.

However just as we were about to enter we heard voices, and stopped again. An argument was going on in French, a man's voice and a woman's. The man's had an almost hysterical, rising note, but in a suppressed whisper. The woman, it soon became apparent, was objecting to something. *'Non! Pas possible!'* But the man went on, insistent, hissing in an undertone, a hint of menace, of threat. The woman had lost her temper and seemed to be laying down the law, but then suddenly collapsed. The tone changed; clearly she had surrendered and I caught a despairing phrase. *'Alcide, tu finiras par me faire mourir.'*

We stood turned to stone by this violent exchange. A moment later we heard quick steps, a door slam, then silence. We waited; and then gradually became aware again of the piano in a distant room, and voices.

'Why doesn't Clayton come?' Heather turned impatiently.

I drew a breath. 'It seems to have blown over. Let's go in. I just hope they speak English.' We entered the house. The corridor was dark, though there was a door at the end of it. We passed the kitchen on the right, where there were a man and two women standing round a table preparing a meal. Glimpsing in, I recognized the old lady we had seen weeding the garden. We continued and found ourselves in a spacious hall, furnished with pretty chairs along one wall – French eighteenth century at a guess – rococo mirrors in gilded frames facing one another and an old but polished parquet floor. The house seemed a little worn and had a lived-in feel, but it was charming. I liked it immediately.

Ahead of us the front doors were open and we could see, beneath the veranda, the steps leading down to the fountain, and beyond, through the trees, the sea. To our left tall doors opened into a large reception room, where several people were standing talking. They were holding drinks and we could hear the piano.

At that moment the old lady appeared beside us.

'You must be Clayton's friends. Come in and get a drink,' she said briskly in English, and unless I was dreaming, there was an Irish tinge to her voice.

We were very relieved to be taken in hand at last as she shepherded us into the room, where eight or so people were standing or sitting, and one woman at a grand piano.

I coughed awkwardly. 'We met Clayton down at the harbour this morning and he invited us up.'

'He said,' the old lady remarked dryly as she turned to a sideboard. 'Here.' She drew a bottle of white wine from an ice bucket and poured us two glasses. I had time to notice that she had changed her clothes and was now in a long black skirt and indigo silk blouse with an impressive gold brooch at the neck. Her abundant white hair was taken up loosely round her face, and secured behind with a variety of combs, stuck in somewhat at random. She gave the impression (indeed everything we had seen since we arrived gave the impression) of wealth carelessly distributed.

We took the wine and waited, frozen for a moment with uncertainty. She had a pleasant but decided manner.

'Now, dears, introduce yourselves, why don't you?'

I took the lead. 'May I introduce my friend Heather Grey. I'm Margaret Stephens, but please call me Meg.'

She extended a hand. 'Pleased to meet you both, and you're very welcome. My name is Abby but only people over seventy are allowed to call me that. Most people call me Madame

145

Leary, in deference to my advanced years.'

There was a twinkle in her eye as she said this, and we shook hands. I had no idea how old she might be, but her manner was vigorous, energetic and decisive.

The brogue was even more recognizable now. I was working very hard trying to figure out what an Irish lady was doing in St Tropez in such a lovely villa. And these people, many of whom were older than us – who were they all? We were both feeling very intimidated. In addition, as I was struggling to take everything in, as we had been talking and I had been glancing round at the other people in the room, I was wondering whether I was going to see Werner again. I realized, the second we entered the room, that he was not here and it occurred to me for a silly moment that he might not really exist; that I had dreamed our meeting. Or that I had completely misunderstood everything and that he had nothing to do with this house at all.

I had already recognized the tall Arab, Karim, however, and remembered what Werner had said about him. A moment later Madame Leary led us across to him and introduced us.

'*Enchanté*,' he murmured as he took our hands, raised them to his lips and kissed them.

He was tall, willowy, extraordinarily beautiful in a feminine way, and his handshake was like a flower resting in the hand. His head was long and beautifully shaped and I immediately wanted to paint him. Everything about him flowed in beautiful lines, relaxed, effortless. He was dressed Arab-style in a flowing robe, brilliantly coloured with wide loose sleeves, and I couldn't help exclaiming, *'Comme c'est belle, votre robe!'* and his face lit up with pleasure.

There was a tall blonde girl sitting at the piano, who stopped playing as we were introduced. She spoke English, and told us her name was Maia, from Sweden. Later she sang French songs to her own accompaniment in a wistful, soulful way, but phrasing the French with a Scandinavian accent.

Across from her sat a very old gentleman. He was quite formally dressed, in a suit and tie, a white-haired old cove with a walrus moustache, and was deep in conversation with a girl of about our age.

'Pierre!' Madame Leary led us across. 'These young ladies are dying to be introduced. Meg and Heather, this is Pierre Bonnard. He's staying a few days.'

There was a pause as we both stared down at the old man and offered our hands. Not *the* Pierre Bonnard, we wanted to say. The actual famous Bonnard, whose pictures we had seen in the Tate Gallery? There was a frozen moment before we jerked back to life and shook hands. The girl, who was called Chantal, smiled up at us in a pretty way; there was something small and fragile about her. Bonnard moved along the seat a little to make room. *'Asseyez-vous...'*

'Non, Pierre. Je vais faire les introductions.' And Madame Leary led us across to where a man sat deeply sunk in a low chair, whom she introduced as Jacques Lemaître, the poet.

Then Clayton appeared at last and poured

himself a drink. I did not pretend to take in everything about these people, though of course as time went on I got to know them better. We were both working very hard to take it in our stride, as if we had spent our entire lives in beautiful villas on the Riviera hobnobbing with famous painters.

Later, as dusk was fading into a perfect night, an indigo stillness, the trees just barely visible and the terrace lit from the open windows of the house, we moved outside and sat about by the fountain. The Swedish girl appeared from the house carrying a large concert harp and, after playing it a little, called, 'Karim, dance for us!'

It was a sight I shall never forget. She struck some arpeggios on the harp, and the long willowy figure in his flowing robe came forward with a stately grace and began to move across the terrace before us, raising his arms slowly, turning, bending suddenly, then again turning, the robe trailing behind his arm, making a sudden obeisance, a half bend, raising both arms, moving a step backwards, then turning again. It was quite spontaneous as far as I could see, quite unlike anything I had ever seen, and absolutely beautiful. His face was solemn and there was a self-absorption in what he was doing, as if he danced for himself alone. All the time as he moved the harp gave the notes, the chords and arpeggios. At the end he retreated further and further along the terrace before being lost in the shadows.

There was a moment of silence before we broke into applause. As he returned to the light I glanced at my watch, and then nudged Heather. 'How long are we supposed to stay?'

She shrugged. 'Who cares?'

'Clayton said come for drinks. We haven't been invited to dinner, have we?'

'What does it matter?'

'I think we should go. We don't want to look as if we're cadging.'

She grudgingly agreed and I crossed to Madame Leary to thank her for her hospitality. She was sitting in conversation with the poet, and smiled up at us.

'Come again.'

As we were saying our farewells I went up to Karim. 'M'sieur Karim, *puis-je vous demander une chose*?' I whispered. 'I should like to ask you a favour.' He turned to me. 'What I mean is, *je voudrais vous peindre, dans votre robe* – I should very much like to paint you in your robe. Your dancing was so beautiful.'

His face radiated pleasure.

'If I were to come tomorrow, perhaps?'

We were just walking away back down towards the town when suddenly lights came on in the trees about us. Looking back we saw that there were Chinese lanterns hanging among the branches. It created a magical effect, and the others all cheered. As we stood admiring the scene, I heard the Swedish girl Maia cry, 'Oh, Werner, you are a genius!'

I stood, struck by surprise, until Heather tugged at my sleeve. 'Come on, let's get something to eat. All that drink has given me an appetite.'

As I was grudgingly dragged away, I could

have kicked myself, and cursed my Mill Hill
manners. If we had lingered on they must have
invited us to dinner and I would have had a
chance to talk to that man again.

The following morning I explained to Heather
about my project to paint Karim. She was quite
relaxed about it and after a moment remarked
casually that Clay had invited her to go swimming. Apparently there was a beach below the
villa, which we hadn't seen.

So after breakfast we walked back up to the
villa, I with my painting stuff, and Heather with
a shoulder bag and swimming costume.

As we stood on the terrace that morning, still
quite early, I looked about me, wondering where
to do the picture, inside or out, and finally
decided that outside would be nice, so long as
we worked in the early morning. Once the sun
got higher it became unpleasantly hot. Or we
could work in the shade of a large plane tree, a
little way from the terrace. I thought of some of
Renoir's paintings of people sitting beneath a
tree, with dappled shadows falling over them.
Then I had to ask myself – was I up to dappled
shadows? Doubts began to creep in. Was I up to
portraits?

As we stood uncertainly, we looked at each
other. Things were very quiet. Are we too early,
I wondered? Had we made some *faux pas*? But
at that moment Bonnard, of all people, appeared
at the door and waved to us to come up. A table
was set for breakfast on the veranda and he
motioned to us to join him. Soon afterwards

Clayton appeared and quite soon he and Heather were in conversation and I was free to talk to M. Bonnard. He was pleased to see that I had brought my painting equipment. 'I too,' he suggested. 'Perhaps we shall work together?'

I told him about my planned portrait of Karim. Bonnard lifted his chin slightly, to signify that he had no idea when he might appear.

I asked M. Bonnard whether I might sketch him – just as he sat eating his croissant, a napkin tucked under his chin, there on the veranda in the shade of the wisteria, and in a moment I got out my drawing pad and had begun. Even on a wonderful sunlit morning on the Côte d'Azur, the old chap was in a three-piece suit, collar and tie.

Shortly afterwards Heather and Clayton departed for the beach and I was left alone with M. Bonnard. There was still no sign of Karim. Jacques and Chantal appeared together, sat and helped themselves to croissants and coffee. They appeared to be wrapped up in each other. Chantal was petite and wore a beret on the side of her head and a blue and white striped top and espadrilles. She seemed to be devoted to Jacques Lemaître, leaning in to him and talking quickly in an undertone.

This cramped my style, and I wished I had never thought of starting a drawing.

Jacques and Chantal drifted off in the direction of the town and an hour later Karim appeared. He was in a simple shirt and trousers this morning and seemed very subdued, quite unlike the previous evening. He sat quietly, across the table from me, and did not look up as he picked at his croissant. I was worried; he appeared not to notice I was there, and I was too uncertain to remind him. I hoped that as he ate his breakfast he might begin to cheer up.

After a little while I gently reminded him of my request. At this he looked up and his face broke into a smile.

The veranda seemed the perfect spot for the picture and he disappeared to put on his robe. We moved away from the breakfast table to the other end of the veranda. 'Are you comfortable?' I asked as I arranged him, setting the folds of the robe about his feet, and the sleeve hanging over the arm of the chair, so as to show off its intricate needlework. In order to have some of the terrace and the fountain in the background I placed him with his back to the breakfast table.

When he was comfortable and I had arranged him to my liking I began to draw. I had decided to do a number of preliminary sketches before putting paint on canvas. I was very unsure of my ability, in any case, and thought I had probably been rash even to suggest it.

However, we had not been working long before Karim began to glance over his shoulder. If there was a noise from inside the house he would turn; he had something on his mind, it was obvious, and this in turn made me nervous. But he was such a sensitive soul that I hesitated to remind him and preferred to wait until he recovered himself and turned again to his pose. This meant that my work progressed slowly. I was drawing on a large sketch pad, which I held

152

up on my lap. I was mainly concerned with the big outline, the shape of his body and the robe on the rectangle of the paper surface, and how I could fit in behind him some of the terrace and a glimpse of the fountain.

Just as I was concentrating on the fountain, a man crossed the terrace with a box of tools and a ladder. It was Werner. He set the ladder against a tree, climbed it, and began examining one of the Chinese lanterns.

At that moment Alcide appeared from the house and sat at the breakfast table, examined it for what was left of the breakfast, and then sat back in his chair and rapped with a slender walking cane against the silver coffee pot.

At this Karim wrenched round and stared for a moment at him. *'Bonjour!'* he called weakly.

A woman appeared and Alcide gestured at the coffee pot, which she then took inside. Alcide was fully dressed in a light suit, collar and tie. Like old Bonnard, who had long ago gone down into the garden, Alcide was dressed for the city, but in an old-fashioned style, in a stiff collar and waistcoat, with a watch chain and walking stick.

He ignored Karim's good morning and took up a newspaper. Karim at last returned to his pose, but I was aware of thoughts going through his mind.

I glanced down into the garden. Werner was still up his ladder and I wondered whether I was ever going to have a chance to talk to him again.

Fourteen

I was still trying to draw Karim, but he would keep turning to glance at Alcide. Finally he could no longer control himself, started up from his chair and crossed to the breakfast table.

'Where were you last night? You didn't come in until two o'clock!'

Alcide continued to read his newspaper, then murmured without looking up, 'You were awake?' There was a casual, spiteful quality to his voice.

Karim was hunched over him, clearly embarrassed that I was sitting at the other end of the veranda. 'You know I was.'

Alcide turned a page of his newspaper. 'I know nothing of the sort.'

Karim was already close to tears. 'Alcide! Why do you do this to me?'

'Do what?'

The Arab threw himself into a chair beside Alcide and clutched his head with one hand. 'Oh! How can you be so heartless?'

'Don't be so theatrical. You should be grateful to be here. It's not costing you anything. Do you think only of yourself?'

Karim swung on him. 'I think of you! All the time. And most of all when you go away.'

'Go away? I didn't go very far.'

There was a pause, then Karim went on more quietly, 'I know where you went.'

'Well then.' Alcide drew a long-suffering breath, and turned another page of his newspaper. 'If you know where I went, why do you get so upset?'

'*Alcide!*' Karim stood up suddenly and screamed down at him. 'Why do you humiliate me? I was here all last evening without you! Everyone could see you were not here and they *all* knew where you were. Can you imagine how that made me feel?'

'Don't be so tiresome. Who cares about your feelings?'

Karim looked stunned. 'Don't you care?' He faltered.

'I don't care for you when you behave like this.' Alcide threw down the newspaper pettishly and at last glanced up at the tear-stained face of Karim. 'Control yourself, and then I might like you better.'

Karim was thinking hard, but at last he smiled bravely, and muttered in a choked voice, 'You do – you do like me a little, still, Alcide?'

Alcide, in a manner half playful, half bored, took his hand. 'Of course I like you. So long as you do not get jealous. I cannot bear it. Now be a good, obedient Karim, and we can be friends.'

Karim, galvanized with energy, pulled up a chair beside Alcide and held his hand. A moment later he raised it to his mouth and kissed it fervently. Alcide permitted this, then pulled his hand away. 'There, that'll do for now.' He glanced at me and raised his voice. 'The girl is waiting to do your portrait.' He was giving me an appraising look. 'If it's any good, I might buy it for you.'

I dropped my gaze to the picture. I did not know Alcide, had not even been introduced to him, and had no desire to make his acquaintance. But clearly I was going to have to sooner or later; I decided it might as well be sooner. I set down my drawing board and went across to him. 'I am afraid I have not had the chance to make your acquaintance,' I said. 'My friend and I were invited here yesterday by Clayton, and Karim very kindly offered to sit for me. My name is Meg.'

He cast his eye over me in a casual – and, I thought, unfriendly – manner and glanced back to Karim. 'Well, go on then. *Meg* is waiting to paint you.' He turned away and picked up the paper. He had managed to inject an extraordinary quantity of disparagement into the one small syllable of my name, but it was not my place at that moment to take offence at anything he might choose to do. I only wanted to get on with the picture.

However, as he took his seat again, Karim seemed too wrung out to concentrate. It was obvious we weren't going to get any work done.

'Why don't you go and join the others on the beach?' I suggested, and he looked at me gratefully. He glanced back at Alcide, who at that moment stood up suddenly and went indoors.

I could see that Karim was about to burst into tears and reached for his hand.

'Karim, please don't cry.'

'I'm sorry,' he mumbled through his tears. 'He is so unkind to me; he doesn't know how I feel and how his words hurt me.'

I held on to his hand, willing him to be comforted, though it was plain that nothing I could say could help him.

'Sometimes I wish I had never seen him.' He drew a shattering sigh.

'Where did you meet him?'

'In Paris,' he said, looking down. He paused as if uncertain whether to go on. 'At the Lido. I had not been in Paris long, and it was my first job there, so I didn't know anyone. The girls are very kind but they have their friends, and after the show they all disappear. So I had no one until Alcide was kind to me. He came to my dressing room one evening after the show and told me how much he had loved my dancing and that I was to hurry up and change because he was taking me out to dinner. He didn't ask whether I wanted to go with him, he just told me, and I was so grateful at last that someone wanted me that I was very happy to go with him. And he is very rich; he took me to a very elegant restaurant. You see, Meg, I was brought up in Oran, and my parents were very poor, so I left school when I was thirteen, and first went to work in a circus, then in a vaudeville in the city. A man saw me dancing there and offered me a contract in a touring ensemble and for four years I toured round France. Then I was offered the work at the

Lido, which is very prestigious, much more than I ever expected, and I was able to send money home to my parents and my sisters. So I was very pleased, as you can imagine.' He paused. 'But since I came here, I don't know anyone except Alcide, and he makes me very unhappy. I know where he goes. He goes to the harbour, and pays men ... He doesn't care so long as they do what he wants. Sometimes I think he has no feelings at all.'

I was looking down as he told me all this. It was outside my experience; I had never met a homosexual before – not knowingly – but I understood his unhappiness. It was clear, palpable; he had no protective carapace, no hard shell, and everything he felt shone forth as if he were transparent. How could I not sympathize?

'Karim,' I started, 'why don't you leave? Go back to Paris?'

He shrugged, turned his head and looked away through the trees towards the sea. It was a silent gesture and, even as I sympathized with him, I could not help thinking it was a beautiful movement, a miniature work of art. Even in his unhappiness he was incapable of an ugly movement or expression.

A moment later he rose without speaking and went into the house.

As I was packing up my things, thinking about what I had just heard, Werner came into sight, this time with a plank of wood over his shoulder and a tool box in his hand. He stopped as he saw me, sitting alone on the veranda. As we looked

158

at each other he called, 'What happened to you last night?'

'I don't understand.'

'You went off with your friend.'

'Oh.' I tried to explain. 'Well, you see, Clayton invited us for a drink. I didn't think it polite to linger on in the hope of being invited to dinner.'

He laughed. 'How strange you are.' He put down the plank, came up the steps and sat opposite me in the chair Karim had left. 'To be fair to you, Meg, you don't yet know Madame Leary or you would see how unnecessary your tact was. She is always inviting people to dinner, especially if they have any artistic ability. You would have been very welcome to stay. She is very pleased you are doing Karim's portrait, I can tell you.'

'Really?'

'Oh yes. She told me about it. And you deprived me of the pleasure of your company.' He gave me his ambiguous smile, but I could not hold his gaze and was forced to look away.

'I had to give up the drawing for the time being,' I said in a rather muffled way. 'Alcide was here.'

'You see then, what I mean?' he replied softly, and I knew he was watching me carefully.

I nodded. I do not know why but I felt curiously constrained in his company. When we had first met I had been quite happy to chat but now I felt awkward and found it difficult to look into his eyes.

'Meg? What is it?' I glanced up at him. 'What are you thinking?' he went on.

159

'I don't know. Nothing really. But it seems a pity to be in such a beautiful place, and to see Karim so unhappy.'

At this moment Werner's attention was distracted and, glancing round, I saw the tall Swedish girl come out of the house. She was barefoot and wearing a long beach robe. Her blonde hair was put up in a loose, lazy way about her head so that it framed her face, softening the edges. She poured herself a cup of coffee and at last came slowly, lazily, towards us, swinging her hips.

As she came up to us she bent to kiss Werner – on the lips, which he was quite happy to respond to, it seemed – then turning to me she laid one hand on my shoulder and bent and kissed me too. As she leaned forward I could see inside the front of her bathing robe and noticed she was wearing nothing beneath it. In the meantime she was kissing me on the lips with a casual freedom. I tried to take this in my stride.

'*Bonjour*, my dears,' she remarked at last, turning again to Werner, and letting her hand linger on my shoulder. 'Are you coming for a swim?'

'I might later,' he said, glancing back. 'To tell the truth it's a bit too late for me. I can't take the heat. And there's that light to put right.'

'Oh. And you promised. You're such a good swimmer, Werner. You have such a good motion.' She chucked him under the chin and laughed softly.

'So they tell me.'

She turned to me. 'Come along, Meg. We'll

leave him to it.'

This surprised me. 'Oh – yes. Only, I haven't got my things.'

'That doesn't matter. Neither have I. Come along.'

And she set off down the steps. I wasn't quite sure what was happening so, uncertainly, I followed and we made our way through the trees along the sandy path down towards the beach. I glanced back to the terrace and Werner waved.

'Don't stay in the sun too long!' he called.

As we made our way through the pines, we could see the sea right in front of us, glinting in the fierce light.

'We'll go to a nice little cove I know where we won't be surprised,' Maia said over her shoulder and soon we found ourselves scrambling down a little rocky gully between large rocks, then jumping from rock to rock, and eventually were in a little landlocked cove, as Maia had said. It was deserted. The sand was golden; the water lapped lazily and looked deliciously inviting.

'I prefer swimming without anything on, don't you?' Maia asked casually. 'And here no one will disturb us.'

She let the robe fall from her shoulders and ran immediately into the sea. With scarcely a moment's hesitation I joined her. And she was right. I revelled in the unaccustomed feeling as the warm water swirled about my body and could have stayed there all day.

Maia was a powerful swimmer and made her way with strong overhead strokes; no ladylike breast-stroke for her but a powerful crawl.

I was still floating lazily, looking up at the pine trees above the rocks which fringed the shore, and then further away at the mountains of Les Maures, dusty green in a faint haze. Closing my eyes, I concentrated on the sensual feeling of the water rippling and eddying about my body. When eventually I opened my eyes again, I saw Maia had gone ashore and, spreading out her beach robe, now lay out on it. I too eventually came ashore, spread my blouse on the sand and sat down beside her. Maia was lying with her eyes shut. It was a somewhat odd feeling, which I did not altogether understand, to find myself there with no clothes on beside this naked goddess. Maia said nothing and after a few moments, idly glancing about at the distant outline of Ste Maxime across the bay and the scattering of yachts on the water, I began to speculate whether there was anything going on between her and Werner. It had suddenly struck me that he must have a girlfriend or woman nearby, and who more likely than the naked beauty beside me? They had certainly seemed on the closest of terms on the veranda.

Maia appeared to be asleep so, as I began to feel the relaxing effect of the heat, I too stretched out beside her and closed my eyes. I had a feeling something was going on but didn't know what it was. So when I felt a hand on my thigh my eyes opened with a snap. I turned my head to see Maia looking intently at me. She was still lying beside me but her hand was now on my thigh. I moved imperceptibly, meaning to dislodge it. 'What's the matter?' she asked softly, touching me again.

'Nothing,' I said weakly and coughed. 'I ... I just wasn't expecting it, that's all.'

'What are you afraid of?'

'Nothing!' I repeated, quickly and unexpectedly loudly. 'No – it's not that – er...' I was hopelessly bewildered. 'It's just...'

'Doesn't it feel nice?'

I didn't know how to answer this. It didn't actually feel like anything. I didn't find her attractive in that way and the thought of her touching me or embracing me was utterly confusing.

'Don't think,' said Maia, as if reading my mind. 'Don't think. Just close your eyes and relax. Let what will be, be.' And she placed her hand over my thigh again and ran it up caressingly over my belly. A huge shiver ran through me, which the other woman must have noticed.

'It's good, isn't it? Don't be afraid. It's nothing but good. It can only be good. Close your eyes again and wait.'

Hypnotized, I closed my eyes, uncertain, embarrassed, and confused. What was she doing? What was going on? Was this woman trying to seduce me?

'Isn't that good?' the voice went on hypnotically, sweeping her hand up over my belly and over one breast. A shudder ran through me and I couldn't help a sharp intake of breath.

'It's good, isn't it?' Maia whispered.

I opened my eyes to see Maia over me leaning on one elbow, her other hand running again over my breast. I could feel a tightening in my chest, and breathing was difficult. Our eyes had locked and I felt like I was drowning.

It was only as she bent over and was about to kiss me that something deep in me reacted and I sat up abruptly, reaching for my blouse.

'Excuse me, it's not what I'm used to,' I muttered thickly, my head swimming from the heat, the intensity of the glare from the sea, and the strange feelings which Maia had induced.

'Please excuse me,' I repeated, 'I think I'd better go in. The sun's too hot.'

I was just getting up when Maia reached for my hand. 'Why are you afraid?'

I flicked her hand free and, standing up now, looked down at Maia, who was still leaning on one elbow and looking up at me.

'I am not afraid,' I said clearly. 'I just don't think it's a very good idea, that's all. I hope I'm not hurting your feelings.'

Without looking back I scrambled back up the rocks to the path above and set off up the path towards the house.

When I reached the terrace again there was no one to be seen and without waiting I continued towards the town, went up to our room, and threw myself on my bed.

I was completely bewildered. First there was Alcide and Karim. I had absorbed that. And now there was this six-foot blonde Swede who could have wrestled me to the ground if she had chosen. I stared at the ceiling and tried to sort out my thoughts. Was Maia right? Was I simply afraid? Suppose I had just lain there and let her do whatever she wanted to do? In fact, as I

164

thought it, I realized I had not the first idea what would have happened.

It was further complicated because I could dimly imagine what it would be like to be attracted to her. And after thinking about it, I began to think that in a way it wouldn't have been the end of the world. It was just, I think, that I didn't want to go down that particular road.

But then a thought suddenly came to me: what did that make Werner? Was everyone at *Les Cigalettes* like that? *Different*?

Fifteen

There was a clattering on the stairs and Heather burst in followed by Clay. She stopped as she saw me.

'Oh, you're here?'

I stared up at them, not understanding the question.

'Yes,' I said uncertainly at last. 'Why shouldn't I be?'

'Nothing – only...' Heather was embarrassed. 'I thought you were on the beach. I saw Werner and he said...'

There was another embarrassed pause. Somehow I seemed to have no energy, but finally I glanced at Clay. 'Hello, Clay, come in.' He had been hovering in the doorway watching me over

Heather's shoulder.

For another moment the three of us stared at each other. Heather was frowning. Then she crossed to the window and closed the shutters. As she turned she bent over me and whispered, 'Darling, do you think you could get lost for an hour or two?'

The truth dawned on me and I pulled myself heavily off the bed.

'Don't worry,' I mumbled, 'I'm going out. Leave you in peace.'

I stumbled down the stairs and found myself outside the restaurant. At that moment everything in me jarred. I was ill at ease, confused, muddled, angry at myself, angry at Heather, angry in general, and I couldn't put any order on this. I didn't have the faintest idea what to do: whether to come or go. And where was I to go, in any case?

I sat heavily on one of the cane chairs. It was near the end of the lunchtime rush and tables were emptying. I looked up, as if through the canopy, to the room above as the image of Heather and Clay intruded grossly on my imagination. Heather and Clay naked on Heather's bed. There had been something so brazen about the way they had come in and, in so many words, chucked me out. My body was still humming with the intense heat from my sunbathing. I remembered Maia's importunity, the casual, careless way she set out to seduce me, as if she could scarcely imagine me putting up a resistance. The confusion, and in a strange way, the excitement I had felt when she had touched me, as if I wanted it, yet didn't want it from her. I was muddled, on fire with everything. I *wanted* but didn't know *what* I wanted.

In the end, when I had lost all track of time and seemed to be sleep-walking, purposeless, I found myself drawn back to *Les Cigalettes*. I remembered my paint things, left on the veranda and completely forgotten after my encounter with Maia, and it seemed the only thing I could do at that moment was to concentrate on my work. It was why I was here, after all, and perhaps by concentrating on it, I could soothe all the emotions that jarred in me.

Making my way up to the house I stopped suddenly, thinking of Maia again. Would I run into her? What would I say if I did? And then it all began again: suppose I hadn't got up and left when I did? What would have happened? It would scarcely have been the end of the world. Perhaps I had overreacted. Perhaps I should have just let myself sink into some passive, receptive state, and – in so many words – let her do what she wanted. After a moment, I took yet another grip on myself and continued on, through the gates, through the pines, until I found myself on the terrace looking up at the house. All was silent; it was mid-afternoon by this time, all the blinds were down and the house looked asleep. Everyone was resting and I was awake, full of inexplicable desires, confused, the blood burning in my veins. Everyone was in their place, Heather was in Clay's arms and only I was outside. I had never felt more alone.

As I stood wallowing in this orgy of self-pity I

noticed the sound of a violin from somewhere inside the house. I listened. It was not music I had ever heard before. I stood still, concentrating. Then it stopped. There was a silence broken only by the rasping of the cicadas until the violin began again. There was something at times quite harsh about it, something raw, straining, yearning, painful to hear. Then the tone would change and it would reach up with ravishing sweetness, vaulting over itself in rising steps, straining every nerve to reach and hold on to the highest, before coming tumbling down again in a cascade of notes. Now it seemed every string was being played at once, raw, open chords. It was as if the player were trying to make the instrument say more than it was intended to. It was the most difficult music I had ever heard and yet, strange as it was, it actually corresponded to something in me, that unsettling, wrenching need to reach into the heart of ... whatever it was.

It was this music that now drew me into the house. The door stood open and as I went in I noticed my paint things had disappeared from the veranda. The broad spacious hall was deserted and I stood looking about me until the music started again. I felt myself drawn irresistibly upstairs until I found myself at an open door.

The room was in near darkness; only thin slits of light stretched across a bed from the shutters. The music came from a gramophone, I now realized, and on the bed, his eyes closed, lay Werner. He was in his old sailor's trousers, but bare-chested and barefoot. He seemed asleep

168

but, as the record came to the end of the side, his eyes opened. He saw me immediately and for a second we were staring into each other's eyes as the needle continued to revolve in the groove.

Then with a snap he bounded to his feet, crossed to where the little portable gramophone stood on a chest of drawers and lifted the needle.

'What was that?' I asked uncertainly, feeling constrained.

'Bach.'

There was another silence as we continued to look into each other's eyes. I felt completely helpless. I lifted a hand, then let it flap again at my side.

'I came to get my things – forgot them this morning. Then I heard the music. I wondered...'

Silence, as if he was waiting. He seemed quite relaxed and he was still looking at me in that considering way as he crossed to me, looked down, and carefully moved a lock of hair away from my face.

'You've caught the sun,' he murmured.

I was staring into his eyes and could feel myself swallowing, and a slight tremor in my leg. 'Yes,' I said.

At last he broke away and with a slightly awkward gesture he seemed to remember himself and indicated a chair opposite the bed.

'Sit down – if you like.'

He turned back to the gramophone and turned the record over. He was about to put the needle down when I said, 'You said – Bach?'

He nodded. 'The chaconne in D minor. Do you like it?'

'I'm not sure.' He turned back to me as I made another helpless gesture. 'I mean, it's very ... raw, isn't it? Harsh. Even though it's beautiful,' I added quickly. I felt very awkward. 'I mean – I suppose I've never heard anything like it before.'

He nodded slightly, set down the needle, returned and sat at the head of his bed with his knees up, facing towards me. The violin started again, filling the little room with sound. It had a dance-like quality sometimes but often veered off on its own way, like a kite at the end of a string, perhaps, or a bird floating on a current of air high in the sky, a single little dot against the immense blue of the firmament, gliding, then swooping, doubling back, free. I listened, looking down at first to concentrate on the music, but at last I lifted my eyes and found that Werner was studying me. In the gloom of that almost-dark room, with the thin strips of light falling through it, he was sitting still, almost Buddha-like in a way, with his bare chest, strong and muscular, resting his arms on his knees, his bare feet on the bed, looking calmly at me. And I found I couldn't take my eyes from his. Our eyes seemed to lock and as the music soared and swooped, clawing its way up sometimes by some titanic act of will, and at other times swooping effortlessly again, we sat motionless, looking into each other's eyes.

Now all the agitation that had been accumulating in me through the day, the heat from the beach and Maia's roving hand, was magnified a thousand fold. The emotion generated by the

170

music was so intense that I felt myself helpless, in some magnetic field, pulled by a huge un-knowable force towards him.

I was drowning, desperate for something to break the spell. And all the time as I struggled to stay afloat, I was trying to fathom *his* thoughts. He watched me, looked into my eyes – into my soul it seemed – and I wondered *what is he thinking? What is he going to do?*

The record came to the end of the side, and he leaped lightly across in his bare feet to change it. I didn't think I could go on like this and he must have sensed it because he turned, with the record still in his hand.

'Had enough?'

'I think so,' I croaked, 'for the moment.'

'Not your *cup of tea*?' he said teasingly in an exaggerated English accent.

'It could be,' I said, reacting to this. 'I'm willing to try anything.'

He looked up at this. 'Oh? That sounds inter-esting.'

'It's not meant to be.'

The atmosphere between us was unbearable. It was as if the words we uttered were merely the surface, while underneath another separate con-versation was going on. The trouble was, I didn't know what this other conversation was. But I wanted to know more than anything. I had no idea what he was thinking or what he thought of me and I was afraid he was just playing with me.

I stood up. 'I really ought—'

'You have to go?'

I nodded. 'There are ... I don't suppose you

know where my painting things are? I left them on the veranda this morning.'

'They are in a shed behind the house. I put them away. Do you want them now?'

I swallowed. 'Well, not really...' I took another grip on myself. 'No. Tomorrow will do.' I became brisk. 'Thank you for letting me hear the Bach.'

As I was at the door he laughed and I was arrested.

'Oh, Meg! What's the matter?'

I turned, bewildered. 'Matter? Nothing. Why?'

He stood in the middle of the room, his hands on his hips, looking at me. He shrugged and at last said, 'You'll come back for dinner?'

I nodded. 'Thank you. At what time?'

'Six.'

I went out of the house and found I was shaking and couldn't go a step further. There was a large cane chair on the veranda. I sat down and just burst into tears. I wasn't sad, or upset really. There was nothing wrong at all; but I was hopelessly churned up inside, happy and bewildered. For a minute or two I wept helplessly and didn't know why. As the tears drained to a finish, I suddenly felt terribly tired and, leaning back, fell asleep.

As I drifted back into consciousness, I realized immediately that the sun had moved round, was lower and the air was cooler. I sat for some minutes, drowsy and relaxed as the memory of our meeting came back, then gradually I became aware of a conversation going on in low tones. I made out Werner's voice.

'I'll speak to him,' I heard him say.

A huge sigh. 'I don't deserve it. I don't really.' It was Madame Leary.

'Look, if necessary, why not make him an allowance – on condition he finds somewhere else to live?'

'I tried it.' Madame Leary drew another subterranean breath, as if her whole body shook. I could hear her attempting to blow her nose. 'It didn't do any good. It's just something I have to bear.' A pause, and she started again. 'Anyway, you don't understand; I gave an undertaking—'

'That was when he was a child. He's not a child any more. You have a right to a life of your own.'

'Werner, you're very kind, and I shouldn't be unloading all my woes on you.'

'Don't be ridiculous.' He paused then went on quietly, 'But if I hear him shouting at you again like that I may have to drive some sense into him.'

'What? No! Werner, I forbid you!'

'I won't have it.'

'No! Not another word. You're very kind, but this is something I shall just have to sort out on my own. Now, give me a hand.' A pause. 'Sometimes, I don't know where I'd be without you. Let's have a drink. I feel quite done in.'

'Come on then, if you want. But I tell you now, you can't let this go on any longer. And I won't let it go on any longer. Another row like that could kill you.'

'Hush now. I'm over it. Come on.'

173

I glanced into the hall just in time to see them disappearing into the drawing room.

Perhaps I could now pretend I had just strolled in from the garden. However, before I could move I heard a door open above me and a second later down came Maia, dressed in an ankle-length robe; I imagined it was something like the sort of thing she wore when she was singing. It didn't leave much to the imagination; as she moved I could easily make out the shape of her breasts moving. It was in character, at least. She stopped at the foot of the stairs.

'Well,' she smiled. 'We meet again.' We were facing each other across the hall. 'Why did you rush away this morning? It was so lovely on the beach and you left me all alone.' She paused and then went on, in her deep Scandinavian voice. 'It seemed such a waste...'

Then Jacques Lemaître appeared behind her. He was in a long silk dressing gown over a white shirt and slacks. His hair was greased back, and there was a touch of the matinée idol about him. He only lacked a long cigarette holder to make the picture complete. Maia went on across into the drawing room, and he passed me with a nod.

Seeing them in these cocktail clothes made me suddenly aware that I was still in shorts and a blouse and feeling distinctly unwashed. I turned immediately back to the town, and a moment later ran into Heather and Clay. Seeing me, she motioned Clay on and turned back with me.

'Darling,' she whispered. 'I'm mortified. Will you ever forgive me? It was only Clay, really and truly – he was so pressing. And thinking you were on the beach, you see...'

'It's all right,' I sighed. 'Don't give it another thought. Only next time you might give me more notice.'

She ignored this and went straight on. 'Anyway, where've you been?'

'Sketching,' I said casually.

'Sketching?' she echoed with disbelief.

'Wasn't that what we were supposed to be doing? You know, when we left London? I seem vaguely to recall. You know, come to the South of France to paint – or some such?'

Heather sniggered. 'Instead of which...'

I wanted to change the subject. 'I must go and change. I'll be back as quick as I can.'

Sixteen

When I returned nearly an hour later, washed, my hair combed, and in a dress, the drawing room was full. What I wanted most of all was to get near to Werner again. I didn't even want necessarily to talk to him. I only wanted to feel his nearness, just be aware of him in the actual solid flesh. There was something about the chunky masculinity of him that had triggered something in me that afternoon. But in the hubbub as people talked – and Chantal had now entered, so there were eight of us in the room – it was difficult to be near Werner. He was still

175

with Madame Leary and after what I had over-heard I didn't want to interrupt them. There was, in any case, another interruption: a knock at the open door of the drawing room. I glanced round and saw two people I had not seen before. It was an elderly couple dressed in the style I imagine the English middle classes wear for the Riviera: he in an alpaca jacket, striped shirt, stiff collar and regimental tie, holding a panama hat and a walking stick; she in a soft flowery dress and holding the leads of two terriers, who fussed and strained in excitement at the strangers about them.

At that knock, Madame Leary glanced round and, recognizing them, came quickly over. They were near me so I heard everything.

'Anthony – and Maud, darling. You're just in time.'

'Fact is, Abby,' he coughed, 'we've come to say goodbye.'

There was something stiff, formal, something rather dignified about him and soon the attention of the others was turned on them. There was a pause as Madame Leary registered this.

'Goodbye? I'm sorry to hear it. Have a drink anyway.'

Shortly afterwards, a glass in his hand, and before he had taken a sip, he turned to her seriously. 'Truth is, Abby, I've had a telegram from the F.O. Old chum of mine. To put it bluntly, old girl, it's time to go. We thought you ought to know. Something for you to think about, anyway. We've spoken to the Taylors and the Brabazons, and they're going too. Looks like everyone's packing up.'

'Back to England?'

'There's something in the air – he wouldn't say what exactly. But it's serious.'

'What about your house?'

He shrugged. 'We're closing up. It's been a wrench, to be sure, after fifteen years. No point in trying to sell; nobody's buying in this climate, as you can imagine.'

The others had all been listening to this and the atmosphere had become sombre.

Maud joined in, in an attempt to lighten the tone. 'It's only a temporary thing, Abby. Until we can see our way forward more clearly.' She hurried on as if to convince herself as much as us. 'It's probably only a false alarm and we'll be back in the autumn. In any case I'm sure the French and the Germans don't want a repeat of the last show. Much more likely Hitler will attack the Russians.' She hesitated. 'Have you had any thoughts about—'

'Closing the house? And where would I go? In any case I'm Irish; we've no quarrel with Hitler.'

'Ah.' There was a hiatus.

'Well, let's hope it all blows over, and you'll be back soon,' Mme Leary went on encouragingly, and the old couple, who had been standing in the middle of the circle looking a little forlorn, perked up a little.

'We'll keep in touch,' were their parting words as she escorted them to the veranda.

After their departure the conversation broke out on the subject of war and what Hitler's intentions might be.

'I thought he said last March he had got all he wanted,' I muttered disconsolately to Heather. 'After Czechoslovakia.'

She shrugged. 'I agree with the old fellow: they're more likely to go for the Russkies. Hitler's always going on about the Bolshevik menace, isn't he? Anyway, we've only just got here. I don't want to go home yet, do you?'

'Certainly not.'

'It's all rumours. Anyway, they're old. Nervous. Oh damn, I want another drink and I certainly don't want to talk politics. Where's Clay?' She looked round and we both saw him across the room talking to Chantal. 'Look at that! Let him out of your sight for two minutes ... Excuse me...'

'I for one have no intention of fighting for my country,' said Jacques Lemaître. 'Fortunately,' he went on, languidly, but quite clearly, 'I have medical exemption.'

Maia was near him, and she placed a hand on his arm. 'Yes, darling, you are such a delicate flower,' she said in her deep Scandinavian voice. 'We must take very good care of you.'

'In any case, they are exaggerating, if you ask me. I don't believe there is going to be any war. Oh, it is all tiresome! Change the subject, somebody, please!'

Then Werner was beside me. 'Meg, will you give me a hand with the Chinese lanterns? There are just two more to fix up. Then we'll have dinner. Oh, sorry,' he interrupted himself, glancing down at my wine glass, 'do you want anything else to drink?'

'No,' I said hurriedly.

'Good. Come with me.'

Without looking round I followed him out of the drawing room across the hall and out to the back. Not far away was Clay's studio, but there were several other outhouses and sheds, and Werner now led me into one and lit a storm lantern.

It appeared to be a carpenter's workshop. There was a workbench with tools scattered along it, others hanging on walls, pots and boxes, a scythe, saws, axes.

On the workbench stood two orange paper Chinese lanterns.

'Oh – I saw you putting these up last night. They're lovely!' I picked one up. 'Where did you get them?'

He laughed. 'Well, thank you! Where do you suppose I got them?

I shrugged helplessly.

'My dearest Meg,' he explained, almost as if to a child, slowly and patiently, 'I *made* them.'

'You made them! But...' I stopped for a moment. 'They're *beautiful*!'

'Oh yes,' he said in that funny way he had and which I can still hear so clearly in my mind – that teasing, caressing way. 'I'm very good with my hands.'

There was a long silence as we looked at each other. Again, it was that look, that message which I could not interpret. Did he want me? Yet it was something so much more than just physical attraction; it was like a recognition of each other. Something that didn't need to be spoken. I dropped my eyes to the lantern, almost embarrassed, and tried to change the subject.

'I heard you talking to Madame Leary,' I said.

'Yes?'

'I mean this afternoon. You were in the hall, and she was sitting on a chair.'

'Ah yes. That.'

He was measuring out some electric flex, and reached an electrical plug off a shelf. He put down the flex, and began to unscrew the back of the plug.

'Was that – what you told me about?'

He nodded. 'As far as I understand, the situation is this: Alcide is her grandson. She used to live in London before the Great War and was married to someone very rich.' He looked up. 'By the way, you really ought to ask her about her young days. She used to be a very fine horsewoman and astonished everybody by riding through the park on a great stallion. She was a beauty, you know; I think she had quite an exciting youth.' I couldn't imagine Madame Leary on a horse, but he went on, 'Well, she had a daughter who married a Frenchman. They had a son, Alcide. There are other children, but I don't know where they are. Unfortunately both parents died in the Spanish flu epidemic of 1919. And as the mother was dying, Madame Leary promised to care for the child. He was about eight then, as far as I know. And she's been caring for him ever since.'

'Well...' I tried to work it out. 'If he was eight in 1919 that makes him twenty-eight now. Surely she doesn't need to go on keeping him?'

'That's what I tell her,' he sighed, as he continued fitting the ends of the electric flex in the plug. His movements were deliberate and neat. He had soon finished. 'There! Come on! Can you carry those?'

I picked up the paper lanterns while he balanced a step ladder on his shoulder and took up a tool box in the other hand. I followed him round the house to the terrace, and he set the ladder against a gnarled old tree. He was busy up the ladder leading the flex among the branches as I paid it out to him, and pulling a nail from a pocket he hammered it in and hung one of the lanterns in place.

'Just tell me how that looks.'

'You can't tell until the electricity is turned on. I think it looks fine.'

'OK, I think that'll do.'

We moved to another tree and put up the other lantern. Werner descended again from his ladder as I watched and, rooting among the low aromatic bushes, found another cable and connected up his plug. I watched him. Everything he did seemed graceful and compact; he was never clumsy. He was obviously an expert. I admired him for his graceful strength. As he worked I was content simply to gaze on him. I was so used to admiring people for their minds, for their clever thoughts and ideas, their ideals, their commitment, as if everything that mattered was intellectual and moral. It had never occurred to me that a man could be important and – I didn't know exactly how to phrase it – significant, perhaps, for the work of his hands. Werner had the loveliest pair of hands I had ever seen, and as he worked there was a careful, loving relationship with the things he was holding. He was a real craftsman.

Fortunately he was unaware of all this. He now called, 'Meg my dear, there is a switch in the hall. Will you go and turn it on?'

As I went in the others were all still in the drawing room talking.

'Is it this one on the right?' I called.

'Yes!'

I switched it on, and immediately all the lights in the trees came on. The effect was magical against the fading light, and several of the others came out on the steps.

'Werner, they're beautiful!' Maia called. 'What a clever fellow you are!'

In the meantime I noticed a table had been laid out on the terrace, and a lady who I afterwards found out was called Marcelline was setting out bowls and bottles. The table cloth was a blue and white check, and the pots and bowls were all in the light, bright colours of Provençal pottery – orange, sunflower yellow, cornflower blue – painted in deft, deceptively casual strokes.

Werner had finished, and I was uncertain. The others were coming out of the house now and settling themselves round the table with lively conversation. 'Come and sit by me!' and 'No! I want to talk to Pierre tonight!'

I still felt uncertain and looked about for Heather; she was already at the table talking animatedly with Clay.

Werner had come up behind me. 'You're not going to disappear again, I hope – like you did last night?'

'To tell you the truth, I'm not sure – Madame Leary hasn't invited me.'

'Oh, you English! So proper! So correct! Wait there.' He left me and crossed to Madame Leary who was in the doorway talking to Pierre Bonnard. As I watched, the old lady beckoned to me.

'Of course you'll stay to dinner, dear, won't you?'

The housekeeper Marcelline and another girl had set out bowls of salad, and wine was being poured into glasses. Bread had been chopped into rude hunks. This was not the ubiquitous baguette, but a large chunky *pain rustique*. Now people were helping each other to salad, and there were bowls of olives. There was another bread too – *Pissaladino*, hot, oozing with olive oil, and containing anchovies and olives.

Since I had not had any lunch, and after what had happened this afternoon, I now realized I was extremely hungry. The others had all sat down and most of the seats were taken so Werner and I found ourselves sitting across the table from each other, and I was beside Chantal. Jacques Lemaître was on her other side, and she devoted all her attention to him. I had not taken much notice of Chantal up to now. She was a tiny girl of about my age as far as I could guess, who wore a beret on the side of her head and bright red lipstick. She was engrossed in her companion. I was not exactly sure what was going on because I had distinctly seen him come out of the same room as Maia that very afternoon. In any case Chantal was no match for Maia – in fact they were opposites. For one thing Maia was twice the size of Chantal and for another, at a guess, she was ten years older. And as well as that, Maia had a commanding presence, a regal bearing, a touch of the Grande Dame. Chantal by contrast seemed almost to shrink in Jacques' presence, looking up at him with adoring eyes.

The food was delicious beyond description and in my hunger I was drinking too, perhaps faster than I otherwise would have done. Wine was poured into my glass as fast as I cared to empty it. It was a relief after the afternoon's events – or lack of them.

'Where's Karim?' I heard someone call. Only then did I notice he was not among us.

All eyes turned to Alcide who looked up in faint surprise and shrugged. 'He was tired, I believe.'

There was a murmur about the table. 'That's a shame; shouldn't we take something up for him?'

'Wouldn't *you* like to take up something for him, Alcide?' Werner asked innocently.

'I am not his keeper,' he replied tartly.

'I'll take him something.' I jumped up. There was something about Alcide that I instinctively hated and I did it to spite him. I remembered the way he had behaved to Karim that morning. 'I'll just take him some of this wonderful stew and some bread and a glass of wine.'

'He does not drink wine – as anyone knows,'

Alcide observed sourly. 'He would prefer to be left alone.'

I glanced around in puzzlement.

'*C'est un Arabe,*' Chantal whispered.

'Even so, I'll just ask him.' And I hurried inside before anyone could say anything.

Once inside, I asked the way to Karim's room, but of course when I got upstairs, I found that Karim did not have a room. He slept with Alcide. I had rushed into this without thinking and now felt rather a fool. Karim might be embarrassed for me to find him in Alcide's bed.

It was a large double bed, with silk sheets. In the half light I saw Karim lying on the bed naked except for a sheet half drawn across his waist. He was lying face down, one arm cradling about his face. He did not move, even after I had knocked very gently on the door. He must be asleep and I was about to leave the tray on a table when he moved slightly and looked up at me. Once again I was struck by his extraordinary beauty and the colour of his skin, his long slender back, the shape of his head.

'Karim?' I whispered. 'I've brought you something to eat.'

He hauled himself on to one elbow. '*Quoi?*'

'I thought you might be hungry.'

He looked bewildered. The thought seemed not to have crossed his mind. He looked down at the tray, which I now brought across to him, the bowl of Provençal stew, the olive bread.

'We wondered where you were,' I went on helplessly.

He looked up at me again, the picture of

misery.

'Do at least eat something,' I went on. 'Won't you?'

'*Je n'ai pas faim*,' he muttered.

'Oh please do. I brought it especially for you.'

He was leaning on one elbow, staring at the tray in silence.

'Karim, I know you're unhappy about Alcide. But everyone's missed you. They hate to see you unhappy. Won't you eat something? Then you might feel better and come and sit with us.'

He said nothing, still looking down. It was awful to see such a beautiful, tender boy – for he seemed scarcely a boy at this moment – muddled and confused by the strength of his own feelings.

I stood up. 'Well, I'll leave the tray. Try to eat something, and then come and join us if you like.'

I went out.

Seventeen

When at last I returned to the table a row was in progress. Alcide, who had a facility for enraging everybody, had decided to annoy Clay. As I rejoined the table Clay was on his feet, pointing at Alcide.

'It's the art of the future – something you wouldn't know *anything* about!' He was furious.

'The future?' Unlike Clay, Alcide, who was

sitting back in his chair, was cool and spoke collectedly. 'What do you know about the future?' He gestured with his slender hands, gracefully. 'You have not the faintest idea about the future. That is merely an excuse and, by the way, it is also a phrase you have stolen from someone else. Even your language is derivative! "The art of the future" – what a futile expression.'

'Your world ceased to exist in 1914!' Clay struck back. 'Look at you – dressed like Marcel Proust! What affectation! The walking stick, the cigarette holder. Where's your lorgnette?'

'No, no,' Alcide shook his head wearily. 'Do not try to escape. I am talking about something very, very simple. I am talking about the quality of a work. The quality! Something you are terrified of, *hein*? You know your – well, I cannot call them paintings; your *daubs* – are devoid of meaning or sense so you hide behind these catchphrases, these clichés of modern life. Ha.' He scarcely deigned to raise his voice. *'C'est pathétique.'*

'Alcide! That will do!' Mme Leary cut across him. Alcide scarcely noticed her, leaning back in his chair and resting a leg across his knee.

'America, it is a cancer,' he went on, looking round at the others and shrugging at the obviousness of what he was saying. 'Everything it touches it destroys. Everywhere it spreads, it eats into the things that matter. All the real things, the true things of life.'

'What true things?' Clay was a fighter; his face was red tonight, and I guessed he had had a lot

187

of wine. 'What true things? *Old things* – that's what you mean! The old world – France especially – is terrified of America. You'd die rather than admit it because if you did, you'd have to admit the United States has got you beat on every count – *every count, baby* – and you can bet your sweet life on it!'

'Hah.' Alcide's expression of contempt was barely a sigh. 'Just so, the Goths beat down the gates of Rome. And after two thousand years, let us remember the achievements of the Goths. Which were? A great capacity for destruction! Their sole contribution to the history of Europe: They came, they saw, they destroyed. Bravo! A man might labour a lifetime on a marble, a picture, a sonnet; but to a Goth with an axe, it is the work of a moment: blip! And it is gone.'

'So?' Clay was contemptuous.

'You fail to understand?'

'I don't know what you're talking about,' Clay said loudly, looking round at the others.

'He does not know what I am talking about,' Alcide echoed coolly. *'Et voilà tout.'*

'Unless – unless,' Clay picked him up, 'unless you are trying to make some kind of *stoopid* comparison between the Goths and the United States. Which is really *stoopid*! Because if there is one thing about the United States, one thing you sure as hell don't want to admit, it is this: the United States is the most creative country in history! Creative, baby! Not copying stuff done centuries ago, not mesmerized by the past, but actually makin' stuff. New things! *Different things!*'

'Hear hear,' Heather piped up. She had been sitting beside him, looking up at him as he half stood, half leaned across the table pointing at Alcide.

'Jacques!' Mme Leary cut through this argument, which to tell the truth had become tiresome. It was the deaf preaching to the deaf; a barren argument which could go nowhere. 'Jacques, read us a poem!'

Heads turned and Clay, looking round slightly dazed, sat down after a moment. There was a feeling of relief about the table.

'Yes, go on, Jacques,' echoed Maia. *Ce jour je reveille sans toi.* That's my favourite.'

He turned to her. 'Very well – if you will play your harp.'

'Bien sûr.'

They both rose and went into the house. Maia brought out her big concert harp, and shortly after Lemaître appeared with a folder. Maia settled herself with the harp; Lemaître stood beside her, flicking through the loose leaves in his folder. As they prepared themselves, I glanced about me. Night had long fallen, and the Chinese lanterns glowed among the branches of the pines and cork oaks. A light shone at the open door of the villa above us. The air was warm, the cicadas whirred in the bushes and very distantly I could even hear the sea. It was quite magical.

Jacques glanced down at Maia beside him. She began to strum a few arpeggios, and then he read aloud:

Ce jour je reveille sans toi,
Ce matin les nuages
Que je vois de mon lit
– au-dessus des toits
Où les fumées de mille cheminées
Se perdent dans le vent d'automne –
Ces nuages, pâles, tristes,
Portent le deuil de mon amour.

He spoke his words like an actor, relishing them, giving every vowel its full value, drawing out the sounds like a musician as if he were playing his poem on a violin. It was very much a performance. I was stunned, though I didn't catch every word, and resolved later to ask him if I could copy out some of them.

I had drunk several glasses of wine and the dinner was wonderful; the people round the table seemed to me the kinds of people I had always wanted to be with – we talked of important things. A poet read his work, a musician played. Even the odd-job man was an artist and beautified the garden with magic lanterns. Thinking this I looked across to catch his eye. Although he was listening to Jacques Lemaître, he must have sensed I was looking at him because he glanced up and gave me a wink. It was a tiny private sign and I glowed within.

As the poem came to an end, we all clapped but Chantal raved with enthusiasm, clapping her hands rapturously, straining up to him, her eyes alight with admiration. I was sitting beside her so I caught it full in the face.

* * *

Chairs were clattering and people were helping to carry the dishes inside in a general atmosphere of tidying up. I too collected plates and carried them up into the kitchen.

As I was coming down the steps I passed Jacques and Maia; he was carrying her harp. Then a moment later at the table Chantal was pretending to load glasses on to a tray, looking down as if to hide her face. As I passed her she glanced up after them and I saw the most poignant expression, her face ravaged, wet with tears. I didn't know what to do. The situation was clear in an instant. After the applause with which she had greeted his poetry, I had no doubts about her feelings for Jacques. I wanted to say something, though in truth there was nothing I could say.

The table was cleared, the party had gone inside and Chantal made her way in with the last tray. I had made my adieus and was about to return to *Chez Constance* when I saw Werner sitting on the terrace beside the fountain smoking a cigarette. I hesitated for a moment then went down intending to say goodnight. Werner looked up at me without speaking then gestured to the low wall beside him. I sat.

The night was inexpressibly beautiful. The fountain plashed gently in the darkness behind me and insects flitted past us. I saw glow worms in the trees. I looked up, and the sky had never seemed so black, the stars so bright. I drew a deep breath of contentment.

I was still full of Jacques Lemaître's poems, their autumnal mood, world-weary, wistful, sad;

so adult, so sophisticated.

'Is Jacques well known in France?' I said at last.

'Very. He writes film scripts too.'

'Really? I'd like to get some of his books.'

Werner looked at me in the darkness. I could just make out his eyes glinting in the distant light.

'I loved his poems,' I went on dreamily, 'though I didn't understand every word.'

He chuckled.

'Why? What's funny?'

'My dear Meg, they're preposterous. Have some sense. Maudlin twaddle.'

'*What?*'

'I will forgive you for tonight – because you did not understand every word.'

'How dare you!' I punched him playfully on the arm. He didn't reply.

I had no idea what the time must be. I stared up at the stars again. The air was so clear that they shone with preternatural brightness, winking brilliantly, the sky thickly studded with them.

'The stars are so bright,' I murmured lazily, feeling beautifully relaxed and sleepy. 'They're never bright like that in England.'

Werner did not reply, and the end of his cigarette glowed in the dark. I turned towards him.

'Do you know,' I said unexpectedly, 'I don't know anything about you.'

A long pause, then at last he said, 'I work for Madame Leary. She needs a man about the house.'

Somehow this didn't seem the whole story. I pushed on.

'You're not French, are you?'

'No, my little flower, I am Austrian. You know, the land of song – the one below Germany.'

I dug him playfully in the ribs. 'I know where Austria is!' Then I added wistfully, 'You speak perfect French – unlike me.'

'Your French is fine.'

'But, Werner,' I continued, rather more energetically, 'there's something I don't understand. You work for Madame Leary yet you seem so clever. I can't believe you are only the odd-job man about the house.'

Werner laughed. 'Well, sorry to disappoint you!'

I had the distinct feeling that Werner was hiding something. It was frustrating, and vexing too; I wanted to know everything about him yet felt inhibited from asking direct questions. I was amazed I had got as much out of him as I had. After a long silence I tried again.

'Werner?'

'Mm?'

'Do you think there's going to be a war?'

There was a long silence. Werner was looking away from me and up towards the house. At last he said softly, 'I hope not.'

'But do you think there will be?'

Another long silence. At last, in an even lower voice, he said, 'Yes.'

My mind was racing now. I was suddenly afraid.

'But, you're Austrian, aren't you? I mean...' I

193

didn't want to spell it out. 'I mean – if there was a war...'

He turned to look at me. I could just make out his eyes, glinting in the distant light. 'You mean, will I return to do my duty?' He paused, and then looked up at the stars. He sighed. 'That wouldn't be such a good idea.'

I was chilled into silence.

'Come on – it's getting cool.' He stood up and offered me his hand.

At the door he offered me his hand again. 'Goodnight. Perhaps we shall meet in the morning?'

'I hope so.'

When I got back to *Chez Constance*, there was no sign of Heather. It was easy to guess where she was, however, and I undressed. Before getting into bed, I opened the shutters and leaned out of the window. The lights glittered along the waterfront and were reflected in the harbour. People were still strolling along and the sound of voices rose to my window. I breathed deeply, smelled the fresh sea air, and again I felt a deep sense of happiness.

As I was having breakfast the following morning Heather appeared. She was slightly shame-faced.

'Hope you didn't miss me,' she said as she sat at the table where I nursed my bowl of chicory coffee.

'Hardly,' I replied coolly, buttering a piece of bread. 'I assumed you were with Clay.'

Heather giggled.

'Fast worker,' I murmured.

'And we've only just got here.' She paused, puzzled. 'I say, how long *have* we been here?'

I shrugged. 'Forgotten.'

'Me too. It's just a wonderful romantic blur. Let's hope nothing goes wrong.'

'I was glad to see Clay give Alcide such a beating last night.'

'Didn't he just!'

We both laughed at the memory of Clay on his feet at the dinner table. The thought of the previous night, however, seemed to prompt a thought in Heather. She looked at me inquisitively, narrowing her eyes.

'By the way, didn't I see you deeply *tête-à-tête* with Werner?'

I glanced away and shrugged. 'We were just chatting.'

The last thing I wanted to do was to discuss Werner with anyone, even Heather.

'And nothing came of it?' she asked lightly.

'Nope. I just returned to my lonely bed.'

'Hard luck. Because, I must say, he is *eminently* desirable.' She looked about us at the morning scene. 'What are you going to do today?'

'Go on with my portrait of Karim. What about you?'

'Strange to say, I think I might paint too. Clay wants to get on with his imperishable masterpiece, so I thought I might as well stay here and dash off one of my own little gems.'

I returned to *Les Cigalettes* where Karim was waiting for me, and we resumed our work. There was no sign of Alcide yet and I hoped to get something done before he came down and put an end to my work.

After a while Maia appeared in her beach robe like the day before. With a cup of coffee in her hand she meandered her way up to where Karim and I were sitting face to face, manoeuvred a cane chair into position with one bare foot, and made herself comfortable.

We made very small talk in English as I worked. I wasn't going to spare her much attention but she prattled inconsequentially about the dinner the evening before and I concentrated on my brushes.

'You know, my dear,' she said after a while, 'when you have finished Karim's portrait, I want you to paint me. I should very much like that. Then I shall hang it on my wall in Paris. It will be a lovely memory of our happy summer together in St Tropez and when I look at it I shall remember my little English friend.'

I could scarcely object to this.

'I should like you to paint me in the nude,' Maia went on. *'The Naked Maia*! Then when I am old and my body is an embarrassment, I shall be able to look at your painting and remember how I once looked.'

She leaned in confidentially. 'Don't worry about Karim; he doesn't speak a word of English. By the way,' she interrupted herself, 'how did you get on with Werner?' She looked close into my face and chuckled a low conspiratorial laugh as she ran a hand over my shoulder. 'He is a very attractive man, don't you think?'

She leaned back in her chair. 'You see! I am not jealous! Not one little bit. I do not have an atom of jealousy in my body!'

I was still pondering the prospect of Maia spreading her long limbs for my inspection again. And the last thing I wanted was to discuss Werner with Maia. Yet it seemed she knew more about him than I did. I was torn.

'Such an interesting man,' she sighed as if reading my mind, then rose and went to the table to refill her coffee cup. By the time she returned I had had time to digest this.

'You seem to know a lot about him,' I said lightly as I concentrated on my painting.

She waited and I sensed that little tug of power she now exerted over me.

'He hasn't told you about himself?'

'Very little. Why should he?'

'Well...' She drew a breath. 'That is a very interesting man. Very interesting. Did he tell you about losing his post at Vienna University?'

I looked round.

She smiled sympathetically, and shook her head. 'My dear –' she leaned in ever more confidentially – 'he was professor of Moral Philosophy and lost his position.'

I had to put down my brush at this.

She nodded. 'The authorities didn't like the articles he wrote in the Vienna papers. The Nazis forced them to sack him.'

The world was reeling about my head. Professor of Moral Philosophy! Vienna! The Nazis! I was speechless.

'It's much worse than that,' she went on in a

197

matter-of-fact voice. 'His wife left him, and took their little girl with her.'

There was a long pause as Maia watched me digesting this astonishing revelation. I was suddenly suspicious.

'How do you know this?'

'It was in the papers. I was quite fascinated to meet him when I came here. Apparently he went to Spain at first and worked as a journalist for an American paper. When he first came here he was writing a book. I think it's finished now. So he's been making himself useful around the house.'

I closed my eyes. 'And I thought he was the odd-job man!' I murmured. 'What must he have thought?'

'Did you tell him that?'

I nodded, and she threw her head back and burst out laughing.

Eighteen

Maia's words overshadowed everything. All day long, in everything I did, even as I talked with Werner, answered his questions, helped him in the garden – for he was the gardener too – her words drummed in my brain. Together we watered the giant urns, trimmed bushes, forked the dry sandy soil, and all the time I was stealing looks at him, remembering what she had said. A university professor! Sacked by the Nazis! Was he on the run, then? Hiding in France? A hundred questions welled up. But dominating all of them was one thought: he was married and he had a daughter. I knew I could not be calm, could not relax, until he had told me about them. I knew however that I could not ask, at least not yet. I had to wait until I knew him better – if I ever would.

I shelved the questions for the moment and for the following few days my life settled into a pattern. Alcide stopped tormenting Karim, who continued to sit for my picture. I won't say it was great art. It was inspired by Matisse's North African pictures. I wanted to get some of his brilliant colour in my attempt to capture Karim's beautiful head. There was a passive quality about him, very feminine, as if he retreated into himself and was content simply to be – and to be admired. There was a narcissistic streak in him too. So far as I could understand, it was a glowing self-absorption in the idea of himself as a physical being. This was what made him such a superb dancer.

As I worked and came near to finishing the picture I had already made up my mind that I should ask Werner if I might paint him. Maia I tried to put off, though she mentioned her own portrait frequently. She flaunted it, to be exact; she would lean over me as I worked so that her beach robe hung open and gave me an uninterrupted view of her large breasts. At other times she might be found sunbathing on a towel on the terrace and wearing nothing but a tiny pair of briefs.

I found I was now a permanent guest at *Les Cigalettes* and Heather and I dined there every night, except once a week when it was Marcelline's night off and we went down to *Chez Constance*. Every night we talked round the dinner table. It would grow gradually dark, the intense glare of the sky would soften, softer tints of violet coloured the sky and the dark shapes of the pines became outlined with brilliant sharpness. Marcelline would place a kerosene lamp on the table and huge moths would flit in and out of the light.

We talked about the usual things – art, sex, death – but sooner or later, the discussion always came back to the same place: what was Hitler going to do? This would widen into the responsibility of the western powers to stop him and the role of the working class.

'You didn't stop him in thirty-six,' said Clay laconically. Being American, he was in a sense outside the discussion and could take a dispassionate view. 'That was when you should have stood up to him. Now it's too late.'

'Politicians,' Heather joined in enthusiastically, 'all old men. Frightened to tell the people the truth.'

'The writing was on the wall in Spain,' Clay went on. 'We all saw it. Hitler and Mussolini crushed the republicans. It's your own fault. Now it'll be Verdun all over again.'

'Mustard gas. Aerial bombardment.'

A gloomy silence descended on the table.

'Unless Uncle Joe can save us. He's our only hope,' said Maia at last.

'This will be the final struggle between capitalism and the proletariat,' Jacques said learnedly. 'The thesis, the antithesis and now the final synthesis – the transformation of society through the armed struggle.' His voice rose and he set his clenched fist on the table before him. 'The workers ranged side by side – massed together to overthrow capitalism!'

Unexpectedly Werner spoke up. 'France could have stopped Franco – in Morocco, before he crossed the straits.'

'We could have sent troops to fight,' I added. 'So could France. Neutrality – what was it, except cowardice?'

'The League of Nations should never have stood for it,' Chantal said suddenly.

There was a huge laugh round the table, and she looked embarrassed.

'The League of Nations?' Jacques pontificated sarcastically. 'What use was that? It didn't stop Mussolini invading Abyssinia. A toothless tiger.'

'Yup,' said Clay. 'Once Mussolini and Hitler saw that, they knew they could do anything.'

'Well, I for one will be very glad if the Nazis take over,' Alcide said at last, in his languid way. Everyone turned on him with expressions of outrage. He was not perturbed.

'What have we had since Versailles? *Voyez* – demonstrations, *manifestations*, strikes, the *Fronte Populaire...*'

There were more explosions of outrage but he

201

continued coolly, 'You see, *mes enfants*, what Jacques never wishes to admit – and this is the most important point – the workers always clamour for more wages, for shorter hours, for this, for that, but the one thing they never ask for is the responsibility. Oh no, that is someone else's role – someone else must decide where and what is to be done. They are like children – always making demands of their mother and father but never thinking of all the problems their parents must grapple with every day to provide for them.'

'Come, come, Alcide,' Werner cut in. 'Be honest – it's the uniforms that fascinate you. The boots, the leather belts, the helmets.'

The table roared with laughter.

Meanwhile there were more shouts of dissent, especially from Maia and Chantal. Jacques again rose to the surface.

'No no, my friend.' He pointed across the table to Alcide. 'The workers have no fear of responsibility. And once the means of production are in their hands, production will be managed for the benefit of the masses – and not for a privileged few!'

'Bravo,' Werner interjected again as he took out a cigarette. 'There speaks the authentic working man. *Voil*à, Jacques Lemaître, his hands calloused with honest toil, his back bent with labour, the sweat on his brow. The voice of the proletariat.'

I noticed during these discussions that Werner preferred to sit on the sidelines and interject these cynical remarks from time to time. He seemed to derive a sceptical amusement from it. I found this very puzzling, since the things we discussed seemed life and death issues, and they contrasted so strikingly with what Maia had told me about him.

Then, one morning a few days later, quite unexpectedly, I overheard Werner and Alcide. Werner it seemed was carrying out his promise to Mme Leary. I was on my way through the passage to the back of the house with its ramshackle group of outhouses and sheds where Heather and Clay had their love-nest, when I heard Werner's voice. The tone stopped me.

'I – will – not – have – it,' I heard him say in a low suppressed tone, emphasizing every word and accompanying each by a heavy thud.

I drew back into the passage, waiting, but immediately heard another voice.

'Take your hands off me!' It was Alcide's voice, strangled, breathless.

'I have told you before.' Still the low concentrated voice. 'And I will tell you once more for the last time.' Another thump. 'If you cannot learn to treat your grandmother with courtesy and respect, I will personally teach you. She is nearly eighty years old and she deserves your kindness.'

'Who the devil are you to tell me how to treat my grandmother – or anyone else? Are you her son? Are you any relative at all? You are her self-appointed guardian, are you? You have no right to be in this house, except as my grandmother's guest. So take your hands off me before I call for help, insolent *canaille*!'

Another thump. 'I am not going to repeat myself. You have heard what I said. Watch out for yourself if you want to escape a beating.'

A short mocking laugh from Alcide. 'A beating from you, Werner *mon cher* – is that a promise? I am not sure it would not be worth it. You are so *strong*, so *virile*—'

'You disgust me.' Another thud, and a moment later I caught a glimpse of Werner stalking away towards his workshop. I tiptoed back out on to the veranda when Alcide appeared, adjusting his cravat. His face was red and he was still breathing hard. I caught his eye briefly as he went upstairs.

For the time being there were no more rows with Mme Leary, no more dramatic scenes; Karim continued to sit for me and his portrait was finished. I was in a hurry, to tell the truth, because I had extracted a promise from Werner to sit for me and I wanted to make a start on his portrait. This was also partly because I still had not plucked up courage to ask him about his wife.

My thoughts now gravitated automatically to Werner, and one morning, when I had finished painting, I was drawn unconsciously in search of him.

I found him at the back of the villa among the outhouses. He was surrounded by planks of wood, a roll of wire netting, and armed with a hammer and a tool box. He was stripped to the waist, in his sailor's trousers and espadrilles. He

204

glanced up and smiled when he saw me but went on with his work. He was very busy hammering and sawing and clearly knew what he was doing. For a moment I wondered whether Maia had made up the story of the philosophy professor. I watched him for a while and finally couldn't help asking what he was making. He stood up and stretched his back.

'Since war is imminent I thought it would be a good idea for Madame to keep her own chickens. Things are going to be tight. At the moment there are plenty of eggs – you can buy them in the market – but—'

'You think it is definite?'

'Of course.' He turned back to his work.

Despite this gloomy thought, the idea of a philosophy professor building a chicken run suddenly made me laugh.

He looked up. 'What is it?'

'I can't explain – I'm sorry – there is just something so funny—'

'Funny?'

I tried to stop myself and drew a long breath. 'Forgive me – it's awfully rude.'

He did not laugh and there was a silence. I thought I had offended him.

'My dear Meg,' he said mildly, 'it is very satisfying – in fact one of the most satisfying things I have ever done.'

Now it was my turn to be mystified. 'What do you mean?'

'Look. What is this?' He indicated his half-built chicken run.

'You said it is going to be a chicken house,' I

said, staring down at the panels of planks nailed together, the tool box, and various tools lying about on the dusty soil.

'And what was it yesterday?'

'I don't understand.'

'It's very simple. Yesterday it was pieces of wood – lots of them. A pile of planks.'

'Yes?'

'And now in addition to being a pile of planks – because all the planks are still there – it is a useful house for chickens.'

'True,' I said uncertainly.

He was thoughtful, staring down at his half-built chicken run.

'I suppose it is what I would once have called a *Gestaltsverwandlung*,' he murmured, and then, recovering himself, turned to me. 'What I am trying to say, my dear, dear girl, is that I have made a real, though small, difference to the world. Yesterday there was no chicken house. Today, there is one. This is a source of satisfaction to me.' He snapped out of this mood, picked up a saw, and readied a plank across a block. However, before he began sawing, he straightened again and turned back to me. 'If you could imagine what my life used to be, staring into the page of a book and trying to think out a conceptual problem until I thought my brain would blow a fuse. Then, looking up at the rows and rows of books, shelves stretching to the ceiling, I would think – *it's all for what?* Nothing I can ever do in here will make the slightest difference in the world. It will make less difference than this chicken house.'

We were looking into each other's eyes. He was serious.

'Then I realized that it is worse than that because ideas *can* make a difference. It is through perverted philosophical ideas that monstrous regimes have been erected. In the end I came to believe that philosophers were a source of evil. They were out of contact with the real lives of the people and their ideas were taken by unscrupulous men and turned round and used against the people with dreadful results.' He looked down at the half-finished chicken house, smiled, and went on lightly, 'I think I would rather build things, make things that can be used.'

This all related to what Maia had told me about him, but I had nothing to say. He looked at me again.

'People will fight for an idea, Meg,' he said carefully. 'They will die for an idea.'

'Is that bad?' I asked hesitantly. 'Surely some ideas are worth fighting for?'

'Name one.'

'Freedom?'

'Name another.' But he went on before I could answer. 'The triumph of the workers over capitalism; the master race.' He went on, quicker, 'The decadence of the west, the need for a new beginning – revolution! Men are seduced, lulled, hypnotized by ideas. They take their eyes off the everyday life they lead and gaze up into the clouds, where ideas live.' He paused. 'As for freedom, excuse me, but what a threadbare word that is. Are you free?'

'I think so,' I said hesitantly.

'No you're not. Neither should you wish to be.'

'I don't understand.'

'Think, Meg! It's very important!' He was terribly earnest. 'You are linked to life by a thousand threads, some irksome it is true, but many of incalculable value! Who is free? A baby! A lunatic! A man who throws himself off a bridge! But all the others – every one of us living, breathing people – we are not free. We are surrounded by people who depend on us, and whom we depend on. Every day we do things which demonstrate the thousand little threads that bind us together. Thank God – for that is what sanity is.'

Where was this going? I thought of him constantly; my whole vision was filled with him. Everything he said seemed filled with significance. I laughed at his jokes, I pondered his thoughts and opinions; there was a perfect *rightness* about him, and about us together. We spoke, or we were silent, I didn't mind which. I stayed with him all that afternoon, watching as he constructed his chicken house, passing him his planks, handing him his nails...

Nineteen

That night after dinner Werner suggested we go to a *guinguette* and dance. Of course I agreed, though I had no idea what a *guinguette* was.

We walked down into the port and on the quay-side we came to *Chez Fredy* which advertised itself by a neon light as a *Bar Américain*. Tables stood outside where men and women sat drinking *pastis*, *marc*, and all the other kinds of drink I was getting to know. It was barely nine o'clock and the bar was only lightly crowded. Cigarette smoke, from the harsh Algerian tobacco that I was growing to like, hung in the air and conversations went on round me in the patois I barely understood.

Werner spoke to the bartender and I soon found a drink in my hand.

'What is it?' I asked as I sipped it.

'*Fine à l'eau* – Cognac and soda.'

We stood at the bar – *le zinc* – and at first said little. I was glancing about me, taking it in. It was rather a shabby place, with some faded railway posters on the walls, and I wondered why Werner had chosen it. However, soon afterwards someone put a record on the jukebox, an accordion played a tango and then a woman's voice took over. She sounded hoarse of voice, weary and sad; she dragged that song out of God knows what cynical and disappointed experience. What she had suffered to achieve that drink-sodden equilibrium, I could not even guess at.

Werner reached for my hand without smiling and laced his arm about my waist. I had never imagined him as a dancer.

There seemed no need to speak. To touch was all, to be in his arms – I wonder whether he realized that? The tango stamped out its staccato beat and Werner, for all the harsh precision of the orchestra, swirled me round in a version of his own that wafted me to and fro among the other dancers. Sometimes we would catch each others' eyes and he would smile down at me, singing along with the record:

Le plus beau de tous les tangos du monde
C'est celui que j'ai dansé dans vos bras...

'The loveliest tango in all the world is the one I danced in your arms,' I whispered in his ear.

He glanced to his feet; I looked down too and, quite spontaneously, we invented a little step of our own. It was deliciously carefree and I didn't mind if it went on all night.

'Werner, you're such a good dancer!' I couldn't help saying.

He shrugged. 'So are you, my Golden Girl.'

'You're just so talented at everything,' I persisted. 'Your beautiful Chinese lanterns—'

'My beautiful chicken house,' he joked, as we circled in another dance, less energetic than the tango.

'Werner...'

'Yes, *ma chérie*?'

'I hope you don't mind my asking. It was something Maia said...'

'About me?'

I nodded. 'It was ... she said you were married.' I was tense. I didn't want to spoil our evening but I had to know.

The music came to an end. He seemed to think for a moment.

'Let's go outside.'

Without saying anything I followed him out on the quayside. It was dark now and the lights of the bars and restaurants glowed along the quay. The big millionaires' yachts out in the harbour were lit up and voices could be heard echoing across the water.

We strolled along the waterside. I was content to breathe the clear cool air after the hot smoky atmosphere inside. I didn't want to say anything till he chose to speak.

'Maia couldn't resist telling,' he said at last. I waited nervously. 'Well...' He was looking down at his feet now. 'She is right. I am married and I have a little girl, who is six.'

'What's her name?' I whispered.

He glanced up in surprise. 'Albertina.'

'Oh, that's pretty!' I exclaimed. 'When did you last see her?'

'Two and a half years ago.' He was thinking. 'Two years ago last March twelfth.'

'And – your wife left you?' I began hesitantly.

He nodded, but then turned. 'You don't want to hear this!'

'But I do!' I exclaimed. 'I do! I want to know everything about you. I want to know every little thing there is to know!'

I thought I had said too much, and he stopped. I could make out his face in the distant light from a restaurant, which spilled out on the quayside near us. People were crowded at the tables and waiters in long aprons hurried between them holding silver salvers aloft. We turned again along the quayside and at last he began, reluctantly. 'I was a lecturer at Vienna University, a *dozent*. I had my *doktorat* and had published my work on *Die Kritik der reiner Vernunft*—'

'What was that? I didn't understand.'

'The Critique of Pure Reason. Immanuel Kant. And to think I once thought it all *mattered*!'

I was bewildered by this. He sounded so bitter that I wished I had never started on it.

'We won't talk about it if you don't want to.'

He shrugged and in a moment seemed to calm himself. 'Oh it's all right. Sorry I shouted. Well, *mein kleines Täubchen,* where shall I begin? How can I begin? How can I even *begin* to describe the path my life has taken over the last three years? Only three years ago I was a successful man. Very successful! I had my post at the university, I had published my book. I was married and my wife had presented me with the most beautiful baby the world had ever seen, my little Albertina. Everything was beautiful. Of course sometimes I chafed a little at the regime at the university, the unbending routine, the prospect of waiting for my professor to die before I could expect advancement, but generally I was not greedy. I had more than most men could expect. My parents were blissfully content. I had a beautiful wife – much admired by my colleagues, by the way. But as you know the political situation was getting blacker by the minute. Austria is a very small country and it is next to a very large country – a country, moreover, ruled by the most monstrous tyrant the world has ever seen and one that, I understood as clearly as anything, was going to send his troops to invade my country. It was inevitable. Everything he said pointed to it. I was incensed. It cost me sleepless nights. I argued with my wife about it. She refused to see my point of view. In particular she did not find Herr Hitler by any means as black as I made out. He had done much that was good for his country, she said; above all he had instilled *discipline*! And he had destroyed the hated Bolshevists, the enemy of the German people. As far as she was concerned Austria and Germany had a common cause, to keep out the Bolshevists and to preserve discipline! *Zucht!* I cannot tell you how I hated it when she uttered that word. It seemed so strange coming from her. She had never said anything like that before we were married, never said anything like it until after Hitler had marched into the Rhineland. And now when I raised it with her, out she came with this hateful, militaristic doctrine. We were far, far apart. And when I submitted an article to the newspaper warning of the danger of Hitler, she was furious. Furious and – you know – afraid. Oh yes, that was what it was. And even more so when my professor indicated – in the most diplomatic way possible – that it was not my place as a *dozent* to write inflammatory pieces for some left-wing newspaper, that words had been spoken in high places. I foolishly told my wife about this. Well, I had no rest from that moment on. I was endangering my position at the university; I was a married man; I had a daughter; how irresponsible could I get, and so on and so on. I tried to explain that at this moment there were perhaps issues more momentous even than our family, that the future of our whole country was in the balance. I can see now, looking back, that I was too full of righteous indignation, too carried away. Because the next thing I knew – and it happened quite quickly – was that (a) I had been suspended from my position in the university, and (b) my wife had gone to her mother's, taking Albertina with her. When I went to see her she categorically refused to return to me or let me see Albertina, and she said that as far as she was concerned I was no better than a Bolshevist myself.'

He had been talking quickly, vividly, passionately; now he paused and looked down at me.

'Are you listening to all this?' he asked slightly suspiciously. I nodded.

'Well. A few months later the Germans did invade Austria. Saturday March twelfth 1937. A friend called on me at three in the morning, and told me I had better get out of the country if I didn't want to be arrested. Oddly, he was not the man I would ever have expected to do this. He was a friend from undergraduate days who had ended up in a dusty job in a ministry. But some papers had passed through his hands and my name was on one of them. I was in a terrible state; for one thing, I had no money and no time to go to a bank, even supposing the bank would have given me any. My friend offered to buy my books. Can you imagine what it is like to have to abandon your flat, all your things, your books, everything, and take only what you can carry easily?' He paused. 'So, what did I do? I had my rucksack, and I simply walked over the border into Italy. I looked like any other hiker and the border guard nodded me through. I went to Genoa, and found a ship going to Barcelona. Are you still listening?'

I nodded again. He stopped and took out a packet of cigarettes. We sat at the waterside and smoked for a while.

'What happened then?' I asked eventually.

'My most pressing problem was money. I had none. But since the Spanish Civil War was raging I had the idea to offer some pieces to a newspaper – an American one. A man I met in Barcelona put me in touch with the European office of Associated Press and they offered to look at anything I sent in. I got as near to the front as I could and simply wrote down whatever I saw and sent it off. And after a bit some money came back and I found I had a job. The main thing was to get within the sound of the guns. The more dangerous the situation, the more likely I was to get paid – that was how I reasoned. So, I was at Guadalquivir and Jarama, working as a stretcher-bearer mostly, and writing furiously. But there again I found myself in

215

difficulty.'

'How?'

'Well, I was on the Republican side and the comrades wanted to know what I was sending off. I realized things could be as difficult there as they'd been in Vienna. By this time, however, I had learned my craft. I simply wrote two texts – one for the comrades, and one for the office. This was quite easy actually, since few of them spoke English. There was an English contingent there, but I kept out of their way.'

'Did you speak Spanish?'

'I learned it.'

I was listening intently, hypnotized by this story. It all lay so far outside my experience that I had trouble grasping it.

'Go on.'

'There's not much more to tell. The Republicans were beaten, thanks to Hitler and Mussolini, and I came to France and ran into Madame Leary. I had to write my book as quickly as possible, and I needed somewhere to do that. She offered me a room.'

'How long have you been here?'

'Six months.'

There was a moment's silence.

'So – have you written the book?'

He nodded. 'Finished it a few weeks ago. That's why you found me putting up Chinese lanterns.'

'They're very beautiful Chinese lanterns.'

'Thank you.'

'And is the book going to come out?'

'No idea. I hope so. A man I know has put me

216

in touch with an American publisher. That seemed my best bet.'

'And your wife – have you contacted her?'

'I tried. I wrote to her, telling her what had happened, asking for news of Albertina.'

'Did she reply?'

He shook his head.

'I'm sorry,' I whispered.

We both stared out across the harbour, looking idly at the yachts with their lights, listening to the laughter and music wafting across the dark water, and the long streaks where lights were reflected in the water, glittering, shifting in the occasional swell.

'What do you want to do now?' I whispered at last.

'I want to go in and dance!'

He was suddenly cheerful, so we returned to *Chez Fredy* and he took me in his arms. The bar was crowded now, filled with couples drifting about to the music, and we drifted with them. Werner seemed to be more at peace and I was glad I had been able to help him in some way. So we danced and later we had another drink and talked about unimportant things like Jacques Lemaître's poetry, and he teased me about it. Then we talked about Maia. I told him she wanted me to paint her nude. He teased me about this too. 'She is quite shameless. That is her charm, if you ask me,' he said thoughtfully. 'You really can't feel offended by her. Can you?'

He was looking at me with a twinkle in his eye.

'Offended? On the beach? I don't know what I thought. Bewildered, mainly. I had no idea how to respond.'

He laughed. 'No, that is your charm.'

Then suddenly, behind Werner, I saw Alcide. He was talking to a man I did not know and who might have been a builder or someone like that. Alcide, dressed in his immaculate suit and stiff collar, seemed out of place, but I remembered hearing Karim mention that he used to come down into the port at night and this must be where he came. Our eyes met for an instant but I quickly looked away. He was the last person I wanted to talk to.

Perhaps twenty minutes later, Werner and I left the bar and strolled slowly along the waterfront. The only thought in my mind was how I could make it up to him for the misery his wife had caused, but I had no idea how to do it.

We turned off the waterfront into the dark street leading out of town, not far from where the little lane led up towards *Les Cigalettes*. It was a narrow street without pavements and quite dark – just one dim light fixed high up on a house further along.

Then suddenly a lorry came roaring down the road behind us. In a relaxed, slightly sleepy way I expected it to slow down or to swerve to avoid us, but with a sudden scream I realized it wasn't going to. The driver had not seen us and in a second would have driven us against the wall – or driven right over us. I screamed as Werner, his arm about my shoulders, crammed us into a shallow doorway, sheltering me, pressing me against the door as the lorry rushed past with only inches to spare.

It disappeared round the corner, was gone in a moment, and I remained locked in Werner's arms, quivering with the shock.

'There, there,' he whispered, stroking my hair. 'It's all right now. Don't worry. Everything is all right.'

I said nothing, still trying to control my breath, and at last as I moved a little we were looking into each other's eyes. It was as if some gleam of recognition flashed between us because he kissed my forehead and a moment later he kissed my cheek, then he found my lips and we were soon kissing hectically, frantically, clutching each other, unable to help ourselves, kissing as if all the weeks we had known each other were crammed up together into a span of a few seconds and we had to make up for it all now, in this instant. All the nervous tension of the near miss was translated into our kisses as we clawed and hugged, clutching each other, and I could hear him gasping, 'Oh, my darling, oh, my darling, oh *du liebe Gott!*' I was the same, holding and kissing him anywhere I could get at, his face, his cheeks, his neck, frantic to hold him.

In a moment we broke free.

'Meg!' He was out of breath. *'Du liebe Gott!* It is *you*! And all this time...'

We clasped hands facing each other in the street. 'Yes, my only darling, my only, only darling...'

He took my hand and we walked and almost ran back through the dark street and up the dusty track, through the gate and the dark pines to the house, and then we were in his room, and in breathless haste we tore our clothes off and fell on to his bed.

My heart was thudding in my throat. I didn't say anything, neither did he. He was over me, pressing down as we clasped each other, kissing, fighting, pressing; a hectic need washed through both of us and our bodies, already glistening with sweat, slipped, slid, my breasts pressing against him, his thigh between mine, pressing up to me. Although I had never done this before I knew exactly what to do; my instinct was completely sure and my trust in him complete. I stretched my legs wide, grasping him about the waist, drawing him to me, gasping, biting, gripping. All the frustration, all the need that had churned in me was now expressed. I wanted him more than I had ever wanted anything, wanted him on me, in me.

But he wouldn't come in. Not yet. I moaned, 'Werner, please...' But now he slid down my body and I cried out as his tongue found my centre, flicking, teasing. I cried out again, it was too much, he must be inside me, I couldn't stand it, I would die.

'Werner, please...' I reached up to him, grasping, clinging. And still he wouldn't. Rising up over me he ran his hands over my breasts up and down, slipping on the sweaty skin, and I ran my hand up from his belly over his chest, up and down.

Then finally he entered me. It was so sudden. I was ready and yet it took me by surprise. He was in me, tight, deep. Somehow he was bigger than I had imagined. But what had I imagined? I cried out and my back arched up to him, wanting him right in me. I gripped his back with my heels, tight, thrusting upwards. Oh, it was so good – more than good, more than words could say. It was all I had ever wanted, ever expected. All my life had been leading up to this moment and now that it had arrived, it was more than I could possibly have dreamed of. All my insides, my centre, had melted and I was liquid, flowing outward to embrace him. But words failed, and I could only fight, thrust, yearning up to him as he pierced me. I was dying, all self gone, annihilated, exploded into a million stars...

Silence as we lay. He was inside me but still now, spent, quiescent. He was leaning on one elbow looking down at me and gradually I became aware of him. 'That was beautiful,' I whispered.

He said nothing.

'My dearest Meg,' he murmured at last. 'My Golden Girl, my girl of the Golden West.' He leaned over me, kissing me gently on the forehead, then subsided beside me, and slid his arm beneath my head. I rested my head on his chest.

Twenty

I opened my eyes, and for a moment couldn't think where I was. Someone was opening a shutter and in a moment a shaft of morning sunlight crossed the room. Werner was standing over me. He was dressed.

'Sleep well?'

Still very sleepy, I nodded, luxuriating in the bed.

'And you?'

'Fine.'

The memory of our love-making flooded back. I reached up to him. 'Kiss me.'

He knelt by the bed and we kissed. As I lay back on the pillow we stared into each other's eyes. 'It was real, wasn't it? That was us last night?'

He nodded. I took his hand in mine and kissed it. 'I love you,' I whispered.

'I love you,' he whispered.

We were still looking at each other when the memory of the near miss came back and I felt quite sick in my stomach. Had it been done on purpose? Could it have been that Alcide had bribed the driver to knock us down? It sounded preposterous, except that I remembered the argument between Werner and Alcide and the concentrated hatred in Alcide's voice, his mock-ing, taunting, tone.

'Werner, my darling – last night...' I held his hand looking up at him. 'Last night – you know – it occurred to me...'

'Mm?'

'You know we saw Alcide in *Chez Fredy* – talking to that man. You don't think...'

'Think what?'

'I know it sounds silly. But – you don't think it was him in the lorry?'

He laughed. 'Who – Alcide?'

'*No!* Of course not! The man. Werner, don't laugh!' I lifted myself on one elbow. 'I heard you once rowing with Alcide. You threatened him.'

'Heard me – when?'

'Oh it doesn't matter – but once you were both out the back, and you told him to be kinder to Madame Leary.'

He sat on the side of the bed. 'Meg, what happened last night was a complete accident. It's much more likely that the driver had had a few drinks and wasn't looking where he was going. Surely you don't imagine Alcide would want to murder me?' I was silent, and after a moment Werner tilted up my chin. 'Do you?'

'I don't know. But I worry – that's all.'

He chuckled. 'Please don't. Come and have breakfast. I'm hungry.'

Sounds of movement were coming up from the kitchen, the clanging of coffee pots and the clat-tering of crockery and as I heard this evidence of normality and reason, I tried to shake off my thoughts. But the memory would not go away.

When I thought that Werner might have been harmed, might have been killed – would have been killed but for the providential doorway – and then remembered that the truck had had no lights on. Surely that was most dangerous? Should a heavy truck have been roaring through the narrow street without lights?

However there was something else. I had spent the night in Werner's bed, and Werner was about to take me down to breakfast.

'What is it?'

'Well – I mean – look, here I am, and – the others – Madame—'

'Come on! I'll speak to her. Haven't you learned anything yet? No one will even notice. Hurry up and get dressed; I'm going down.'

And with that he left. I pulled myself out of bed, found a jug of water and basin on a wash-stand and, huddling naked, hastily washed myself. I pulled on my dress from the previous night. Every one of them would watch me emerge; every one of them would see my dress – in glaring contrast to their morning casual wear, their shorts, their dressing gowns. I felt very conspicuous.

By this time, as I have said, Heather was also installed in *Les Cigalettes*. She shared a sort of outhouse or shed next to Clay's studio. When I arrived at the breakfast table on the veranda, just as Werner had told me, no one made any remark, and I simply took my place.

Heather had not yet appeared. I didn't like to disturb her and Clay, but then Clay himself appeared and said Heather was on her way. Seizing this excuse I went out to their little love nest and found her still in her underwear dragging a comb through her unruly hair and inspecting herself in a bit of mirror standing on a window ledge. A large dishevelled bed occupied most of the room.

'I don't know how you manage to stay so neat and presentable,' she said as she surveyed me in my dress. 'Or indeed why?'

'I'm not sure why either,' I replied at last. 'Parental discipline, I suppose. Long years of training.'

I told her about the row between Werner and Alcide, about Alcide in the *guinguette*, and our near miss with the truck. Heather was disposed to make light of it, though she was intrigued by the thought of a fight between Werner and Alcide.

'As far as the truck is concerned, I'm certain it meant nothing—'

'*Nothing?*'

'*Chérie*, all I meant was I don't think there was any plot to murder you and Werner. Sounds too melodramatic.'

'So Alcide was there by pure coincidence?'

'*Absolument*. We all know Alcide's tastes by now. And why Karim cries himself to sleep every night.'

'Hmm.' I thought for a moment. 'If I were Karim, I would have left by now.'

'*Moi aussi*.'

'Why doesn't he?'

Heather merely raised her eyebrows knowingly and shrugged.

'Anyway, thanks,' I said after another moment, relieved by Heather's common-sense approach. 'I'm sure you're right. It was just such a terrible shock, that's all. When I think – if anything had happened to Werner...'

Heather glanced up at me from the mirror. There was a moment of silence as she studied me and in the end I had to avert my eyes.

'I say, Meg, were you here last night? You were, weren't you?'

I was still unable to meet her gaze.

'It's serious, isn't it?' I could hear the surprise in her voice.

'Nothing was ever so serious in my life,' I muttered.

'Strewth, and you've only known him a few days.'

'I knew from the instant that we met.'

She chuckled. 'A romantic moment indeed. Me chucking up into the harbour and you spouting Keats.' She finished her preparations. 'Coming for breakfast?'

As we ate breakfast I felt distinctly cheered by what Heather had said. It helped to put things in perspective and I looked forward to making a start on Werner's portrait.

There were eight of us round the table – myself and Werner, Heather and Clay, old Pierre Bonnard, Jacques and Chantal, and Madame Leary. It was another exquisite morning: warm, clear, with the promise of heat to come, light filtering through the pines and throwing dappled shadows across the breakfast table. The checked table cloth, the Provençal bowls and cups, the heavenly smell of fresh coffee, the happy relaxed atmosphere as we chatted and joked. It seems at this distance like some golden age, when there was no sense of time and never any hurry to do anything or get anywhere.

We were still at breakfast when a large black Citroën police car appeared in the drive and came to a halt. Three *gendarmes*, in their *kepis* and boots, got out and came across to where we were all sitting round the table.

'*Excusez-nous, Madame, de vous déranger,*' one of them addressed Madame Leary respectfully. '*Est-ce-qu'il y a ici un Jacques Lemaître?*' The other two *gendarmes* looked down at us as we gawped up at them. Their expression was of complete impassivity and they were not friendly. They loomed large over us and exuded an air of authority, of implied violence, of menace. They might have been made of stone.

Jacques, in his dressing gown, was frozen to his seat. For a moment he could say nothing as we all swivelled our gaze round to him. He stared up at them; they focussed on him.

'*Vous êtes Jacques Lemaître?*'

Jacques nodded, then swallowed, still without having spoken.

The officer had a piece of paper in his hand. He glanced down at it, refreshed his memory, then spoke, still with this complete impassivity.

'You are apprehended.'

'*Mais pourquoi?*'

'You were ordered to report for mobilization at

the *depôt* of the third military district of the City of Paris on the eighteenth of May last. You failed to appear.'

Chantal gave a little gasp and threw herself across Jacques' chest, clutching him round the neck. Jacques was speechless. Madame Leary was on her feet now. 'You cannot arrest him! He has a medical dispensation.'

'We have no knowledge of that, Madame. He was ordered to appear. That is all we know. *Venez, M'sieur, s'il vous plaît,*' he went on in that voice of stone.

Jacques looked imploringly, speechlessly, round at us all. Madame Leary had not yet given up. 'Let me see your authorization,' she said firmly. The officer shrugged and handed over the papers. She glanced briefly over the papers, then spoke more quietly to the policemen. 'Messieurs, *s'il vous plaît* – if you will step into the house one second...'

They glanced quickly at one another then followed her into the house. As they disappeared, we all started talking at once. Jacques, still with Chantal clinging to him, had crumpled and was weeping. 'What shall I do?' he mumbled, one arm about Chantal, his face streaked with tears, looking wildly about him. 'What shall I do, Chantal? They have found me. Oh, *mon Dieu*, I shall die, I know it. I know it, I shall die!'

A few minutes later the three policemen reappeared, Madame Leary following them.

'Jacques, don't worry about your things,' she said calmly. 'Chantal will pack them up and bring them down to the *Gendarmerie*. You had

228

better go with the officers now.'

He stood, flapping his arms wildly. 'But – I cannot go like this. Oh, what shall I do? Chantal, help me! Oh, *mon Dieu!*'

'*Venez, M'sieur.*' The *gendarmes* were beginning to get impatient. 'Evading conscription is a serious offence. *La Patrie* is in peril. She has need of all her sons.'

A few minutes later Jacques disappeared in the black Citroën. I caught a last glimpse of him between two large *gendarmes* in the back of the car. He seemed visibly to have shrunk in those few minutes. Chantal had already dashed into the house. 'I must pack his things.'

As we looked at each other, still gathered about the breakfast table, Werner at last spoke. 'So the medical dispensation...'

Madame Leary raised her hands and let them fall. 'Poor Jacques. I did what I could. God knows what use he will be to *La Patrie.*'

'What did you say to them?' I couldn't help asking.

'I merely asked whether they couldn't come back again tomorrow. I have always kept on very good terms with the *gendarmes* and they know me well. I even contemplated offering a *douceur.* But they were in their most ferocious and patriotic mood this morning, as you could see. I had to be careful. They might have arrested *me,*' she added with a wry grimace, and then added, 'Poor Jacques.' She shook her head.

For the rest of our breakfast we were in a sombre mood. The world had intruded into our idyll in a very unpleasant manner, and the thought of war now hung over the table and invaded all our thoughts. The idea of Jacques in uniform – a *poilu* – seemed grotesque. I glanced at Werner. If Jacques could be picked up like this at such a distance, was even Werner safe? After all he was – very nearly – an enemy alien. If war broke out Werner would certainly be arrested. But even if war did not break out, might they not arrest him anyway? Might they not send him back to Austria?

Soon a taxi appeared and Chantal came down from the house dragging a huge suitcase. Werner helped her load it into the taxi and it disappeared into town.

As breakfast was cleared away, I tried to catch Werner's attention. 'I was hoping to make a start on your picture today,' I began tentatively. This was not as frivolous as it sounds. The sudden arrest of Jacques reminded me of Werner's fragile situation and the need to do my picture, to have a tangible record of him, something that bound us together, became suddenly very pressing. To my relief he was quite amenable, and twenty minutes later we were installed on the terrace, my canvas ready and Werner relaxed in a wide cane chair with a dappled effect of light over his face, and the brilliant sea behind his head. I planned also to put a pine tree in the picture with a Chinese lantern suspended in the branches.

'Did you know he was wanted for the call-up?' I asked.

He shook his head.

'Do you think Madame Leary did?'

'I think so.'

'So she was running a risk – I mean, letting him stay here?'

'Yes.'

'Do you think Jacques could have got her into trouble – I mean, the fact that she knew he was running away?'

'Possibly.'

'Werner...'

'Yes, my little pea hen?'

I concentrated on my picture for a moment, sketching in the basic outline of his head and shoulders with a stick of charcoal. There was a silence with only the scratching of the charcoal to be heard.

'Yes, *mein Schatz*?'

There was another silence. I simply could not put my question into words. I concentrated on my drawing. Finally he said, 'You were going to ask me if the *gendarmes* are going to come for *me*, weren't you?'

I nodded without looking up.

'Well, since France is not at war with Austria, I am not *yet* an enemy. Still, I am registered with the *gendarmes* as a resident alien—'

'Resident alien?' It sounded horrible. 'Do you have to do that?'

'Oh yes. And if I hadn't, my dear, you may take my word for it, they would have been around soon enough to check up on me.'

'So they know you're here?'

He nodded.

'And do they know about ... about what you did in Austria – and being wanted there?'

231

He shrugged. 'Who knows?'

I concentrated on my picture and there was silence for several minutes, broken only by the scratching of my charcoal. Looking at the few marks I had made on the bare white canvas I was suddenly assailed by doubts, suddenly reminded of my very limited abilities. How was I ever to catch the essence of Werner in a picture? A few dabs of colour, a few brush strokes on a canvas – who was I fooling?

Another thought now sprang at me. 'Werner...'

'Yes, *darlink*?'

'I wonder – wouldn't it be safer for you to go to England for the time being?'

'Perhaps – if the situation gets any worse.'

'Have you made any enquiries – I mean, do you have to have a visa or something?' My brain had begun to focus with frightening rapidity when Werner's safety was involved. 'I mean, if Frenchmen are being called up, the French must think the situation is very serious, mustn't they?'

He nodded again.

At this moment Chantal reappeared, slowly crossing the terrace, going up the steps and into the house. She said nothing, did not even appear to notice us; I wasn't sure but I think she was in tears. I turned again to my canvas but a few moments later I set down the charcoal.

'Excuse me,' I muttered. 'I must just go and see that she is all right.'

However when I got upstairs to Chantal's room, the blinds were down, and I could dimly see the girl on her bed, face down and, sitting beside her, Maia, stroking her back and speaking

232

in a low and soothing voice. Maia glanced up as I appeared in the doorway and smiled. After a moment I withdrew and returned to the veranda where Werner was still sitting.

'It's all right, Maia is with her.'

I picked up my charcoal but put it down again a moment later. 'I've done enough for the moment,' I muttered brusquely, unable to look at him.

'What's the matter?' He took my hand and, leaning forward, looked up into my eyes. 'Meg? What is it?'

'I'm sorry,' I said after a moment, 'but Jacques' arrest has upset me. And there's Chantal upstairs in tears ... And then, thinking of you – I can't concentrate.' I paused again. 'This morning we were all so happy sitting at the breakfast table, and it was so lovely, everything was so beautiful, and then, when those *gendarmes* came it was just horrible.' I could feel tears starting in the corner of my eyes. 'And if anything happened to you...'

He took me in his arms. 'Meg. Hush. Hush, my little cabbage. This is when we must all be strong. And you *are* strong, I know.'

I looked up. 'Am I?'

He nodded.

I drew a long breath, took out a handkerchief, and dabbed at my eyes. 'Sorry – it all came at me suddenly.'

'We'll go for a swim,' he said suddenly. 'Get some towels.'

I jumped at this, and soon we were making our way along the dusty path through the pines.

Werner did not take the straight path down to the water, but kept on further along the low cliff overlooking the water.

'We'll go to Maia's private beach,' he said over his shoulder. I followed and soon we were clambering down over the rocks and came to the little patch of hot bright sand where the water lapped slowly in tiny waves and the sun was already glinting on the water. We took our clothes off and in a second were in the water. It was a stroke of genius of Werner's: the shock of the fresh cool water stimulated me and drove off in an instant the gloom that had swamped me after Jacques' arrest. Werner was near, grinning, and teasing, diving and coming up near me, taking me round the neck and kissing me. He was like a dolphin or seal, sporting about me, until I couldn't help joining in, and was diving down and swimming between his legs, coming up and clasping him from behind. He would twist round and kiss me; he took me by the waist and half lifted and half threw me into the air, and I fell backwards, coming up again and laughing. We were like two water babies, revelling in our nakedness. It was a second childhood.

Then we were on the sand again and he was caressing me, running his hand over my breasts, kissing and touching them, and I was caressing him too, running my hands up and down his hard man's back, loving all the tough strength of him. We concentrated on each other, serious, staring into each other's eyes, as if to find there some fathomless meaning, some profound significance, some ultimate answer to the riddle of life, utterly focussed on each other. Then we made love – not fast, not violently or aggressively as we had that first time, but slowly, languorously, deeply, me lying flat, my head thrown back, my arms flung out, as he raised himself above me and slowly ran up into me, deeper and deeper, until I was transfixed, holding him in me, wanting to keep him there for ever and never wanting to lose this moment, this moment of perfect harmony between us, this complete peace and understanding, knowing that this was what we were for, that this was what was intended for us, that here was our centre, that all our lives had been leading to this and, now that we had it, it could never be taken away from us.

Twenty-One

The following morning, I was awake early and for once Werner was beside me, still asleep. I was able to study him, his sturdy square jaw, the face in repose, his blond hair flopped across his broad forehead. I reached and carefully moved the lock of hair away from his brow, touching his hair lightly; I did not wish to wake him. Just to lie and look at him, just to take in the precious reality of him here with me in this most intimate of places, us two together in his little bed. If only I could freeze this moment. In the end I could not resist bending over him and kissing him lightly on the brow. At that he stirred slightly, turned, and his eyes opened. For a second he looked up at me as he returned to consciousness, then that quizzical smile curled his lovely lips, and I could not resist bending over to kiss them, his beautiful soft lips that I will never forget as long as I live.

As we lay, relaxed, quiet, with his arm round my neck, my glance was drawn to an inscription on the wall. I had seen it before but had never really taken notice of it. This morning I did.

It was in German – of which I know not one word. I asked what it meant.

Grau, teurer Freund, ist alle Theorie
Und grün des Lebens goldner Baum.

'It's Goethe: "Dear friend all theory is grey, but the golden tree of life is green".'

'What does that mean?'

'When I came across that, I suddenly realized what my life had been up to that moment: all theory, getting life out of a book.' He turned over and looked deep into my eyes. For once he seemed serious. 'You see, Meg, the trouble with theory is that it always reduces life, it simplifies it. It looks at life from only one angle, in only one aspect, and in so doing it drains it of colour. It is grey. That was what my life was like at the university: standing in the lecture hall, facing the rows of my students, each with his note pad ready, listening intently and taking down words that had been dictated to generations upon generations of students before them. Whereas I had only to turn my head and there outside the window, in the street, there was life – life, in all its variety, all its complications, its contradictions; life in all its colours, life in its refusal to be bound down by any rule or system, making itself up as it goes along, with its eternal ability to reinvent itself, to surprise us – well, that's the gold; that is what is truly valuable. And I felt that the Master had expressed the thought so well, it deserved a place on my wall – just in case I was ever tempted to open a text book again.'

'Won't you ever open a text book again?'

'Not if I can help it.'

'You mean you wouldn't want to teach in a university again?'

'Never.'

'Well – what will you do?'

'At this moment I can't be sure. If I can get my book published, I might try to work as a journalist. If there is going to be a war, there will be work for journalists.'

There was a silence between us. This was the thought that hung over all our heads constantly. Every conversation seemed to come round to this point.

'Why don't you go to England?' I said suddenly.

He thought for a moment and at last said slowly, 'I have been thinking of it.'

I sat up on one arm, full of energy. It was suddenly the obvious and right thing to do.

'You must!'

He smiled. 'Would you like that?'

'How can you ask? I'm going home in September – we must go together!'

It was that simple. I had a blinding vision of myself and Werner in a flat in Charlotte Street. I could continue with my art – or not, it didn't matter. I could just as easily get a job if necessary and Werner could go round the newspapers and get work.

'You speak French – and German and English. You're unbelievably brilliant, you know absolutely everything – you are perfectly qualified! And you sent all that stuff to Associated Press from Spain, you told me. You'd only have to tell the editor what you've done and they'd give you a job immediately! Then we could—'

It had been on the tip of my tongue to say we could get married.

'Well, that doesn't matter...' I stuttered. 'But the important thing is you must come to England. You must!'

'OK,' he smiled, amused at my exuberance. 'I am convinced.'

I kissed him.

'But there are the formalities.'

'What do you mean?'

'I am an Austrian citizen, Meg.'

'So?'

'Well, I shall have to apply for a residence permit, I expect.'

'Will you?'

'I think so. And that will depend on whether I have any money, or a job to go to.'

'I don't see how that matters. You will get a job soon enough once you're there.'

'No. I have to show proof.'

238

'But you can do that once we're in London.'

'No, *mon petit chou*, all this must be done *before* I come to England.'

'What? Well, how?'

He shrugged. 'At the British consulate.'

'Is there one in St Tropez?'

He laughed. 'We'd have to go to Nice – or Marseilles.'

I leaped out of bed. 'We'll go today. Oh, Werner, we must! I can't wait another day!'

And that is what we did. We took the little narrow-gauge train to St Raphael, and changed to the express to Marseilles. And eventually, on the fifth floor of a dusty office block in the centre of the city, we did find the British consul. He was actually the employee of a commercial import-export company, but he could do the paperwork.

As Werner had explained, the whole success of this depended on his ability to maintain himself. In a word – did he have any money or the promise of a job?

'My book on the Spanish Civil War is with an American publisher at the moment,' he explained. 'If it is accepted I shall receive an advance.'

At the end of our discussion it had come down to this: a residence permit depended on either money in Werner's pocket (i.e. the advance from the American publisher), or a signed piece of paper promising Werner a job in England. As we sat there in that dingy office, another idea had struck me. I was full of ideas, then; my brain was racing on Werner's behalf. Surely I could help Werner to find a job, and like a fool, the very first possibility that occurred to me was with Edward's father's printing business. After all, it only needed a letter from him to convince the consul. I would write today. A reply could be with us within a week. It was only later that I unravelled the complications likely to arise from such a scheme.

Then we were out on the streets of Marseilles again. It was a hot dusty afternoon by now, traffic rumbled by, shops were closed for the afternoon siesta, and it was a dismal, shabby change from the peace and loveliness of *Les Cigalettes*. I took Werner's hand.

'Let's get back.'

In the train we were quiet. Suddenly the world was full of complications and my brain felt stuffed. First of all, the idea of writing to Mr Tremayne. Supposing he agreed, how was I to introduce Werner to Edward? It seemed a crackpot idea. Then we didn't know how long it would take the American publishers to reply to Werner's manuscript and whether they would take it. I was sure they would, of course. But I had no idea how long these things took. And suddenly I was in a frantic hurry. I wanted answers. I wanted Werner's permit. I couldn't be at peace until he had it in his hand.

It occurred to me that a surer way would be for my father to wangle a job for Werner at Marshall and Snelgrove. Even if he only had some menial job in the postage and packing department – or maybe translating overseas correspondence –

it would get him the all-important residence permit. I decided to write home that night.

However, by the time we returned to *Les Cigal-ettes* it was the middle of the evening, just after sunset, and all these thoughts were suddenly driven from my mind as Marcelline greeted us in the hall.

'*C'est madame...*'

'*Quoi? Qu'est-ce que s'est passé?*'

'*Elle est malade...*'

'*Où est elle?*'

'*Dans sa chambre.*'

We raced upstairs, but stopped at her door. I motioned Werner to be silent and knocked lightly. Maia opened the door. The room was in near darkness. Maia came out of the room and closed the door behind her.

'My dears, let's go downstairs. Madame is asleep for the moment.'

Without saying anything we followed her down to the saloon. Pierre was sitting there alone. We greeted him, then Maia made us sit down.

'My dears.' Maia for once was perfectly serious and spoke softly and calmly. 'Madame has had a slight attack – or seizure. *Une crise cardiaque*, the doctor called it. He was here this morning and has given her a sedative. She will sleep till morning and will have to remain in bed for some time.'

'How long?' Werner leaned forward insistently.

Maia shrugged.

'Where is Alcide?' He persisted.

'Alcide has not been seen – not since...' She paused. 'Not since...'

Werner now grasped what had happened. 'You don't mean they had a row that brought on the seizure?'

Maia was very serious, said nothing at first, but finally answered, 'It would seem so.'

Werner could scarcely contain himself. 'Where is Alcide?' Maia didn't know. 'Was he here today? Have you seen him?'

'Not since breakfast.'

The following morning we found Madame Leary awake, though very frail. We said nothing about Alcide or the row, and concentrated on helping her to recover.

'Don't worry about me, my dears,' she said at one point. She was lying in her bed, her head on the pillow, looking up at us standing round the bed. 'I've had my life. The future is yours. I'll just lie here quietly. Now – run along – I'll be all right.'

The doctor called during the morning. He said there was nothing to do except to lie quietly, and wait for the body to recover itself. Light food, no excitement.

'And, Werner,' She laid a hand on his arm. 'Say nothing to Alcide.' He started, but she tightened her grip. 'For my sake, my dear. Say nothing. Promise.'

Werner gave a grudging promise.

Even so, the old lady soon tired of the enforced inaction, and barely a week later insisted on being brought down to sit on a *chaise longue* on the veranda.

Karim was at the breakfast table, but there was no sign of Alcide. Poor Karim looked ever more wretched. I resolved to speak to him and, when Werner went off to his hut, I moved to the chair beside Karim's.

'How are you today?' I asked innocently.

He did not reply, staring down at the croissant on his plate.

'Karim...' I laid my hand on his arm. 'Karim, I do so wish there was something I could do.'

He shook his head again without speaking.

'Surely,' I said softly, 'anything would be better than this, wouldn't it?'

He looked up at me at last, waiting.

'Have you thought,' I struggled on, 'have you thought of just going back to Paris?' I asked at last, as gently as I could.

He shook his head. 'I would rather be dead.'

'Oh no! Surely not! You must never think like that!' I took his arms in my hands, and made him look at me. 'You have so much! Think of the pleasure you give to people by your dancing! You must go on – just for them. When does the season reopen at the Lido?'

'Middle of September,' he muttered.

'Well why not go back a little early, to prepare for the season? What does your agent say?'

He shrugged. 'I don't have to return yet.'

'Go back to Paris now,' I said more urgently. 'Now, while Alcide is not here. It would be best. Then he couldn't hurt you any more.'

He shook his head. 'I would rather be with

243

him, even if he hurt me,' he muttered.

'Even if he hurt you?' I repeated.

He nodded, and took a tiny nibble from his croissant.

'I don't understand...'

My voice faded. I was clearly not going to succeed. And who was I to criticize? Karim was in love. It didn't matter what Alcide did, I could see that now. It didn't matter at all. Karim loved him; he would endure all.

I suddenly felt the impertinence of what I had been saying and how juvenile I had sounded. Who was I to intrude between them? Karim would work out his own salvation, in his own time. I said no more.

I went up to see how Madame Leary was. I found her awake, and after I had asked her how she felt, it was clear that she was going to survive. She didn't want to talk much yet, but was happy to listen to me. I told her something of myself, my family, and life in London.

'One day, when I am feeling a little stronger,' she promised, 'I will tell you of *my* time in London.' She smiled weakly. 'It might amuse you.'

'I shall hold you to that.'

That morning I wrote a letter to my father. After a bit of thought I realized that I didn't have to make anything up. I simply explained that Werner was a university lecturer who had been driven from his post because of his anti-Nazi views and needed to get to England. To do that he had to have a sponsor – someone who could give him a job. And I felt sure that Marshall and

Snelgrove could find room for him. It would be a patriotic act, I hinted. I was growing up fast, I realized as I read this letter through.

For the moment there was nothing else to do except to get on with Werner's portrait, and so we set up the easel on the veranda and I set to work again. I had sketched in the outline with charcoal, and it was time now to set paint to canvas.

Alcide finally reappeared in the late afternoon, when the sun was lower, and the air had cooled a little. Werner was in his workshop-cum-study and I was sitting with Pierre Bonnard in the drawing room looking through a book of reproductions. Alcide glimpsed us and stood in the doorway looking insolently down at us. He was dressed immaculately as always, and seemed completely at ease.

'Where is my grandmother?'

'She is in her room,' I said in a low voice, without expression. 'The doctor was here this morning.'

He glanced about him coolly. 'Good,' he said at last, and made his way upstairs.

After a moment I excused myself from Pierre, and followed Alcide quietly upstairs. I hesitated at the top of the stairs, listening, and could hear voices speaking low in Mme Leary's room. Not quite sure of what I was doing, I tiptoed to the door and tried to make out what they were saying. They were speaking in French, in whispers, and I could make no sense of it. I could make out the tone, however, which was gentle and soothing on his part, and complaining and sighing on hers. After a little while I crept downstairs again.

Later I began to wonder what had become of Werner. I had now reached the stage when I missed him almost immediately and was uneasy unless I could account for him every minute of the waking day. I wandered out of the house to his study. He was not there, so I continued round the side of the house and there, for the first time since I had come to *Les Cigalettes*, set a little further off, and shielded by trees, I came across a tennis court. It was made of compacted red earth, and Werner was occupied with a rake, clearing off pine cones, leaves from the oaks nearby, and dust. For a while I watched him. He had not noticed me, standing among the trees, and continued with his work. He had the same careful, methodical manner I had admired in him at first, raking the dusty red earth neatly back and forth across the tennis court.

'You might have told me before,' I said casually, coming forward.

He looked up. 'Told you what, my little flower?'

'That there was a tennis court.'

'All in good time. Besides, I did not know you played tennis.'

'What do you mean?' I said, coming closer. 'I adore tennis. Only, I warn you – ' I smiled teasingly – 'I am very good. I would not wish to embarrass you.'

He paused and leaned on his rake. 'Now I am

glad to hear that. It is so tiresome to play against inexperienced amateurs, don't you think?' There was a small smile now on his lips, and I had an instinct, not well hidden, that Werner was probably very good himself.

'When are you going to give me a game?'

'Now.'

I glanced round. 'Are there — ?'

'Racquets? I'll see what I can find.'

A moment later he had returned and offered me a choice of two old racquets. I took one at random.

I would not say that Werner slaughtered me, but he certainly played very aggressively, and I had to run about the court very nimbly to stay in the game at all.

'Am I going too fast for you, *ma petite*?' he asked innocently at one point.

'Not at all,' I said, somewhat out of breath. 'Only it's a while since I played. I'm just getting my eye in.'

'I understand. It's the same with me.' He slammed another serve past me.

'Besides, I'm not used to a clay court,' I panted as I ran after another ball. However there was something about the athletic way that Werner was eyeing me and limbering himself up that provoked me and I determined not to be a doormat. It was my serve and I gave it every ounce of strength I had. It was a good one, and he failed to return it.

'Not too fast for you?' I asked innocently.

'Just getting into my stride.'

The day had cooled, the sky was just a shade

darker, and the pines threw their shadows across the tennis court. Werner threw off his shirt.

'Warm, isn't it?' I remarked, readying myself for another serve.

'I suppose it would seem so to a cold-blooded northerner,' he remarked.

'Is that meant for me? I haven't taken my shirt off yet, Werner, *mein Liebling*,' I added in imitation of his accent.

'Perhaps,' he murmured, as he stood ready to return my serve.

I served as hard as I could, but this time he was ready. He slammed it back over the net and I failed to return it. I had not been keeping a score, but he remarked, almost at random, 'Love all.'

At that moment I remembered the game I had once played with Edward against the fading light. How far I had come from that north London tennis club, that haven of suburban respectability. How far I seemed to have come from my old self, and how far I had come from Edward. He seemed a dim and distant figure, a long way away that evening.

Twenty-Two

'I let you win, otherwise you'd sulk all night.'

We were in Werner's study-workshop. I set the racquets on the bench, and as I did so I looked casually over the typewriter and the mass of loose correspondence, letters opened, envelopes franked, scattered about it. I picked one up casually as Werner was changing his clothes. It was from Austria. This took me slightly by surprise.

'Who are you writing to?'

He didn't want to answer.

'Werner...' I stared at the letter and as I turned it over a photograph fell out. It was of a little girl. My heart stopped and I stared in silence at this picture for some seconds.

It was a perfectly normal photograph, the sort of thing one carries about with one. The girl was in her best frock, it seemed, and was standing in a garden facing the camera.

'What is that?'

'It's your daughter, isn't it?'

'Meg?' He took me up sharply. 'Where did you get that?'

'I happened to pick up this envelope and it fell out,' I answered hoarsely. I was still trying to come to grips with the implications. 'Is this a letter from your wife?'

He crossed to me, took the photograph, and put it back in the envelope.

'No,' he said seriously, 'it is not. And even if it were, she would not send me a photograph of Albertina. It is from my brother. He stole the photograph – since you ask.' He could not look at me, and set the envelope back on the desk.

There was a long silence between us. At last I timidly touched his arm. 'I'm sorry – I should never...'

He shrugged, but still could not look at me. Then unexpectedly he leaned forward on the bench, staring down. 'Meg, I think I must be mad. What am I doing here?'

I was terrified by this sudden change in him. I waited, frozen, for him to continue.

'I have thrown *everything* away. Can you imagine that? I can never return home. I shall never see my daughter again.' He shook his head. 'Never,' he repeated. 'I have no home and no job. And no money. And here are you – you are young, you are like one of my students – is it not grotesque irresponsibility of me to love you as I do? To allow you to be so kind to me?' He turned to me at last looking with an almost beseeching look. 'Don't you realize, I should send you home tomorrow!'

'What?'

'You are just a student! You are living with your parents. You have your life in London with all your friends. What am I doing behaving like this?'

'*Werner!*' I screamed. 'Don't think that! Don't say it!' I grasped him by the arms. 'I may be a student, and I may be living with my parents, but I know what I am doing! I know! And I love you, I know that too. I know what I am doing! Why do you think I suggested that you should come to London? Because I don't want to lose you!'

'Oh, God, and I don't want to lose you,' he sighed as he took me in his arms.

'We'll go to London,' I said as I reached my arms about his neck, 'and you will get a job. Then we'll be together. That's all I want.'

'And that's all I want.'

He kissed me and out of that anxiety, that uncertainty and that need we had for each other, the chemistry began to work in us instantly. In a moment I had shuffled off my shorts, he had lifted me on to the desk and, standing in front of me as we kissed frantically, he was already inside me, and we were wriggling and clutching each other in a hectic, spontaneous rush of desire. All the energy of the tennis match was converted into a spontaneous heat, we were grasping and clutching and I was sighing and calling his name as he drove into me.

It was over very quickly and we clung to one another in silence; my heart was thudding wildly in my chest, I could see nothing, could only know the intensity of my need for him.

Then gradually he released me and I was set uncertainly on the earth again. My legs were shaking, I could see nothing, only conscious of him near me. I touched him, touched his face, and he bent to kiss me. 'My darling,' he whispered. I felt as if I were in another time, or rather out of time, out of all known and familiar time or place, set apart in a special place with Werner.

I bent to pick up my shorts and, as I pulled them on again, my glance strayed over the letters and envelopes with their Austrian stamps. I could not help thinking *he writes an awful lot of letters* and a tiny knot of worry began to grow in me, gradually, until I would have to question him about them. He wasn't simply writing to his brother for some crumbs of family gossip.

That evening we were quiet at dinner. Amazingly Alcide and Karim were both at the table. Werner gave him a quizzical glance.

'You must be relieved to see your grandmother recovering?' He glanced at Alcide.

'And so must you,' Alcide retorted sharply. 'Otherwise you would be out of this house. And then where would you go?'

'Let us hope for all our sakes that she makes a swift and complete recovery,' Werner replied suavely.

'Yeah,' Clay joined in. 'Let's all hope your grandmother lives to a very ripe old age, and is cared for by her *loving* grandson!'

One afternoon I was sitting beside her on the veranda as she reclined on the *chaise longue*. She was asleep but eventually she began to regain consciousness, saw I was there, and that we were alone together. It was here that she finally told me the story of her life.

Madame Leary was philosophical.

'I don't mind dying, my dear. I think about it often, you know. I have had my life,' she went on simply, 'but you have yours ahead of you.' She smiled benignly and then reached for my hand. She was a very old woman and her hand was distorted with arthritis, blotched with spots. I was conscious of mine, new, young, clear, lying in hers. She held it tightly as she looked into my eyes. 'But don't fall in love with Werner *too* deeply.' She was looking carefully at me. I could not reply, and she went on, 'It is not wise ever to attach yourself too deeply to anyone or anything. Everything passes, you know. I was so in love with my Nick – and then he died, quite suddenly – after the birth of our daughter. I was destroyed. He was the first man to be kind to me, and I owed him everything. My dear Nick – Werner reminds me of him sometimes – he was so funny and observant, always bringing me little presents. He really loved me. When he died, I was destroyed. Then my dear son William was killed in the war, so I attached myself to my daughter. She married a Frenchman and went to live near Paris. They died in the 1919 flu epidemic. So all I have left is Alcide. Perhaps that is why I put up with his unkindness – oh, I know he takes my money. He only wants my money – I know that.' She was silent for a moment, then went on, 'My brothers went to America and I lost touch with them. My sister married a British MP and would not speak to me – on account of my *past*.' She chuckled.

'Your past?' I asked uncertainly.

Mme Leary smiled slyly. 'Well, my dear, you see when I was your age I was what they called in those days a *demi-mondaine*. I did not have your sheltered life in the suburbs. I had come from the west of Ireland with nothing and had to survive as best as I could. Fortunately I used to be a very good horsewoman and this drew me to the attention of a certain class of men with money in their pockets and the flavour of the turf about them. And so...'

She paused, and then went on dreamily, 'I must say in all modesty I did look very good on a horse. And those were the days when one wore a riding habit cut very close to the figure. It left nothing to the imagination, believe me. Oh, how I had yearned for that riding habit. Nick bought me my first one. I so wanted to please him, to look good for him! I told the dress maker, "Make it fit good and tight, Madame Brocquet!"' She laughed, then after a moment sighed. 'Then he had to leave me – because of his wife – and I fell in with a crowd. They had money, they only wanted a good time – I wasn't very pleased with myself, to tell the truth. When Nick left me, it hurt me badly. So, in a way, I didn't care what I did. They paid me well, we went to the races, we had endless parties, we enjoyed ourselves – and all the time, all I could think of was Nick...' She looked away, distracted, and was silent.

'Do you still think of him?' I asked gently.

'Every day, my dear.'

'I'm sorry,' I muttered. 'I should not have asked.'

'That's all right. But that was perhaps why I

said what I did – about Werner. I know, you see. The French have a saying – trite perhaps, but true all the same: *On n'aime qu'une fois.* You only love once.' She looked at me again. 'You don't mind me saying this?'

'Oh no, it is most interesting, really!' I exclaimed. 'You should write it down.'

She sighed. 'And it is all such a very long time ago, my dear. Looking back now, to the eighties – how the world has changed. The clothes we wore. Can you believe I wore a bustle?' She laughed. 'A bustle! Imagine! I had a lady's maid to do me up in it. It took me half an hour to dress in those days. Every little detail had to be right. And my hair! And the jewels I wore!' She shook her head in a sort of amazement. 'You know, I can hardly believe that that was *me*. If I see a picture in a book now of the clothes I used to wear, I can scarcely believe that it was really *me* dressed like that.' She looked at me again and at last said thoughtfully, 'And to think I was just your age.'

The next thing I remember, something that drove all other thoughts aside for the moment, was that posters went up all over the town advertising a *Bal Masqué* on August 15 – the feast of the Assumption, which was of course a national holiday. All shops would be shut, there would be a religious procession through the town in the morning, in which a figure of the Virgin would be carried and in the evening an open-air dance, with masks.

Heather and I were on fire immediately over

this. It was a matter of pride – not to say national honour – to create the most original masks in the town.

We laboured for several days, painting, pasting, working with *papier maché*. Eventually we had produced masks, not merely for ourselves but for every inhabitant in *Les Cigalettes* – excepting Madame Leary and Pierre Bonnard, who exclaimed that they were too old for that sort of thing.

We would start with a rough cardboard outline of the proposed mask, on to which we would mould *papier mâché* to create a face. These faces were of every conceivable design. Some were benign, the face of a smiling young girl; a sun face, round and beaming; the face of a happy drunk, rubicund with a fat nose. Others were threatening: the face of an evil queen, cold, beautiful, unsmiling; the face of a satyr, distorted, leering; the face of a devil, with contorted eyebrows, and moustaches twisted upwards in a diabolical laugh. The possibilities were endless. Heather's were the best: she had a real flare for this sort of thing.

The other thing to consider was costumes. Clearly one had to come up with something appropriate for the night. I was intending to go as a gypsy, with a colourful skirt, and a scarf about my head, but Heather again outdid me. She found in the *Mont-de-Piété* – the pawn shop – a drummer boy's uniform, a scarlet jacket with white facings and epaulettes, blue breeches and a tricorn hat. She then made for herself a little boy's mask. She looked terrific in this ensemble, and I resolved on the spot that I had to find something more original than a gypsy skirt. As I was getting near to desperation Madame Leary came to my aid. She took me into a spare room upstairs, and indicated some large travelling trunks.

'I keep one or two old things,' she said, 'for sentimental reasons. Open that one.'

I did as she bade, and found inside old gowns and items of clothing from the past, carefully wrapped in tissue paper. As I lifted them out and laid them on a table, she looked them over. For a long time she was unsatisfied, uncertain, and I wondered whether she even knew what it was she was looking for.

But in the end, after I had opened another trunk, she pointed to one item, and I lifted it out and unfurled the tissue paper wrapped so carefully about it.

It was what she had been telling me about – a ball gown of the last century.

'I even have the bustle,' she smiled, and brought up a contraption of leather straps and a wire frame. 'See if it fits, darling.'

I strapped it round my waist – I was wearing a blouse and shorts at that moment.

'I think it should fit. Bring it into my room, and let's try it on.'

So I carried the dress, which was of white silk with gold trimmings, into her room and laid it out on the bed. This was something quite awe-inspiring, to tell the truth. It was a complicated composition, the bodice only partly joined to the skirt, and containing innumerable ties on the inside which had all to be joined in the right order, she told me, to make it fit.

'Fortunately, I have also the stays – without which the whole exercise would be a waste of time. And the petticoats, and stockings – and shoes too. Though they may not fit.' She glanced at me. 'You're quite happy to go along with this?' she enquired uncertainly.

'Happy?' I was astonished. 'I'm *delighted*! I think it's...' But really, words failed.

'You'll think it very silly of me, but I should like very much to see you in one of my gowns – just for old times, if you like.'

There was now quite a lengthy process of fitting me into these things, the shift, the stays, the bustle itself, the petticoats; we must have been a full half hour before she could feel even reasonably satisfied.

'Now, my dear, take a look.'

She turned me to an old pier glass.

Well, the effect was ... I can't find words for it. It was as if I were looking at a complete stranger. I could never have believed the degree to which clothes could alter one's appearance.

'It's only a pity I can't find you a wig too. In the days when I wore this dress myself, my maid spent a full hour putting my hair up, and setting jewels in it. You girls nowadays just don't have the hair any more – you don't have the time to dress it either, of course,' she added phlegmatically. Finally, she asked, almost apologetically, 'Do you think it'll do?'

'I think it's the most wonderful thing I've ever worn,' I said simply. I could see the dress

258

properly now that I was wearing it. As I said there was this strange bustle at the back which had the effect of making me lean forward a little. The bodice was fitted tightly over the stays, making a neat, narrow waist. It then exploded round the bust in lace running up on either side to narrow shoulder straps. The bust was sculpted very *décolleté* and there was a rose in gold silk sewn on as a corsage.

The skirt was like an apron to the knees, then fell in a series of lace flounces to the ankle. It was a complicated design which must have taken seamstresses weeks to make.

Finally she produced a black ribbon. 'Tie this round your neck, and let it fall behind. That's all you need.'

I'm almost sorry I shall be wearing a mask, I thought as I surveyed this vision in the mirror. *No one will know who I am.*

Twenty-Three

August 15th soon arrived. I had never known much about the feast of the Assumption – never known *anything* about it, to be honest – but I quickly came to realize that in a Catholic country it was very important indeed. It is the date of the Virgin Mary's death, and the word 'Assumption' refers to her being carried up to heaven. Some of the guests at *Les Cigalettes* went to Mass during the morning. Even Madame Leary was conveyed in a taxi. I accompanied her. Others – Chantal, and to my surprise, Alcide – walked into town to the church of St Tropez. I sat beside Madame Leary through the Mass, kneeling when she knelt, crossing myself when it was time to do so. I am not religious myself but it seemed only courteous to go along with the others. Then there was a procession through the town. A statue of the Virgin was carried on the shoulders of four men and the crowd followed through the narrow streets of the town, many of them barefoot. The narrow streets were crowded by the throng, packed in between the old faded whitewashed walls, and over their heads, bobbing like a raft on the sea, the Virgin heaved and swayed in white and blue and clasped the infant to her breast, her glazed eyes staring sightlessly ahead. Eternal beauty, I thought, never to grow old, preserved through the generations. Families had come and gone, men and women had been born, had grown to adulthood and gone to their graves, and still on the fifteenth of August the Virgin floated, timeless, unseeing over their heads. How old was that statue? I had no idea.

The town was *en fête*. Already in the morning preparations were underway everywhere. Shops were closed; lanterns were strung among the plane trees in the Place des Lices; café owners were sweeping terraces and wiping tables and chairs in preparation. Makeshift market stalls were being erected, sweet sellers – especially of the wonderful southern nougat, compounded of white of egg, honey, nuts and candied fruits – flower sellers, and across the square men were putting up a platform for the band. There were to be fireworks at midnight at the Port de Pêche, in the shade of the old *Vieille Tour*. The town was busy and there was an atmosphere of excitement and anticipation.

Heather and I had completed our masks and late in the afternoon there was a ceremony of assigning them to their prospective wearers. My masterpiece was the sun-god, aflame with gold, and with a benign smile. That was for Werner. Chantal had a cat mask, in blue, which suited her very well. Maia declined at first to wear a mask. 'It is not for me, *chérie*,' she said. I was very surprised, however, when Alcide unexpectedly made his appearance and demanded his mask.

'You are going to wear a mask?'

'Certainly. Why not? Is there some reason why I should not go, Meg? Besides I have chosen my mask – I shall wear the golden one. It will suit me perfectly. The Sun King – *Le Roi Soleil.*'

'You can't,' I stuttered, taken completely by surprise. 'That one is already taken.'

He appeared astonished. 'But I insist. That mask is obviously meant for me. It *is* me.'

'I'm sorry,' I repeated. 'I cannot – I have promised it...'

'To Werner, I suppose,' he said frigidly.

'Well, yes, if you want to know.'

'*Eh, bien, ma chère*, you will have to make me another.'

I was in difficulties. 'I'm sorry. I haven't time.

Besides, if I had known – Alcide, I swear, I would have made you another.'

There was a moment of embarrassed silence, but in the end he shrugged his shoulders irritably and picked up a devil mask.

'Very well. Since I am not allowed to be the Sun King, I shall simply have to be the other thing, *Le Diable*. Perhaps that is appropriate.'

He held the mask to his face and laughed in a suitably heartless way and went off. I was particularly annoyed by this scene. This was supposed to be a day of festivity, but inevitably Alcide had been able to inject a note of poison into the fun.

We all appeared that evening at the dinner table in our costumes and as each woman appeared there was a little round of applause as she came down the steps from the house on to the terrace. Heather got a huge laugh in her drummer boy uniform and I drew my share of applause too as I stepped down, gracefully I hope, taking up the fullness of the skirt as Madame had instructed me. She was watching carefully as I made my entrance.

But it was Clay who really drew gasps of astonishment. He had been very secretive about his preparations. Now, as we sat round the table, he appeared in the doorway and came down towards us. He had come as the Minotaur! He had created a complete bull's head, superbly made, with horns, and beautifully shaped face and hair. Beneath this he was in a shirt and knee breeches and bare feet. There was a gasp of astonishment at this apparition.

Some of us weren't in fancy dress at all. Alcide and – surprisingly – Werner, couldn't quite enter into the spirit of the evening, and were attired in *tenue de soir* – white tie and tails. In all fairness, I have to say, Alcide was dressed faultlessly, like some *fin-de-siècle* Oscar Wilde character, and I felt perhaps just a shade of disappointment that Werner and Alcide – of all people – should be dressed alike. But then, I reasoned, they were neither of them artists and allowances must be made. At least Werner had my sun-god mask.

Maia was dressed in a man's grey lounge suit, with spats and a trilby hat, the brim turned down. As she was wearing dark glasses too, it would have been natural to take her for a man, especially as Chantal went everywhere with her, arm in arm. Chantal was in a striped top, short skirt and fishnet stockings, black beret, and wore my cat mask.

When we arrived at the Place des Lices around ten, it was already crowded, and the band was playing on their platform, an accordion, a trumpet, a saxophone, a drummer and bass, and they had even managed to heave a piano up, too. Below them the crowd swirled round. Beneath the music there was the loud buzz of chatter, and in a moment I was in Werner's arms as we swung round in the crowd. A little later I noticed Maia dancing with Chantal, towering over her and guiding her with complete assurance.

Round and round we went. In the plane trees coloured lights winked, throwing leafy patterns across the heads of groups of friends at café tables nearby. Beyond the lights, the inky black sky was velvet dark, soft, caressing. Werner was in my arms; I wanted nothing more.

'Are you happy, darling?' I asked with an idiotic smile on my face. Why did I ask? Because even in my supreme moment of happiness, I needed reassurance. Was he as happy as I?

Werner in his golden sun mask nodded.

It is an extraordinary thing: masks change your appearance. Obvious perhaps, but it comes as a surprise too. Here in my arms was Werner, yet because of the mask it was as if I were dancing with a stranger – dancing with a god. 'The God of my idolatry,' I murmured, but I think he missed it because he said nothing.

Later I saw Alcide in his diabolic mask at a table with Karim, Heather and Clay.

Other people wore masks, but they were mostly little factory-made, bank-robber affairs, and could not compare with our artistic creations. Several times Werner was congratulated by perfect strangers on his mask, and he would introduce me into the conversation. 'Credit where credit's due,' he said afterwards.

Eventually Werner and I found ourselves at the table. The bar was called *Le Gorille*, I remember. Alcide had ordered champagne. We were busy assembling more chairs about the table – the café terrace was crowded – and as I looked round I noticed Maia was missing and, shortly afterwards, as Chantal pointed, I saw that she was now on the bandstand and was talking to the musicians.

So, after a musical introduction, Maia came forward to the microphone. She still wore her dark glasses and her trilby hat. I had heard her many times before at *Les Cigalettes,* accompanying herself at the piano. That had been something quite refined, delicate, nuanced.

Tonight she was a *chanteuse.* Her voice was deep, husky, and had a wayward quality; she did not seem to be addressing the crowd below her, but sang as if she were communing with herself. The song was *Mon Legionnaire*, the usual story of a woman waiting (in vain) for the return of her lover, who in this case is away with the Foreign Legion. The sound was throaty, smoky, the words dragged from her as if she were somehow sleepwalking, or dreaming perhaps, inhabiting a bitter, despairing private world of her own.

The song, which was a popular favourite, was wildly received and, when she returned to the table, Chantal was quick to embrace her and offer her a glass of Alcide's champagne. In the meantime Werner had removed his mask. Unlike ours it was a whole face mask; we girls wore half masks. He laid the mask on the table while he lit a cigarette and took a mouthful of wine.

Maia was now dipping strawberries in her wine glass and popping them into Chantal's mouth.

It was some time later, as we were all talking together, that Alcide, who had been eyeing it, picked up the golden mask and tied it on. He stood up and struck a pose with his walking cane.

'*Le Roi Soleil.* Suits me, don't you think?'

'Yeah, it makes you look almost human,' said

Clay, who had also removed his bull's head and was wiping the sweat from his forehead. 'You should keep it on.'

'I think I shall.' And with that he disappeared into the crowd. Karim, his eyes burning, watched him go and was clearly torn for a moment whether to follow him.

'*Laissez-le.*' Maia placed a hand on his arm. 'Come, Karim,' she ordered, took his hand and led him back into the crowd. Later when Werner and I were dancing again, I saw them dancing together. It was a difficult question to decide who was leading whom.

'They make a perfect couple,' I chuckled.

'He'd make her a good wife, you mean?' We swirled on and then he said, 'She'd certainly make him happier than Alcide.' After a while he went on, 'He has a lot of enemies here, you know.'

'I imagine. He seems to have a talent for it.'

Later I saw Maia again, with her arm in Karim's, strolling back through the crowd. Chantal waited at the table, watching them. Back at the table Maia was putting herself out to cheer Karim up and roped in Chantal to help. There was no sign of Alcide.

At midnight there was an announcement.

'*Les feux d'artifices!*' Fireworks! And the crowd flowed towards the old fish harbour, the Port de Pêche. The mayor and his assistants were on the little stumpy tower to our left, the *Vieille Tour*, where he was overseeing the fireworks, and we all packed forwards to the water's edge in anticipation. The fishermen's boats were pulled up on the sandy slope, while others rode at anchor on the still water. Beyond the little circle of light the sky was black over the sea, but further out various yachts were lit up, and their light travelled in irregular lines across the water.

The mayor insisted on making a speech from the tower, which as far as I could make out was a eulogy to himself and detailed the effort and expense which he and the council had incurred to provide this spectacle tonight, for the honour and dignity of the *Commune de St Tropez*. There were various satirical cries from the crowd and more calls for him to 'get on with it!'

The mayor finally withdrew and, after another pause, there was an explosion and a rocket went up, to explode in a star of brilliant red and gold. The crowd roared its approval and a second later another went up. For some twenty minutes the spectacle went on; the sky was painted in star-bursts of red, green and gold, the crowd was briefly illuminated by the ghastly glare of magnesium and the air was punctuated by explosions.

In the crush through the narrow streets to the port, Werner and I had become separated from the others and as the show came to an end we turned and moved with the others back towards the Place des Lices.

In this mêlée, with everyone shouting across each other, with songs and laughter, I began to make out cries of alarm, discordant shouts cutting through the laughter and chatter.

'*Attention!* Send for an ambulance!'

I turned my head at this, and heard more

shouts. 'Make way there! Stand back! Let him breathe!'

And then, more chillingly, 'Is he still alive?'

At this our curiosity was definitely aroused and as we tried to peer through the crowd to see what had happened, a *gendarme* with his baton in his hand was gesturing to the crowd and repeating, '*Attention!* Stand back there!'

Someone else was shouting, 'Bring him inside!' only to be contradicted immediately.

'No! He mustn't be touched! *Laissez-le!*'

Werner asked among those nearest what was happening, and a man turned.

'*Il est mort! Fusillé.*'

'*Mais qui est-il?*'

The man shrugged and turned away.

'Someone's been shot,' Werner said gravely. 'They've sent for an ambulance.'

The *gendarme* was still trying to get the crowd to disperse, but it was impossible. The mayor now appeared, pushing self-importantly through the crowd.

And then I heard, 'Someone must run and tell her!'

'Tell who?'

'Madame Leary!'

At this Werner pushed violently forward through the crowd. '*Je connais Madame Leary! Qui est battu?*'

And there, spread-eagled on the cobbles, lay Alcide. A doctor knelt by him.

Werner leaned over him. 'I know him, Doctor. Is he alive?'

The doctor nodded. 'At the moment. The shot

passed through the shoulder, and the top of the lung. He is very fortunate. An ambulance is on its way. We shall take him to St Raphael. If he is operated on quickly he should not be in any danger.'

Werner turned to me. I was, as you can imagine, staring down at the figure of Alcide. Near him, trodden in the dust and broken, was my golden sun mask and without thinking I picked it up.

'I'll go and tell Madame,' I said and was about to set off.

'No! If Alcide is not in danger, there is no need to wake her. Tomorrow will be soon enough.'

But now Karim appeared; bursting into a paroxysm of grief he knelt by the inert body and tried to pick him up. He was incoherent. *'Oh, mon pauvre!'* he cried, and was forcibly restrained by the doctor. All the time people were jostling about us, shouting and gesticulating to one another.

Another two *gendarmes* now pushed their way forward, and pulled Karim on to his feet.

'Qui est-il?' They were large and brutal. *'C'est vous? Vous l'avez tué, hein?'*

'Non!'

'Venez, espece de canaille!'

They pulled poor Karim away from the body and dragged him away through the crowd. Werner hurried after them, shouting, *'C'est un innocent! Ce n'est pas lui!'* But they simply elbowed him aside. I hurried along beside Werner, but he turned to me.

'Meg, stay with Alcide, and find out where

they are taking him.'

I turned back to where Alcide was still lying. By this time he had regained consciousness and was staring dazedly up at us. I knelt by him and, pulling out a handkerchief, wiped his face.

'They are taking you to hospital,' I told him. 'An ambulance is coming.'

He grimaced slightly, a shadow of pain across his face, and lost consciousness again.

Soon after I heard a siren and the ambulance could be seen gradually pushing its way through the crowd. A stretcher was brought out and two men carefully lifted Alcide on to it. A dribble of blood had escaped from his mouth and run down on to his white shirt. The ambulance men knew their job, however. As they were stowing him in the ambulance, I climbed in with them.

'*Je suis sa soeur*,' I muttered. They said nothing, and in a moment we were on our way. The ambulance had dark blue glass windows, so I saw nothing of the journey, which lasted nearly an hour. One of the ambulance men sat beside Alcide and wiped his face. Alcide had regained consciousness and I could see the pain passing over his face at every bump of the ride.

Eventually we came to a halt, the doors were opened, there was a door, and Alcide on his *brancard* was lifted out and carried inside. I followed, hurrying behind them, and soon there were nurses and a doctor all around. Alcide had disappeared through a swing door and I was left alone. It was that eerie time of night, just before dawn I suspect, which has an unreal feeling about it; the body is protesting at being still awake. I shivered and realized belatedly that I was still gowned and coiffed for a ball in the 1880s. I looked down at Madame Leary's white and gold silk gown, her heirloom. It was dusty about the knees where I had been kneeling beside Alcide at the Port de Pêche. The hospital was almost deserted. What anyone must have thought to see me like this, I couldn't imagine, but although occasionally a nurse or an orderly might pass, they took no notice of me. No doubt people in fancy dress were a regular sight in the hospital. I found a chair and sat down to wait. I found to my surprise that I was still clutching the broken gold mask.

Waves of tiredness would sweep through me and my head would droop on to my chest until with a jerk I would snap upright. It was light when a doctor came out and told me that they had operated on Alcide. He was out of danger but sedated for the moment. I could return the following day to see him.

I asked for a taxi and drove back to *Les Cigalettes*. The road followed the coast round the bay towards St Tropez. Day had now dawned, and despite, or because of, my tiredness – for I was in that unreal state between sleeping and waking – the bay looked magically beautiful, the water an indescribable light blue and the sky pale and washed out. There was an incredible stillness about the scene, which was only enhanced by a single fishing boat making its way slowly across the calm surface.

Twenty-Four

When I arrived at *Les Cigalettes* I found Werner waiting for me. He had changed, had shaved, and seemed wide awake. I told him about the operation. He listened seriously.

'Madame has not woken up yet,' he said when I had finished. 'As soon as she does, I'll tell her what has happened.'

'Let me, Werner. It might be easier – I went to the hospital with him.'

He looked surprised. 'Don't you want to go to bed? You must be done in.'

'I'm all right for the moment. I seem to have got over it. Besides, I nodded off in the taxi for a while. I'd better get out of this dress, that's all. And I'm dying for a wash. Anyway, she'll be up soon, I expect. What happened to Karim?'

'He's here.' He nodded toward the drawing room. 'The *gendarmes* threw him out once I had explained the situation – and after they'd roughed him up a little.'

I went in to where Karim was sitting, still in his beautiful Arab robes, huddled, pale beneath the dark skin, in a chair, looking shrivelled, frightened. I took his hand and explained that we would be able to go and see Alcide the following day. We couldn't go now – I had to take his arm and restrain him as he attempted to get up – because Alcide was sedated and would not wake till tomorrow anyway. Finally I told him the best thing was to go to bed and get some sleep.

'Sleep?' he murmured, haggard, woebegone. 'How could I sleep?'

I went to our room to change and when I came downstairs again the smell of coffee was wafting from the kitchen and I realized I was ravenously hungry. Werner was waiting.

'She'll be awake by now.'

He nodded and I went upstairs and knocked gently on her door.

'Madame,' I whispered. 'It's me, Meg.'

There was a pause, then, 'Come in.'

She was on her feet though still in her nightgown. Her hair, which was long, was let all down her back and she had been standing in front of the wash stand.

'Meg? What time is it?'

'Oh – about eight, I think. But, Madame, I have some news for you. It's all right, it's not very serious...'

She was more alert now, and turned to me.

'What is it?'

'It's not very serious, Madame, but Werner thought you ought to know.'

She waited. I swallowed and went on.

'It's about Alcide.'

'Yes?'

'I'm afraid ... I'm afraid he's been hurt.' I paused again then went on as calmly as I could, 'Somebody has shot him.'

As she jerked forward I seized her hands and

273

went on quickly, 'It's all right. He's alive; you are not to worry. They have operated on him. I was at the hospital and the surgeon told me it had been successful. He's been sedated and we can go and see him tomorrow.' It all came out in a rush.

We stared at each other in silence. At last she seemed to relax and shook her head.

'I have warned him so many times.' She shook her head again. 'So many times.' She sighed.

'I don't understand.'

'I wish I didn't have to explain.'

'Don't – if you'd rather not.'

She looked at me. 'My dear.' She took my hands in hers now. 'You know what Alcide is like. I knew eventually it would catch up with him.'

I was struggling to keep up with her. 'You mean...' I swallowed. 'A lover?'

'Most likely.' She covered her face with her hand, still holding on to mine with the other.

'I'm so sorry this has to happen to you,' I murmured.

She nodded without speaking.

Soon after that I left her and went down to where breakfast had been set out. Werner was waiting.

'I spoke to Madame.'

'Good girl. Thanks.'

'She said...' I hesitated. 'She said it must have been ... one of his lovers.'

Werner nodded in agreement. 'Very likely.'

He noticed the broken golden mask on the table and picked it up. 'What a shame,' he said, turning it in his hand.

'I made it for you,' I said simply.

He laid it down again and put his arm round my shoulders. 'Time for bed.'

Sometime during the afternoon we woke, and when we went down we found the others sitting round a late lunch. Heather and Clay had surfaced by now and, even later, Maia and Chantal. We sat round the table in the sunshine, sifting through the evening's happenings and recounting the number of times Alcide had disappeared into the town at night, the time Werner and I had seen him in *Chez Fredy*, and generally going over ground we had already trodden. Clearly Alcide enjoyed flirting with danger. Picking up 'rough trade' at a port, however, was bound eventually to bring trouble.

'Extraordinary,' Werner remarked, 'when one considers the kind of thing he writes.'

'Writes?' We all turned.

'But of course. Why do you think he dresses like Marcel Proust?'

'Are you serious?'

'Absolutely. He's terrifically secretive about it, but I looked into his room once. He has a desk, he sets out his paper just so – and it must of course be the finest quality paper – and he writes with an expensive fountain pen – he would not pollute his hands with a typewriter, naturally. He writes very little. Exquisite *pensées*.'

'Have you read anything by him?'

'Once. He had left his folder open.'

* * *

That afternoon a man arrived from *La Poste* with a telegram for me. It was brief:

'Request impossible stop return England immediately stop father'

The telegram was reply-paid.

This came like a shower of cold water and I stared at it in incomprehension as my brain tried to work out all the possibilities. Finally, I showed the telegram to Heather. I had taken her into my confidence concerning Werner's visa.

'Does he know something we don't?' she asked as she read the few blunt words.

'I don't see why.' I was plunged into the dumps. At last I said tentatively, 'You weren't thinking of going home yet, were you? What am I going to say? He wants a reply.'

Heather shook her head. She was thrown by this too, I could see, because a moment later she erupted. 'It's all talk! I don't see anything will come of it! OK, Hitler marched into Prague in March. But that doesn't mean he's going to attack France, does it? He knows what happened last time, and there's the Maginot Line as well. In any case, everything points eastwards. If he's going to attack anyone, it's going to be Stalin; it stands to reason.'

I still had not shown the telegram to Werner. I was afraid to, because I was still so unsure of the outcome. I simply could not bear the thought of being parted from him. But I also thought that he would know better than I what to do.

That evening I showed it to him.

He was surprisingly light about it. He simply

shrugged and said, 'Well, my dear Meg, I shall simply have to throw myself on the mercies of the British people. I shall ask for political asylum.'

'Political?'

He smiled, and put his arm about my shoulders. 'I told you, I had to leave Austria in rather a hurry at the *Anschluss*. I cannot return to Austria. I should not think the British will turn me down.'

He made it sound surprisingly simple.

'What about the money?'

'I am still waiting to hear from the United States.'

'When do you want to go?'

'Why?'

I showed him the telegram again. 'My father thinks I should return at once.'

'He is concerned for you – you are his little girl, and you are a long way from home. It is only natural.'

I was relieved. 'What do you think I should say?'

'Say?'

'I have to reply – he's paid.'

'That is kind of him. You are a lucky girl to have a father who is so concerned for you. Well, just tell him you will be coming home soon – you will have to, anyway, won't you, sometime in September?'

'Term starts on September twentieth. We've got weeks yet.' I turned to him, suddenly passionate. 'And I don't want to go yet! I want to stay as long as I can. I never want to leave!'

For a moment we stared into each other's eyes.

'Nor do I,' he murmured and took me in his arms. For a long moment we stood clasped together.

We made love that night – long, inexhaustible, into the dark night. Long hours, it seemed I lay with him, lay beneath him, as he penetrated me, slowly, languorously, lovingly. I wanted it never to end but to go on like this all my life, the two of us in the darkness, exploring and finding each other in a slow, endless dance that ended only with an exquisite tension and then the final arching of my back and the escape of a long aching sigh. I felt as if I had dissolved completely, that I was only Werner's, part of him, fused together forever more.

The following morning I went with Madame and Karim in a taxi to St Raphael. Madame had a bag with a change of clothes, toiletries, and other things. Alcide needless to say had exquisite taste – silk pyjamas, creams and so forth for his skin, brushes and combs, nail scissors.

We found him in a hospital ward staffed by nuns in flying butterfly wimples, swishing up and down the wards in flowing *soutanes*.

Alcide was awake but had little strength and was lying on his back. He had been wounded in the lung and it was painful for him to breathe; hence he could speak only in a whisper.

Madame hastened to show him what she had brought and busied herself stowing the things in a cupboard beside his bed. Karim and I sat on either side. Karim reached for Alcide's hand and, as he took it, Alcide turned slowly to look at him. He smiled painfully and squeezed Karim's hand. He seemed a changed man; shrunken somehow, timid, grateful for Karim's presence.

'Thank you, *mon cher.*'

There were tears in Karim's eyes as Alcide watched him with large eyes.

'You won't leave me, will you? You won't go away now?'

'No! No, never. We are both here to look after you.'

On the other side Madame leaned forward to reassure him. 'It's all right, dear, we're going to take care of you.'

Finally, Madame asked the question I was dying to ask. 'Have you any idea who could have done it?'

Silence. Alcide looked bewildered. After a moment Madame started again. 'Have the police come to see you?'

'The nurses won't let them in yet. *Grande-maman*, you will be with me if they do come?'

She reassured him again that she would take care of him. I had never seen a man so changed. Another pause, and Madame laid the leather briefcase which she had been holding on the bed beside him. She adopted a lighter note. 'I have brought your papers.'

There was a secretive, covetous look as he hastily took it under his hand. He glanced at me. 'You haven't shown them to anyone?'

'Of course not,' she reassured him wearily, as if he were a child. 'You have nothing to worry about. You are quite safe here. The nurses will take care of you and then when you are well enough we will bring you home.'

'Thank you,' he breathed, and relaxed back on the pillow.

On the way home, I held Madame's hand. She was a tough old bird but I knew she had been deeply affected by this experience.

'He's going to be all right,' I said quietly. 'I think he has learned his lesson.'

She glanced at me.

'He will be more careful,' I went on.

'I hope so,' she sighed, and turned to me. 'He's all I've got.'

The next morning I sent the reply to my father's telegram.

'Yours received stop returning soon stop will wire again stop Meg'

There was no question of returning immediately, as he had demanded.

The police came up to the house and asked more questions. No one had anything to contribute and they left empty-handed.

I wanted to get on with my portrait of Werner. He promised to sit for me, but excused himself after a couple of hours, because of letters he had to write.

'Don't go yet,' I pleaded. 'I do so want to finish it. I want to have a souvenir of our time in St Tropez.'

But he was adamant. 'We shall be leaving soon. There is a lot of business I have to finish up.'

'What business?'

He shrugged awkwardly. 'Letters to write – that sort of thing. Besides, once we have gone, Madame will be left on her own – with Alcide to look after. She is an old lady. I must make some arrangements.'

After he had gone off to his study-cum-workshop and I was left staring at my half-finished canvas I fell to thinking. What business? What letters? Gradually, these letters began to weigh on me. They could only be letters to Austria, I thought. Was Werner keeping up some kind of clandestine correspondence? Wouldn't that expose him to danger?

I stared at my picture. We were so happy; my picture was intended to represent that happiness. I would be able to look at that picture and always remember our time here. But it was not yet finished. I was seized with a restless anxiety and worked on, doing the background, putting in the trees, the Chinese lanterns and the distant glimpse of the sea.

Maia appeared from the beach accompanied by Chantal. Since Jacques had been hauled off so unceremoniously, these two had become inseparable. Going upstairs after lunch, intending to have a siesta, I happened to glance into Maia's room and saw Maia and Chantal in bed asleep, little Chantal curled up like a dormouse in Maia's arms.

There was something infinitely touching about this scene and it inflamed me instantly. Why wasn't I in Werner's arms at this moment? I wanted him, I wanted him very, very much; I wanted him now.

I made my way back out and round to his hut. The door to Heather and Clay's love nest was closed; they too were having their siesta. Looking into Werner's hut, I saw him at the far end with his back to me, sitting, bent over his typewriter, the letters and papers scattered thickly about.

'Darling?' I whispered from the door. With a start he whipped round. He stared at me for a second as if he didn't recognize me, then relaxed, and smiled.

'Sorry. I was miles away. I thought you were going to lie down?'

I went across to him. 'I was – and then I felt lonely...' I pressed closer to him and drew his head to my breast. He threaded his arms about my waist and we rocked together in silence. 'Do you want to come up?' I asked softly at last. He replied by gripping me tighter.

'Oh, Meg,' he sighed.

'What is it?' I looked down.

'Why are you so good to me?'

'Werner – what is it?' He was staring up at me almost bewildered, and was clearly upset. 'My darling, what on earth is the matter?'

At last he drew a slow painful smile as I bent over him and we kissed slowly.

'Nothing,' he whispered.

'Then come up now, darling, please.'

That evening Werner brought his gramophone out on to the terrace, and Maia produced some records of popular songs. One I shall never forget. It was Tino Rossi singing *J'attendrai.*

J'attendrai, la nuit et le jour,
J'attendrai, ton retour...

We danced, Werner and I. The Chinese lanterns glowed in the pines, and the others were still talking over the dinner table, but when Werner put on Tino Rossi again and took my hand, there was no one else. And the talking and the laughing seemed very distant and Werner and I were alone, complete to one another. I had such a hunger then, such a hunger to seize every moment together, to hold it and make it mine forever. It was because I was afraid. I was afraid he would be taken from me, and there would be nothing I could do about it...

Twenty-Five

I went with Madame again to visit Alcide; he was already stronger and was now sitting up, propped on pillows, had his notebook open and was writing with his fountain pen as we came in. The notebook and pen disappeared quickly as he saw us.

Days passed, and I finished Werner's portrait. As I stared at it and saw that there was nothing more I could add, I became cruelly conscious of its shortcomings. It seemed such a small thing when I intended it to be an offering to him, a token of my love.

Heather in the meanwhile contented herself with taking photographs of us all.

Once the picture of Werner was completed I had Maia on at me again to begin work on her portrait but now there was a new complication: Chantal was jealous. The morning when Maia finally browbeat me into making a start, Chantal was present in the role of a chaperone, no less. It was quite amusing.

This picture was done indoors; I am quite sure Maia would have been willing to take her clothes off anywhere but I thought the others might not look so kindly on this flaunting of her charms in the garden and passing visitors or tradesmen making deliveries might have received a surprise. So I insisted on commandeering the drawing room and Maia stretched herself on the *chaise longue* in imitation of Goya's *Naked Maja*. Chantal sat nearby in fierce concentration. There was to be no hanky-panky.

She needn't have worried. I was too busy concentrating on the painting. Flesh is the most difficult of all surfaces to render convincingly and I started by making studies, experimenting with flesh tones, whites, pinks, green shadows, and so on.

It was the following day, August 23rd, that the bombshell broke.

'Have you heard the news?' Werner stood in the doorway, completely ignoring Maia and

Chantal, who immediately handed a robe to Maia.

'What news?' I looked up from my easel. He came in and sat down opposite me without speaking for a moment. I was alarmed.

'What is it?'

'It was on the radio just now.'

'What?'

He looked down, clasping his hands together.

'Meg – and you too...' He glanced across at Maia and Chantal. 'It's the Germans – they've done a deal with the Russians.'

We stared at him uncomprehendingly. Finally I blurted, 'What deal?'

'Molotov, the Russian foreign minister, and Ribbentrop, the German minister, have been meeting in secret. They have made a treaty.'

'Treaty?' I was utterly bewildered.

'Meg, don't you understand? The Germans and the Russians have struck a bargain.' He was insistent.

'I don't understand. How...?'

'It's actually very simple. They have agreed not to attack each other.'

We stared at each other in silence. At last I began to fathom out the consequences. 'Well, if the Germans aren't going to attack the Russians, that means...'

He nodded. 'It leaves them free to attack the French. We're back to 1914, only this time the Germans don't have to fight on two fronts.'

It still seemed incredible. And in a moment I returned to the argument. 'Werner, are you absolutely *sure*? Hitler has always attacked the

Bolsheviks, as you know yourself. Why should he strike a bargain with them? Why should Stalin want it?'

He shook his head slowly. *'Realpolitik,* pure and simple.'

I now heard shouting in the kitchen and a moment later someone came running into the house. It was Heather. She burst into the room. 'Have you heard about the Russians and the Germans? It was on Clay's radio.'

Werner turned and nodded.

'What are we going to do?' Heather was looking at me.

I looked at Werner. He was frowning but said nothing. I was helpless. Indeed, the whole room was frozen at that moment. Maia clutched the robe across her, frowning. Chantal moved instinctively nearer to her.

At last, almost under his breath, Werner murmured, 'Damn!' He was looking at the floor, still with his hands tightly clasped.

'Meg,' Heather repeated, 'what are we going to do?'

I was still waiting for Werner to speak, but I could see he was thinking hard. At last he said, carefully, 'We probably have a few days.'

We all turned to him as he pieced together his thoughts. Finally he said, 'The Germans have always been afraid of fighting on two fronts. Now that Hitler has done the deal with Stalin it leaves him free to attack France. It's got to come. However, even so, it is going to take him some time to get his men into position. Weeks probably. We have a little time.'

'Do you think we should leave?'

He nodded, and then added, 'There are a few things I have to tidy up first, that's all.'

'And then we'll go to England?' I asked anxiously.

He nodded again, then rose. 'I'd better make a start.' He went out. Heather was looking at me. 'Don't you think we had better go?'

'I'm not going without Werner,' I said simply. 'Anyway, he said it would be only a few days,' I added encouragingly.

She chewed the inside of her lip and finally said uncertainly, 'OK, but it ought to be sooner than later, if you ask me. We don't want to be trapped in France if the balloon goes up.'

At that moment I didn't care about the balloon or anything else. I cared only about Werner. Wherever he was, I had to be too.

It was difficult to concentrate on the painting after that, and soon afterwards I gave up for the day. That afternoon a man lumbered up from *La Poste* with a letter for Werner and another telegram for me. I knew before I opened it what it would say.

'Return to England now stop father'

With it there also came a money order, cashable at the *La Poste*, for ten pounds.

When I went to find Heather, she told me Clay was leaving. 'The bastard,' she muttered. 'He's down in the town at the moment looking up boats from Cherbourg.'

We stared at each other for a moment.

'Sorry,' I murmured.

She heaved a sigh. 'Oh well, it didn't mean

anything, I suppose. We both knew what we were doing, didn't we? A bit of slap and tickle – don't suppose it would have gone anywhere.' She frowned. 'Damn!'

I reached for her hand. 'You don't want to go with him?' I suggested.

She jerked out a laugh. 'Don't think so, somehow. Clay is a *free spirit*,' she added in a voice laden with irony.

A moment later I showed her the telegram.

'Do you think we ought to go?' I asked uncertainly.

'It might be wise,' she said eventually. 'It's all over here, isn't it? Even if we stayed, it would be no fun. We'd only be thinking of what's coming next.'

'I'll speak to Werner. He said he had business to wind up.'

Heather frowned. 'What business?'

'I don't know. But he's got a desk covered with letters and papers. He was waiting to hear from America about his book, too.'

'You'd better tell him to hurry up,' Heather said briefly as she got up. 'I'm going to start packing. Then I'm going into town to check on train times.'

I went out to Werner's study. When I got there I found him standing with a letter in his hand. I waited in the doorway as he continued to study this letter. After a long moment he looked up slowly at me. He made no motion or sign of recognition and his mind was clearly far away.

'Meg?' he said at last in a hoarse voice. I saw

288

now that as well as the letter there was a photograph in his other hand. I was afraid.

'What is that?' I said at last, timidly, certain
that it was bad news.

'I don't know.'

Silence. 'I don't understand,' I whispered.

'Neither do I.'

'Can you tell me?'

He gestured with the letter. 'It's from my wife.
And she's sent a photograph of Albertina.'

Again I waited and at last, as if dragging it
out, he went on, in this voice hoarse with disbelief, 'She's coming to the Côte d'Azur, to Ste
Maxime, and says I can see Albertina.'

'Isn't that good news?' I asked tentatively.

'I don't know what to think,' he muttered. 'It's
so utterly unlike her. I would even have said it's
fake—'

'Fake?' I interrupted him sharply.

'Except that it is her handwriting,' he went on
as if he had not heard me, 'and she has sent the
photograph.' He stared at the photograph
through a long silence. 'And why should she
think of going on holiday at this time? And why
didn't she give me more notice? She's coming a
week on Saturday, September second.' He stopped again. 'It's very strange.'

He sat heavily on his chair, still staring at the
letter.

'When did it arrive?'

'Just now.'

'Maybe she did send it earlier but it was
delayed?'

He flicked the letter towards me. 'It's dated

last Thursday. No delay.'

I held the letter briefly, but of course it meant nothing to me, being not only written in German but in a peculiar crabbed handwriting. I handed it back.

'Can I see the photograph?'

He passed it to me, and I studied it. It was not unlike the one I had seen before. A little girl of six or seven, smiling at the camera, in her best dress. 'Would it be a recent photograph?'

He took it back from me, and studied it hard. 'I should say so,' he said at last.

I struggled to put a positive interpretation on it. 'Does it have to be bad news?' I asked hopefully. 'Maybe it means exactly what it says? After all, Albertina has probably been asking about you and your wife is doing it to please her.'

He nodded without speaking, his face still heavy with thought.

'All you have to do is go,' I went on. 'Then you'll know. What harm can it do? We can easily wait till then, can't we? It's only a week. Nothing's going to happen in a week, you said so yourself.'

He looked up at me and a moment later stood up. 'Let's go for a walk. There's something I haven't told you.'

This chilled me. 'What? What haven't you told me?'

'Come on.'

We began walking along the path through the pines. It was getting towards evening and the glare had gone from the sky, though the sea still sparkled far away between the trees. We walked some time in silence, our footsteps silent on the thick bed of pine needles and sand. Then he stopped.

'Meg, I haven't been fair to you.'

'What do you mean?'

'I mean, my Golden Girl, I should have told you everything before.'

I waited as he stood looking down at me.

'You remember I told you I had to leave Vienna in a hurry because I was on a wanted list? Then I told you I went to Spain and carried a stretcher on the Republican side? That I then came here and wrote a book about the war, and sent it to America?'

I nodded.

'There is more than that. I have been in touch with many old friends in Vienna and many outside Austria too now. During the Spanish Civil War I wrote articles and smuggled them into Austria where they were printed on clandestine newspapers and circulated. Since then I have been sending in more articles, about anything I could think of – the state of the world, the economic basis of capitalism, and the unholy alliance between the Nazis and capital. Worst of all, the complete erosion of liberty in the name of security. Do you know something, Meg? In Austria, ten years ago, when it looked as if there might be a civil war, the whole country was forming into armed groups, some of the left, some of the right. They had names like *Heimwehr, Heimatschutz, Schutzbund*. Always this word, *Schutz*. What does it mean? *Protect*. When they want to control you they call it *protection*!'

He paused. 'Anyway, we have been trying to maintain a network of contacts and, as I said, I have been sending articles into Austria for publication by underground organizations for secret circulation. They smuggle things out and I get them syndicated to western newspapers – we keep up a flow of anti-Nazi information so no one over here is under any illusion about what is going on. The *Heimwehr* have long since found out where I live. But they have found it very difficult to get near me. It is always so crowded here and they employ local criminals who are fortunately very inefficient. Still they have made a few attempts – you remember the night when we were nearly run down in St Tropez?'

'No!'

He nodded. 'And, I am afraid, my dearest girl, that the bullet that got Alcide may have been meant for me.'

'Oh my God!' It was clear in an instant. 'The mask.'

He nodded. 'The fact is I should have left after our near miss. It was obvious then.'

'Was it?'

He nodded again, still thinking hard.

'Then,' I hesitated, 'if they knew where you were, why didn't you leave?'

He looked deeply into my eyes, but said nothing.

'Because of me?'

He took me in his arms. 'Meg, I have been a great fool and I may have endangered you too.'

'I don't care.'

We held each other and were silent for a long

time. When we separated at last, he said, 'I still can't imagine why she should have written. It is just not in her character to do it.'

'Then don't go!'

'But that's just it. Suppose it's genuine? Suppose she really does mean it? She doesn't like me, but I can't really believe she would allow herself to become part of a plot to kill me.'

'Oh my God!' I repeated in a shocked whisper. 'Don't say it.'

'Meg.' He clasped me by the arms. 'This may be the last chance I have to see Albertina again, perhaps for ever. I *must* go!'

For a second we clung together. I was unable to speak.

I could feel him relaxing and when I looked up at him he was smiling again, his old mischievous smile.

'You mustn't worry too much. Nothing has changed, really. I shall be careful. If it looks suspicious, I shall simply not go in.'

What could I say? I was helpless, and could only wait.

It was Wednesday evening, and somehow I had to last until the following Saturday week. Ten days.

That evening the atmosphere was very subdued. The only piece of good news was that Alcide was to be brought home next week. This cheered Madame considerably.

'I shall have him where I can keep an eye on him, Meg,' she said quietly, leaning in to me.

Relations between Clay and Heather were

distinctly cool.

'Clay's got his tickets,' she announced stonily over the dinner table. 'He's off in the morning, and sailing on Friday.' She glanced at him. 'Better safe than sorry, eh, old chap?'

'If the old world is about to tear itself apart *again*, I don't intend to stay around to watch,' he retorted. He'd had a few glasses of wine, I saw, and said what he otherwise might not have done: 'Thank God I'm not French.'

Heather raised her eyebrows. '*Charmant*,' she murmured with leaden irony.

'And if you want my advice,' he went on, ignoring her and looking round at us, 'you'd all get out while you can. This country's finished. Living on its memories, washed up, stony broke, and about to sink into oblivion. *Fini! Vive la France!*' He emptied his glass and set it down with an unexpected thud.

'And while I'm on the subject,' he went on, 'the same applies to Britain. Come the day, Hitler will roll over you. All of you. Roll you up. Like a carpet.' He refilled his glass unsteadily.

'That remains to be seen,' I said. I noticed Werner watching me.

'Oh yeah, Meg? You wanna bet? Hey, you wanna know what folks think back in the good ol' US of A? They think...' He leant forward. '*They think*,' he repeated with drunken emphasis, 'that your Mr Chamberlain has done everything he can short of crawling up Hitler's *ass*!'

'Well.' I remained cool; in fact the more offensive Clay became, the cooler I felt. 'What you say has an element of truth in it, it must be admitted—'

'Oh! Your English irony!' He gestured round the table. 'I just love it! You're about to be bombed into rubble, the legions of the *Wehrmacht* are about to trample over your necks, gas canisters will rain down on you, and you're so fucking—'

'Clay, that will do, please,' Madame interrupted.

The following morning Clay departed. The local taxi appeared. Boxes, valises, suitcases, his paint boxes, and his great canvases rolled up, all were carried out from the shed at the back and loaded in.

Heather and I watched him go. No one else was there. We shook hands coolly, nothing much was said. I glanced at Heather trying to work out how she was feeling. But she didn't really seem to be upset at all. There was a brief handshake, a brief, 'Have a safe crossing,' and he was gone.

As the taxi rolled away down the drive, I turned to her, and we stared into each other's eyes for a moment.

'Are you all right?' I asked.

'Never felt better,' she said briefly.

We returned to the breakfast table. Pierre Bonnard was there with Maia and Chantal. Madame had gone early with Karim to see Alcide in St Raphael. The picture of Maia was still unfinished and was not going well; I had not mastered the flesh tones, which came out sometimes pink, sometimes grey, sometimes the colour of cement. Furthermore, I had not caught her expression adequately and my anatomy left much to be desired. In short, my picture was doing less than justice to Maia's statuesque beauty. I was particularly embarrassed since I had been quite pleased with my picture of Karim and even of Werner.

'What are you going to do?' I asked, glancing over to her.

She raised her chin in a classic Gallic gesture. 'Wait and see,' she said in her heavy Scandinavian drawl. 'What else is there to do?'

'You're not going back to Sweden?'

'Oh, Sweden! No thank you! I should die of boredom. No, we shall go back to Paris eventually and wait. Something tells me that, whether the Germans come or whether they don't, the nightclubs will still be open. Besides I have a contract with a record company.' She glanced at Chantal, who by the way spoke no English and presumably understood nothing of what we said. 'The fact is, Meg, that for women like Chantal and me, there will always be work – of one kind or another.' She gave her low, throaty chuckle as she rested a hand on Chantal's thigh.

Twenty-Six

'When are we leaving?'

Breakfast was over and I was about to return to Maia's portrait. Heather was looking up at me without smiling, however, and I sat down again. I would have to tell her – not everything, but something at least. I told her briefly about Werner, the letter from his wife, and the visit on September 2nd.

'The second? When's that?'

'A week on Saturday.'

'I can't hang around till then – it's over a week away.'

'I shan't leave without him,' I said quietly.

'Bugger,' she muttered in a low voice after a long silence.

'Do you want to go back on your own?' I suggested hesitantly.

'Not really.' Another silence. Heather looked thoroughly fed up.

'Look, what's the hurry?' I began again, trying to cheer her. 'Just because Clay panicked, does not mean we have to, does it? Werner said nothing is going to happen immediately. In any case,' I added, 'if there is going to be a war, we ought to make the most of it.'

She looked at me dubiously.

'If war breaks out,' I went on enthusiastically,

'when are we going to get the chance of coming again? Maybe not for years! We don't know what's going to happen. We *must* make the most of it. Do you realize we may never come to France again; we could be middle-aged, burdened down with kids. Look, just wait – it's only till next Saturday. There are lots of things we haven't done – and in any case you haven't done much painting, old girl.'

'I spent too much time under Clay, you mean?' she added with a morose humour but was, as I could see, beginning to thaw.

'I can't talk. Anyway, I've got to finish my picture – such as it is – of Maia.' I heaved a sigh. 'To tell the truth, I wish I'd never started it.'

Heather seemed cheered and reconciled to the idea of waiting until Werner could travel with us and so I returned to my portrait.

Maia was indefatigable, constantly encouraging me, and was adamant that the picture should be finished. I got out my stuff, she displayed herself once again on the *chaise longue*, and I set myself once more to wrestle with the flesh tones. As I worked, however, there was another thought that began to preoccupy me.

I wanted to buy a gift for Werner. I already had my return ticket to London, so the money my father had sent was in a sense free. And from the moment I had cashed the order at the post office and actually held the money in my hand a single thought had occupied my mind: I must buy Werner a present. However, I walked about St Tropez without being in the least inspired. There was almost nothing to buy and certainly nothing that came close to expressing my feelings for him.

But that morning after breakfast as I sat again at my easel and surveyed the magnificent limbs spread before me and then looked at my own paltry effort to do them justice, I muttered, 'What a mess! Now, if Bonnard were doing this picture—'

And then it came to me. Bonnard! Of course! A terrible but simple idea crashed into my mind, inflamed it, and consumed every other thought in a second. Bonnard must paint a picture of *me*! And in the nude! A picture that would convey to Werner exactly what I thought about him and me, a picture that would show him in the clearest way possible that I was his, all of me and for ever. I almost laughed out loud as I thought of it. And after all the rude thoughts I had had about Maia's compulsive exhibitionism! But the thought, once thought, was so complete, so inevitable, and so necessary, that there was nothing for me to do but make the arrangements. To be precise, I had to persuade Bonnard to do it.

I laboured for a respectable spell at Maia's picture, announced that that was enough for the day, and made a great show of packing up my things. Maia and Chantal went off to the beach and I set about my campaign of attack. This needed considerable planning and I was deeply uncertain of success. He was a painter with a hugely successful career behind him. He was very rich. His pictures hung in galleries in every capital city of Europe and lots more in America, no doubt. He still painted – every day, as a matter of fact – but he seemed to have reached a plateau of competence – and confidence – which allowed him an almost nonchalant relationship with his canvas. He was so relaxed. He would sit before the empty white rectangle, his head on one side, glance about him, look at his brushes for a moment and select one, then would dab, a little of this, a little of that, mixing the colours on his old palette, and then, a cigarette in the corner of his mouth, try a little on the canvas. He would look at it, think, then add a little more. It was as if he had all the time in the world and yet, a couple of hours later, the picture was largely finished. It never took more than a day to do a canvas, often less.

He was at work when I found him. It was a simple landscape: the garden, stone steps, the great urns, some mighty succulents, the house above at the back, dappled shadows across the old tiled terrace. Simple elements, but worked with a careless ease into a pleasing and harmonious composition.

Fortunately, I had sat with him before as he worked and I knew he didn't mind.

Bonnard spoke no English, which complicated things. I had to use all my persuasive skills, offer a bribe if necessary – in fact offer every penny I possessed – but I had to do it all in French.

'M'sieur Bonnard—'

'Pierre.'

'Pierre, *je voudrais vous demander quelque chose...*' I began, and went on hesitantly to outline my request, trying as best I could to convey the importance of this picture for me. It was essential, I told him, my heart in my mouth. All the same, it did seem a colossal impertinence, from an art student to one of the giants of European painting. I even offered him money, aware of the laughably small amount I had in my purse.

Bonnard did not hesitate in his work as I talked, as I repeated myself, as I made grammatical mistakes, as I stumbled, as I forgot words. All through my awkward speech he continued to paint, pausing once only to take the cigarette from his mouth and flick away the ash.

Finally he laid down the palette in his lap, turned and studied me carefully.

'*En plein air – ou dedans?*' He nodded towards the house.

I struggled for an instant to understand him. Then, as I grasped his meaning, I explained immediately what I had in mind.

'*Dedans – mais devant la grande fenêtre, avec la vue de la mer. Il y a une grand chaise canné...*'

He nodded and went on in his casual way, '*Eh bien. Il faut en faire. Demain matin.*'

I jumped up and kissed him on the cheek.

The following morning at breakfast I explained to Maia and Chantal that we would continue with our picture in a few days, but for the moment something else had come up.

I had also explained to Werner that Maia was embarrassed by people coming unexpectedly into the drawing room while she was undressed, and would he please keep away while I was busy. He smiled his oblique smile, agreed, and went out to his shed.

I went to our room, undressed, wrapped myself in a dressing gown, then returned to the drawing room. Pierre was there with his easel, his paints. I indicated the big cane chair, with its great half-circle back and wide cane arm rests. I moved it beside the window.

'I thought,' I tried to explain in French, 'I could sit in this chair, and look out of the window.' I slipped off the dressing gown and sat myself as I had envisaged. I sat upright in the chair facing the artist, my legs straight before me, my ankles crossed, and my arms resting relaxed on the arm rests. I turned my head toward the window. I was completely exposed; no artfully placed hand, no convenient scarf trailed across my thighs. Everything was on show. This was important to me. I wanted Werner to understand exactly.

When I looked back Bonnard was studying me carefully. *'Eh bien,'* he murmured. *'Une femme amoureuse.'*

'Oui.'

He made me get up while he moved the chair slightly; he adjusted the position of my head; he rearranged his easel; he set out his paints and jars and boxes and then, when all was ready, he simply studied me for some time in complete silence. I sat. I had never felt so at peace. I knew he was looking at me, though I could not see him, of course, as I was staring out of the window. Then I could hear him at work.

I sat; I looked out of the window; I felt completely free. It was a glorious freedom, everything taken off me. I had no responsibility, nothing to do, nothing was expected of me; I was free simply to be. Free to be a woman. I *was* a woman; I felt it, through and through. I was a woman and I was offering myself to the man I loved. I have never been so happy, before or since.

The painting was completed in three sittings. I was very pleased with it. I could see immediately that quite apart from my personal part in the business and the purpose for which it was intended, it was a lovely picture. I was no great beauty, but I was nineteen and my figure was youthful, not voluptuous but, shall we say, athletic – firm, slim, taut. There was something else too that I understood instinctively, though at first I could not work out why: I was not 'nude' but 'naked'. What was the difference? I don't know. But I felt it, and feel it still. It was a narrative picture too. It invited speculation. The young girl was sitting at peace, at ease. She was completely relaxed. But why did she have no clothes on? Was it the painter's whim? Or was it a very warm day, perhaps? She was looking out of the window. Was she awaiting a lover? Was she indulging a pleasant reverie of what was soon to come?

It was a picture that could sit on anybody's wall and give pleasure; a young woman at ease in a room and gazing out at a view of a Mediterranean garden, with a glimpse of the sea beyond. On a rainy English day it would always bring a happy memory and even for a stranger invite pleasing speculation.

My next problem was when and how to present it to Werner. My instinct wanted this to be a special occasion: at the conclusion of a dinner, perhaps? There had been gossip about what Bonnard and I were up to in the drawing room these three mornings, which was awkward. Werner may even have guessed. But I didn't want to have to display it to the others – not immediately anyway. Its message was unmistakably for him alone.

Where could I hide it in the meantime? I wrapped it in paper, took it to our room and pushed it behind the chest of drawers.

That night in our room, I unwrapped the picture. Werner stared at it for some time. He looked at me, then at the picture, then at me again. There was nothing to say. He knew it and I knew it. Then he kissed me gently, reverently.

'I wish I had something I could give you, my darling. It's beautiful.'

'You don't have to give me anything,' I whispered. 'You have already given me everything I ever want.'

In the darkness we made love. It was not frantic as it often was; there was no striving, no urgency this time. It was all acceptance, all giving. And it seemed to go on for ever. There was no hurry as we moved about each other, over, under, exploring touching, until I was in a state of heightened awareness, as if my whole skin were alive with tingling impulses.

Later we talked. Like a fool, in my preoccupation with Werner and myself I had for a moment lost sight of his daughter, but after a few minutes, after we had digested the picture, and said everything we could about it, he said, 'Once we are in England, once Saturday is over...'

And I remembered immediately his daughter. In truth she had never been out of his thoughts and I felt a fool to have been so carried away with my plan for the picture when all the time Werner could only think of his little girl.

'My darling,' I whispered, 'please forgive me. Of course you're thinking of Albertina.'

There was a silence. 'All the time,' he began at last. 'All the time. I remember the day she was born. I was so proud. Of course everyone knows how a woman feels when she holds her daughter in her arms for the first time. But for me it was such a miracle. I could not get over it. I walked about the streets and murmured the words, "My daughter, my daughter." Then I would imagine scenes in the future: "Have you met my daughter?" She would be five years old, and I would be walking with her little hand in mine. Then she would be a fourteen-year-old, awkward, shy, growing, on the verge of womanhood. Then she would be, say, twenty, a blossoming young woman. "Have you met my daughter?" I would introduce her to colleagues, and they would reply, "Your daughter, my dear fellow? This lovely young lady?"'

He paused, and there was a painful silence. I felt crushed, and cursed my own stupidity at not foreseeing this long ago. My picture now seemed a paltry thing, juvenile. 'So, my dear Meg,' and he drew a shattering sigh, 'you see, when my wife wrote to say I could see her on Saturday, I have been able to think of nothing else. I hope you understand.'

I couldn't even speak for a moment, and only squeezed him gently as we lay in the darkness.

'I had another letter,' he began again. 'She has given me very precise directions – the Hotel Latitude 42 in Ste Maxime – and the time. Three in the afternoon on the second.'

'You're sure now it isn't a trap?' I asked hesitantly.

Another silence, then he spoke in a low hoarse voice. 'I have to go.'

During the days that followed, I tried to concentrate on the future. There was much to think about. First of all, there were the arrangements we would have to make when we arrived in London. I would introduce Werner to my parents. This would not be easy, I saw at once. They would be suspicious of him. If the worst came to the worst and they refused to accept him, well, we would find a room in Soho, somewhere near to Heather, and start looking for work. And if Werner had difficulty at first – it might take time to establish contacts, I could see – then I would go out to work. This held no terrors for me. The art course already seemed an irrelevance that I had outgrown.

But suppose there was a war? During the afternoon I put it to Werner. I had no idea what happened in such circumstances.

'Would they lock you up?'

'Probably. They would want to be sure I

wasn't a spy.'

'A spy!'

'It's obvious, my dear. But don't worry; I think I could persuade them I was quite safe.'

'But then, if there is a war, what would you do?'

'To tell the truth, I am not exactly sure. I might have to go to the States. I might even have to find a teaching job – and after all the rude things I said about the university.' He chuckled.

This conversation did not reassure me. There were going to be big problems when we got to London, that much was clear. But I was not afraid. There was a rock of certainty in me and I knew that together we could overcome any – and all – problems.

The next few days passed in an indistinct haze. All I can remember is that we made love. We seemed to make love continually. Although I felt sure of Werner and myself, this did not stop me feeling anxious. The political situation had become so uncertain, our future so uncertain – above all the visit by his wife and daughter, which took over his every waking thought – that I clung to him as a reassurance and I think, looking back, that our love-making was to some extent a refuge from it all. Together we could be in a state of perfect unity; here in this beautiful garden, with the sea before us, and the villa behind us, we were in a little oasis of innocence, of trust and love. It would not last long, I knew, and we would soon have to leave, but for these precious moments I was free to be happy.

Twenty-Seven

On Friday morning, September 1st, we heard on the radio that at a quarter to five in the morning the Germans had invaded Poland. We listened to this with a mixture of incredulity and a dull consciousness that our worst fears had been confirmed. This had to be war.

All day we listened to the radio. There were continuous bulletins and at first the outcome seemed uncertain. The Poles were fighting back. But as the day dragged on, it became clear – what had been obvious anyway – that the Poles had not a hope. The German thrust was expertly planned. Strange place names – towns and rivers I had never heard before were constantly repeated and we hunted out an atlas to be able to follow events.

Then we heard that the French Government was gravely concerned. There had been a treaty with Poland – the French and the British had guaranteed Poland's security – but what did this mean? Were Britain and France to go to war over Poland? It was not at all clear and all day a cloud of uncertainty and fear hung over the house.

Heather was decided. She confronted me during the morning.

'We've got to go. I'm packed already. We'll

get the train tonight – it leaves at eight thirty-eight from St Raphael. If we can get on it,' she added glumly.

I tried to reason with her. 'France is safe for the moment. If the Germans are in Poland they can't attack France as well, can they? Look, it's only one more day. We'll definitely be on the train tomorrow night. We'll be in London on Sunday night. Without fail. In any case,' I added, 'I'm not leaving without Werner.'

Heather listened with a long face and I could see she was deeply torn.

There was another development, however. At about four in the afternoon a taxi drove up and Heather's brother Jack marched into the house. He was in no mood to compromise.

'Pack your bags, Heather – and you too, Meg. We're leaving tonight.'

'Where have you come from?' We were both staring at him open-mouthed.

'Barcelona, by the first train I could get this morning. As soon as I heard the news I left. Are you girls ready?'

There was a pause as Heather looked at me.

'I am,' she said uncertainly, still looking at me. Jack switched his glance to me.

I was awkward. 'I am going tomorrow night. I don't think there's such a panic as you seem to think.'

'Panic?' He was incredulous. 'Did you hear the radio this morning? There's going to be war within twenty-four hours – forty-eight at the most. We're going.'

'It's not at all clear whether France will go to

war with Germany over Poland,' I went on sturdily. I was determined not to be panicked into changing my plans.

'Oh, isn't it?' he replied sarcastically. 'Well, I'm not staying here to find out. I won't be happy till I've put the channel between me and the Hun, and that goes for you too, Heather.'

'I'm staying with Meg,' she said with an effort.

'Like hell you are!' he exploded. 'Do you think I am going home without you? What do you think our parents would say if I told them I had come back to England and left you in France? I don't know what you're up to, Meg, and frankly I don't care, but Heather is coming to Paris with me tonight, if I have to drag her on to the train by the hair. Which I will do,' he added with emphasis, staring at her.

There was another silence as we continued to stare at each other, trying to fathom each other's thoughts. Finally, Heather turned to Jack. 'Sit down. I'll get Marcelline to give you a drink.'

'What do you mean?' Her brother was taken aback.

'Jack...' She now stood over him. 'What Meg says is true. One more day can't possibly make any difference. She has got to wait till tomorrow for Werner – he's her chap – and I'm not going without her.'

The house seemed quiet and as we sat round the dinner table that evening conversation was muted, sporadic. We were all preoccupied. We had the radio on continuously and hunched over it whenever there was any sort of a news

310

bulletin. There was no movement from the French Government; the war continued to rage in Poland however.

That night when we went to bed we were in no mood for love-making. 'My darling,' I whispered, 'this time tomorrow we'll be on the train to Paris. In two days we'll be in London. And then we can start our new life.'

The following day, Saturday, I could see how nervous he was, distracted, unable to concentrate. I was busily packing our things.

'Meg, do you think she'll still come now that...'

He left the sentence unfinished. I did not know what to say, and eventually he went on uncertainly, 'She hasn't written again.'

I was down to earth. 'You'll just have to go. Just go. If she's not there...'

Poor man, he wiped his hand across his face. 'I just pray,' was all he said. I held him and we stood silently together, praying. I'm not religious but just then I prayed as hard as I knew how. Prayed that Werner would see his daughter, prayed that it would not distress him too much, prayed that it wasn't a trap, and prayed that we would be safe on the train together that evening.

He left at about half past one to take the train round to Ste Maxime. The meeting was arranged for three o'clock. I supposed it might last an hour, and that he would be back between five and six. We would then leave at seven to take the train to St Raphael and the express to Paris.

I made my adieus with Madame and Bonnard.

Alcide would be brought home the following week, she told me, and she and Karim would care for him. I had packed all our things. I had wrapped my canvases, all my painting equipment, and Bonnard's portrait. When I stacked it all together it seemed a lot. Fortunately Werner was with me and between us it would not be a problem.

Werner had also been busy, but mainly burning papers. 'I can't take this stuff,' he explained. 'If it fell into the wrong hands, it could do a lot of damage – and not just to me either.'

There was an old stove in another of the huts and he spent the morning carrying papers to this stove and burning them. That left his personal things, but there were not many of them. A typewriter, a hold-all full of clothes. He never had a great range of clothes – the canvas sailor's trousers, a few shirts, a leather *blouson* jacket.

I was now consumed with anxiety. If he met his wife and daughter at three, and they spent an hour together, then Werner came back, it would be nearly six. We then had to leave soon after seven – at the latest – to be sure to make the connection at St Raphael. The timing was very tight.

That afternoon I watched him go. He became cheerful at the last minute.

'Don't worry!' he said as if he had never told me of all his own concerns and doubts.

'I'll stop worrying when you're back here and we can go to St Raphael.'

I watched him walk off down the track into town. Then I turned and wandered back slowly to the house. It was impossible to concentrate. How could I think of anything except Werner and his daughter? All my preparations had been completed that morning. I wandered into the house, sat down, but after a minute got up again and went out into the garden. It was siesta time. Maia was upstairs with Chantal, Madame was lying down. Bonnard too. But I could not rest.

Silence reigned. The heat beat down, the sea was lying still, flat, glittering like beaten metal, an intense, dark blue. I sat on the steps by the terrace and stared out through the trees towards the sea. This was my last afternoon. Tomorrow morning I'd be in Paris and tomorrow night London. My last day – how could I hold on to this moment, somehow stretch it out? By concentrating as hard as I could, by taking in every element, the stillness of the trees, the incessant rasping of the cicadas, the little fountain, the worn old tiles of the terrace, the giant urns. My eye wandered over it all as I strove to register it for ever in my memory.

In the end I too began to feel drowsy and I went up to our room. The bed had been stripped: we were never going to sleep in it again. A new bed would await us in London.

I lay down on the mattress and closed my eyes. But as soon as I did, a picture of Werner intruded. I looked at my watch. Twenty past three; he was in Ste Maxime by now. Four o'clock came at last and I thought of him in the Hotel Latitude 42 – what a strange name for a hotel it was.

I dozed briefly, then jerked awake again to

313

look at my watch. Finally, when five o'clock came, I went into the kitchen for a glass of water then walked out on the track leading into town. It was no good pretending: I could not relax until I saw Werner again. He should be coming some time before six. I walked up and down the dusty track, that compound of sand and pine needles, looking idly at the clusters of broom in this harsh red earth, the oleanders, the gnarled old cork trees. Now that I was about to leave I found myself noticing everything again, the way I had on my first day here. Half past five came and my unease rose perceptibly. He ought to be here soon. I walked up and down. I wanted to go to the lavatory, and cursed the glass of water I had drunk, but didn't dare leave the track in case he appeared.

Another fifteen minutes and my hands were damp and I was rubbing them against my shorts. It was intolerable: if only he would come and I would know he was all right.

Then he did appear, strolling up from the town quite casually, just as when he left. I ran to him and threw myself into his arms; I had never been so anxious in my life. For a moment I could only gasp over and over, 'Oh thank God, thank God, you're safe!'

We separated; he put his arm round my waist and we turned back towards the gates.

'Did you see her?' I asked at last.

He shook his head. 'It was a trap, as I suspected.' He paused.

'Oh, I'm so sorry. So you never saw Albertina?'

He shook his head again. 'Even before I got near the hotel, I saw a car parked across the road with two men in it. So I sat down on a bench on the promenade to watch them. After a while a man came out of the hotel, crossed to the men and spoke to them, then went back inside. I watched them for a while, half an hour maybe. Then I went to a telephone box and rang the hotel. They said a room was reserved in my wife's name but she hadn't arrived yet. I went back and waited and watched. None of them saw me; I was only two hundred metres away, just sitting on a bench on the promenade with my eye on the hotel. It was very quiet, hardly anyone came out. No one went in. My wife did not go in. I went and telephoned again to be sure. She still hadn't arrived, and there was no message from her. I was now certain it was a trap, so I returned to the railway station and caught the train back.'

We were walking slowly up the track, our arms round each other.

'So she was never going to come at all?'

He shook his head.

'I still don't understand,' I said at last. 'She definitely wrote the letters, didn't she?'

He nodded again, looking down at the track. He was very preoccupied, and I could see the crowd of thoughts in his mind. I hesitated to question him too closely, but it seemed that whoever was planning to kill him had got the co-operation of his wife.

'They knew how much I wanted to see Albertina,' he said at last with a deep sigh.

I pressed against him. 'My darling,' I whispered, 'I'm so, so sorry.'

Behind me I now heard a motorbike, coming up the track towards us. Instinctively we moved to the side of the road but did not turn round.

Then in the blink of an eye, the motorbike roared past us, jammed to a sudden halt, wrenched round in a spray of sand and was in front of us. There were two men on it and the man on the rear held up a pistol and fired it point-blank into Werner's face. There was a deafening explosion, Werner jerked out of my arms and was flung violently back on the path. The motorbike roared into life and disappeared back towards the town. It was over in a second.

I stared down in stupefaction for an instant before flinging myself on my knees beside him. Werner was dead, a hole in his forehead, and blood in his hair. He was completely dead – quite, quite dead. I saw it instantly, yet in crazy incomprehension I tried to lift his head; my fingers could feel the warm blood matting his hair and staining the sand. I was screaming, 'Werner! Werner! Oh my God! I don't believe it!' I was stunned, it was meaningless, unreal. 'No, No!' I screamed. 'It can't be! You're not dead, you're not dead! Oh my God!' I looked about me on that quiet deserted track. 'Help!' I cried stupidly and starting to my feet I ran hard back up to the house.

'Come quickly, come quickly!' I shouted. 'Werner – it's Werner – '

As Heather appeared at the door, I rushed to her; my hands were covered in blood, which she saw immediately.

'It's Werner!' I repeated incoherently. 'He's been killed!'

'*What?* When?'

'Now! This minute – come, for God's sake, come quickly!'

Behind her, Madame Leary and Jack now appeared, caught the end of what I was saying and we all hurried back to the gate and down the track.

As we arrived, Jack said, 'Don't touch him!' He looked at me. 'You're sure he's dead?'

'You can see the hole in his forehead! The man was a foot away!' I was in hysterics. Heather clutched me to hold me still. 'Look at him!' I screamed over and over, 'Look at him. Oh my God! There were these men – on a motorbike – just a moment ago. We were just walking up to the house when they rode up and a man ... Oh my God! A man just pointed a pistol and shot him. I can't believe it!'

Heather clutched me tightly as Jack and Madame Leary looked down at Werner's body. They looked at each other. 'We must phone the police,' said Madame. 'Come inside – Meg must wash her hands.'

I was reduced to silence now as we returned to the house.

'Heather, go with Meg and see that she washes her hands – and tidy her a little.' Upstairs, in another bedroom, Heather poured out some water and helped me wash my hands. I was shaking uncontrollably, couldn't think, could only feel an intolerable pressure on my forehead, as if my brain was about to explode. Heather took charge, washed and dried my hands and made me sit as she ran a comb through my hair.

When we got downstairs again, Madame was waiting with Jack. She now approached me and placed her hands on my shoulders.

'Now listen, Meg, we've talked it over, and this is what we're going to do. I shall report the murder. You will go with Heather and Jack now to get the night train for Paris.'

'What?'

'You can't stay here!' she went on forcefully. 'If you do, you will be kept here perhaps for months while the police are making their investigations. You are the only witness; they will not let you go – it could be for months,' she repeated. 'In the circumstances—'

'I can't go! He's still lying there! My God, don't you understand! He's still...'

Jack was beside her, and together they concentrated on me. 'Meg,' he said, 'you're coming with Heather and me – now. The taxi will be here in a moment. We're going – now, tonight. Everything Madame Leary says is true. It's out of the question leaving you here. You could be kept here for months – and in the meantime anything could happen.'

'*I can't go!*' I screamed in their faces and burst into tears. '*I can't! I can't!*'

They were looking at each other. 'She's coming with us now.' Jack was deadly serious.

It was only a few minutes later that we heard the sound of a car, and Heather called, 'It's the taxi.'

'Right!' Jack became super-efficient. 'Let's get the stuff in.'

I was still standing in a stupor in the hall as the three of them hurried bags and boxes and parcels out to the car and after a moment Jack took me by the arm. 'Let's go,' he said tersely.

'I can't go!' I screamed again.

'Don't worry about Werner, Meg,' Madame said, taking my arm. 'I'll take care of him. Trust me. Everything will be done. I will write and tell you everything. Be calm. It will be all right. But you *must* go now.'

I thought my brain would explode.

'He's lying there dead! Don't you understand? In the dust! We must bring him in! Oh my God! We can't just leave him there! What are you thinking?'

Madame repeated that everything would be taken care of. But that I *must* go.

I didn't know what I was doing, but soon afterwards I was in the taxi and we were on our way to the station.

Twenty-Eight

How did I get home?

It's a jumble of images. We were on a train; Heather and Jack were handling bags and cases; I was good for nothing. The train continued to fill and by the time we left Marseilles – it must have been around ten – the train was packed, with people standing in the corridor. Heather and I were squashed side by side, Jack was opposite, and eventually we dozed off, and I have these crazy dislocated memories as I drifted in and out of consciousness: the dim light overhead, people opposite asleep, their heads hanging on each other's shoulders. A man had climbed into the luggage rack and was asleep. But every time I drifted off the memory returned: the men on the motorbike, the explosion, Werner wrenched out of my arms and flung backwards on to the dusty track. I twisted my head, tried to shake it off, but as soon as I closed my eyes it returned.

It was soon dawn and I awoke again as people stirred about us, stretching, yawning, and snatches of conversation began. People began to pull out parcels, unwrap packets of bread and garlic sausage.

My mouth was dry and I was gasping for water but we had drunk everything and I sat in a miasma of tiredness and wretchedness, still in a state of shock as the light grew imperceptibly and a glorious September morning dawned. I felt quivery, light, stiff, yawning, nervous. I didn't know what I felt – unreal, out of all time.

'Should be in Paris in half an hour,' Jack said as he leaned across. 'We can get some breakfast.'

I had no will and eventually, when we arrived, it was Heather and Jack who handed down all our luggage, arranging and checking things, and eventually we were in front of the station on a bright clear morning. Traffic roared past, travellers were hurrying in and out. Everywhere there were soldiers and army *camions*.

'We've got till ten, that'll give us a bit of time.'

As we ate breakfast in a *brasserie* over the road Jack and Heather talked, about the emergency, about getting back to London. I sat silent, and found that tears were streaming down my face.

Heather took out her handkerchief and, without saying anything, gently wiped them away. 'Don't worry, Meg, Madame will take care of Werner. Trust her. It's all right – and you'll be home soon.'

I said nothing.

We took up our stuff and made our way through the métro to the Gare du Nord where chaos reigned. The station was so crowded we could scarcely get inside and all about us we heard English voices and snatches of conversation. When we fought our way as far as the Calais train it was now a question of whether we would get on it at all. It was already quite full but in the end, after a lot of aggressive pushing and elbowing and many angry looks and comments, we managed to force our way into the corridor. Jack left the luggage in the guard's van.

We stood during the three hours to Calais. I had scarcely slept the previous night and I found myself drifting in and out of sleep, rocking on my feet, held up by other passengers. The talk was all war speculation: whether the government was going to react to the invasion of Poland. It passed in and out of my consciousness without my reacting in the slightest.

At Calais the crush was worse. The luggage was everywhere, scattered on the platform, and people were herding into passport control in a panic, so eager to get on to the ship, which I could see over the roofs of the sheds.

The first thing we heard as we at last were able to get out of the train was, *'C'est la guerre!'*

The cry was taken up all around us.

'It's war!'

'What's that?'

'It's war – Chamberlain was on the radio at midday, apparently.'

It was now after one o'clock.

'What?'

'It's war! He sent an ultimatum at nine this morning; Hitler didn't answer, and it expired at eleven.'

'He thought Chamberlain was bluffing.'

'It seems he wasn't. He came on the radio at twelve and said it's war. One of the sailors just told me.'

'Oh my God!' a woman cried somewhere.

Under the impetus of this long-expected news a frenzy rippled through the crowd, all crushing forward towards the barrier. They – we all – couldn't wait to get on to the ship. There it stood, high above the quayside and once aboard it was just a few miles and we would be back in England: safe. A fever gripped everybody, even Jack.

'Where's our stuff?' Heather was hunting among all the packages and bags and suitcases, which had been tipped unceremoniously on to the platform. Jack, who up to now had been cool and in charge, suddenly became terribly nervous on seeing the ship, the smoke billowing from its stack, and the other passengers crowding towards the barrier – all pushing and calling to each other, a terrible scrimmage.

'Never mind the bags – let's get on the ship!'

Heather was angry. 'I'm not going without our stuff! There's all Meg's pictures! Not to mention mine.'

'To hell with Meg's pictures! War's broken out – didn't you hear? Let's get on the bloody boat!'

'Where's our stuff?' I was as anxious as Heather now, tripping among suitcases and pushing among all the other passengers, all as exasperated as we. But I had to find Werner's portrait. As we were turning over this mountain of luggage, Heather unexpectedly called, 'Here's your picture, Meg,' and thrust the brown paper parcel into my arms.

A wave of relief rippled through me and suddenly the rest didn't matter. All the other stuff –

what was it anyway but some dirty underwear and a few amateur canvases? As for the Bonnard – it all seemed utterly irrelevant. My little gift to Werner – how futile, how juvenile. In the end, with the scrum round us, the gesticulating, the pushing and shoving, Jack shouting at us to 'Get on the bloody boat!' I found myself herded with Heather through the barrier and up the gangway.

As we came out on the deck the horn was already sounding, ropes were being cast off, and water soon appeared between us and the quayside. France was receding, already becoming a memory, a dream that would be embroidered, exaggerated, edited and rearranged.

I had ceased to care or notice. I clutched the picture. I had Werner with me and I clung to it, my talisman. With him I knew that it had really been true. It had really happened and nothing would ever alter that.

Then what? Deflation. Victoria Station in the late afternoon, the newspaper stall closed, everything quiet, people dispersing in a hurry to get home. The three of us on the platform, Heather saying, 'I'm going with Meg.' Hasty handshakes, and then we were on the tube. Heather had very kindly telephoned to my parents.

All about us people had the Sunday papers open; there was such an air of quiet in the late-afternoon sun, a breath of autumn in the air, as we finally emerged at Mill Hill.

A quiet suburban street. My father was waiting at the tube station with the car. He didn't say much and Heather and I were driven home quickly. My mother was overjoyed; she clasped me, but I didn't really take it in; I was very tired and everything had a dull feeling. I was still anaesthetized, clutching my precious package.

As soon as the first effusions had died down, my mother had made a cup of tea and we were seated in the front room, my parents' eyes were on this parcel. I was reluctant to open it. It was my one talisman, and I was afraid they might take it from me – all kinds of irrational fears ran through me – but in the end I had no choice but to cut the string.

When I opened it, I found it was not the picture of Werner after all. It was the Bonnard, the nude picture of me.

While my parents were absorbing this, uncertain whether to expostulate or to enquire how it had come to be, I was reeling. I stared and stared at it. Where was Werner? What was it all for if my one and only memento of him was lost in France? The tears began to trickle down my face and soon, I didn't know how – I saw Heather speaking quietly to my mother – but soon I found myself being led upstairs and put to bed.

Later the doctor called. He asked questions, but I didn't know what to say. How could I tell him about Werner? He left some tablets; my mother appeared with a glass of milk, made me take a tablet, and soon afterwards I was asleep.

The next morning I must have woken late, still feeling drowsy, hungover, my limbs rung out. All in pieces, I lay in bed staring at the familiar ceiling, and the tears began again. I just couldn't help it.

The room was in complete darkness and it wasn't until my mother came in that I found why. She reached up into the window, lifted out a black blind, and set it on the ground.

'It's the blackout. In case the Germans come,' she explained.

My father had gone to work. My mother sat by my bed and, after a few preliminary questions, asked me, 'Couldn't we talk about it?'

I shook my head, just rolled it on the pillow; I couldn't look at her. She placed her hand over mine, I withdrew mine; I couldn't talk. How could I tell her about Werner? How even begin to explain? It was all madness.

Fortunately other people were more concerned about the war. My father came in that afternoon with the *Telegraph*.

'The French are in,' he announced briefly. 'Declared war at five yesterday afternoon. You got out not a moment too soon. I don't like to think what would have happened if you'd delayed any longer. It was a damn fool thing to stay as long as you did. My God, do you realize, Meg, you got out by the skin of your teeth.'

I nodded on my pillow.

'Well, you're home now, and that's the main thing. I owe that young fellow a drink.'

He knocked the rolled-up newspaper against his hand for a moment and soon afterwards went out.

All I could think of was Werner lying on that sandy track, in the shade of the pines. How could I have gone off and left him like that? As I lay and thought of it, I began to feel a monstrous anger against Heather and Jack. It was they who had forced me to flee to the train and to leave him there – to leave that sweet, beautiful man lying on the track with his poor head smashed in and blood matting his hair. I couldn't get over it – to think he was still there, lying there in the open air, with no one...

As the tears continued to paint my face, I tried to tell myself that Madame would have taken care of him. But I could never forgive myself as long as I lived for having deserted him as he lay there like that. Never.

And I didn't even have his picture. That picture I had worked so hard at, to try and capture him, try to hold just a fleeting essence, just the tiniest glimpse of what he was really like. It was too bad. Instead of which there was this irrelevance, which my parents would want to know about, and about which no doubt they would soon be asking the most embarrassing questions. What answer would I make – except the most banal, perhaps, that the famous Pierre Bonnard had wanted to paint me?

Two days later Heather called. I was still in bed, indescribably weak, rung out, and weightless, listless, and unwilling to communicate, scarcely eating. Heather had brought her holiday snaps. I went through them, little two-inch-square images, tiny pictures, glimpses of the sea, the pines, or the house, with us smiling and fooling, Maia with her harp, several of Clay, smiling beneath a broad sun hat. And there was one of Werner and me, arms round each other.

'I had a copy of that one made for you,' she

said quietly, handing it over.

I stared and stared at that picture. I could have eaten it. Werner was in other pictures, in groups, and so was I. This was the only one of just the two of us, together, and holding each other.

'Bless you,' I whispered, and pushed the little snapshot beneath my pillow as I handed the others back.

'Another ten days and we'll be back in college. Are you coming back?'

I didn't know. I didn't know anything.

'Are you?' I asked at last.

'If it's still there, I suppose.' She paused. 'You haven't been out, so you probably don't know, but there's the most frightful blackout been imposed. Absolute. And a whole new race of tyrants has appeared in the shape of air-raid wardens.'

After Heather had gone, I took out the little snapshot and stared and stared at it. As I did so, as I remembered all the times we had been together and the times, too numerous to count but every one precious, that we had made love, I was able to ponder at leisure a new – if not entirely unexpected – development. Something that frankly I should have been aware of from the start but had chosen to ignore. In short, my period was late. In fact it was nearly two months late. All that day I lay in bed, staring at the little picture of Werner and me, thinking of the rightness of my bearing his child and now contemplating the horrible injustice of what had happened. Why? Why me? We were just meant for each other; we would have had our baby and been together. It was the right and proper thing to do! And instead he lay dead in the dusty track, his hair matted with blood, and I was lying in bed in Mill Hill expecting his child.

It got worse. During the morning my mother appeared bearing a letter for me. It was from Edward – whom frankly I had completely forgotten. She explained that she had dropped him a note to let him know I was back. He would be home at the weekend on leave, he said, and hoped he might call and see me.

So now I had to try and square this circle. I was still feeling abominably tired and every time I tried to puzzle it out my brain seemed to overheat and I would just lie back, close my eyes and forget. And then the memories would start again; I would feel the heat of that Mediterranean sun on my neck, hear the cicadas, and see the others round the dinner table in the evening by the light of Werner's Chinese lanterns and the next thing I knew the tears were streaming down my face.

I had been in bed five days when Edward called. He was admitted to my room and stood somewhat awkwardly, shame-faced to find himself here in the intimacy of my bedside. I must say, even in my low state, I could see that he looked very dashing and handsome. He had been commissioned, he quickly told me, in the Ox and Bucks, and was arrayed in his officer's uniform. It suited him, and I could see how it had given him confidence and stature; he exuded a new maturity.

He was very concerned to see me so prostrated.

'A slight fever,' I croaked.

A few remarks passed between us. He allowed me briefly to tell him about the South of France, then broke in, 'Well, I must say, Meg, it was a miracle you got out. That was the last boat from France, you know.'

'Someone said that.'

He shook his head. 'Frankly, I don't like to contemplate what could have happened. You could have been marooned in France with no money. Why didn't you come home sooner, for heaven's sake?'

I shook my head listlessly. 'We didn't know it was going to be the last boat,' I said at last.

'Well, by Jove, surely you could see the writing on the wall? It was obvious to everybody.'

'Was it?' I murmured.

'As for that brother of Heather's, I should just like to give him a piece of my mind. By God, when I think of it, it was damned irresponsible!'

He was working himself into a righteous fury when fortunately he remembered the reason why he was here. He abruptly climbed down from his high horse and became more hesitant, studying me carefully. He pulled a chair to my bedside, leaning forward.

'Meg, I can see you're feeling poorly, so I hesitate to ask you. But you know, I've been thinking of you all the time you've been away. And – ' he hesitated – 'well, the reason I'm here is to ask you – well, the same question as last time. Have you thought about what we said?'

I was silent, staring up at the ceiling. At last I nodded very slightly. He waited and, when I said nothing, leaned forward even more, willing me to give him the answer he wanted. His will was like a great weight oppressing me. I turned at last, and tried my best to appear polite.

'Edward,' I murmured, 'I'm still feeling very tired. Could you come and see me tomorrow? I'll try to give you an answer.'

Twenty-Nine

And what answer was I to give him? I was still so weak that the effort of thinking was almost beyond me. How could I even contemplate the thought of marriage with Edward when the memories of France were still going round in my head? That night I was given another sleeping draught and sank into a deep, dreamless sleep. When I woke the following morning, my head was clearer but my limbs were all loose and rubbery as if my body had been taken to pieces and then fitted together again badly.

My mother tried to dissuade me but I forced myself to dress and awaited Edward in the sitting room. I might still feel like death but I was not going to present myself as some sort of invalid. However I had not the strength to stand and remained seated when he came in. He sat opposite me, crouching forward on the edge of his chair, his elbows on his knees, awaiting my reply.

I could not face him at first and was staring down at the folded hands in my lap. 'I have thought of what you said yesterday afternoon. What we discussed.' I paused and he started forward, but saw the look in my face. I had not finished.

'Edward, I cannot...' I shook my head and dropped my gaze. Another pause. I wiped a hand across my face. Perhaps I should have stayed in bed? Yet I had to get through this.

'Edward,' I began again. 'You have been very good with me and I owe you an explanation. There is something I must tell you first – before you say anything.' I was circling round the point, uncertain where to begin. He waited. 'While I was in France,' I croaked.

'Yes?' He waited.

'While I was in France ... there was somebody.' Still he waited. 'A man, I mean, and we ... Oh, Lord...' I could feel myself crumbling and, before I could go on, the tears started. I covered my face with my hands. 'I'm sorry. It wasn't meant to be like this.'

Edward was appalled by this and started forward, kneeling beside my chair.

'Meg, for God's sake – what is it?'

'There was a man – only now he's dead. He's dead, you see, and...' I couldn't go on.

'Dead?' he whispered. 'How?'

'He was shot while I was with him. We were talking and then a man rode up on a motorbike and just shot him, right there.'

'Good Lord,' he breathed. 'Did they find who did it?'

I shook my head. 'I don't know,' I sobbed. 'I had to leave. I wanted to stay but they wouldn't let me.'

'Who wouldn't?'

'Heather and Jack, they said we had to go or we wouldn't get the boat back to England,' I mumbled into my hands.

'Was this after war had been declared?'

I shook my head. 'No, the day before, on Saturday.'

He sat back, and there was a long silence. I pulled out a handkerchief.

'I'm sorry.' I mopped my eyes. 'It was a terrible shock, you see.'

'You poor dear,' he murmured. 'No wonder you're so down.'

There was a discreet knock at the door and my mother poked her nose in. 'Edward, I was just wondering, would you like a cup of coffee?'

Edward was very good. He got up, went to her at the door and whispered something. The door hastily closed. He came back and sat opposite me. 'I see now that I have been too hasty. It's quite all right, Meg, I won't trouble you now. I'll call again when I'm next home on leave – and we can talk again. When you're recovered.'

'It won't make any difference.'

He waited, and then said, 'Even so, maybe in a few months – once you've got over the shock...'

I must say, the warmth of his sympathy struck me even in my low state.

'Edward,' I began, drawing a long breath. 'You've been very good. I wish I had something better to say.'

'So do I,' he whispered at last. 'Still, next time I'm home on leave I'll—'

'It won't make any difference,' I repeated in a low voice.

There followed an inconclusive, wrangling sort of conversation until he finally rose. 'Well, perhaps I'd better be going,' he muttered awkwardly.

'Yes.'

'Well, goodbye then.'

We shook hands woodenly and eventually he let himself out. I remained in my chair and could hear some conversation between my mother and Edward before the front door closed. After a moment my mother opened the door.

'What did he say?' She looked at me in hopeful expectation.

'He asked me to marry him,' I said sadly.

She darted forward. 'Do you know, I had an idea it was coming. You can always tell. It just needed that nudge to tip him over the edge. Now, it may be tricky to organize. He's away in camp so much. Still, if he's getting married, I'm sure they'll give him compassionate leave—'

'We're not getting married.'

There was a stunned silence while I remained staring at the carpet.

'Margaret?'

'How can I marry him? I don't love him. I will only ever love one man – and he's dead!' I got up, walked quickly past her and went up to my room.

A little later there was a tap on my door, and my

mother looked in. I was lying on my bed, fully dressed.

'Margaret dear, we must talk.'

'There's nothing to talk about.'

'I think there is, dear. You say this man is dead. Clearly it has been a shock. But I'm sure you will get over it. If we leave it for a month or two, then you could drop a note to Edward, perhaps at Christmas—'

'Mum, please!'

That evening when my father came in from work, they pounced again.

'Margaret,' he began, 'I understand Edward proposed to you this morning.'

'Yes.'

'And what answer did you give him?'

'Hasn't Mum told you?' I said listlessly.

'Margaret, I don't think you are being sufficiently serious about this. Edward is a fine young man with excellent prospects. An offer from him is something to take very seriously indeed. Frankly you would be a fool to refuse. Especially now.'

'Why now?'

'Haven't you been reading the newspapers? We are at war. There is no knowing what may happen. Young men will be sent north, south, east and west. All normal life will be completely disrupted. This was an excellent opportunity for you – one which may not recur for a very long time. You may have many years to repent of this if you make the wrong decision.'

I had not the strength to reply.

'Now, I have been thinking. I am going to write a short note to Edward, intimating in a roundabout way that you might change your mind, explaining about the terrible shock you have had—'

'No, Dad! I told him! I cannot marry Edward.' I stood up. 'Oh, God! How can I marry him? Don't you understand?'

I went quickly out of the room and this time out of the house, for the first time since I had returned from France, and walked quickly away.

Nothing more was said, though the atmosphere in the house was tense, fraught with unspoken significance. My parents were clearly very displeased.

Through the next few weeks the other – bigger – problem was looming in my mind and I realized that sooner or later – in fact sooner rather than later – my parents would have to be informed about the fact that I was expecting a baby. The thought almost floored me and I spent many sleepless nights trying to work out how to tell them. I could scarcely imagine the scene yet I could not postpone it for long.

One idea I had, the best I could think of, was to explain what had happened, to emphasize that of course Werner and I would have been married, and then to try to convince them that the best thing for all of us – to minimize the embarrassment and fuss that would be caused – would be that they should make me a small allowance and that I should go and live with Heather in her flat.

I shall never forget the night I finally screwed

up the courage to break the news. If they had been stood against a wall and shot it could not have been worse.

It was after dinner a few weeks later. The nights were drawing in; autumn was upon us and there was a slight chill in the room. I had a cardigan round my shoulders.

'Mum, Dad,' I began, 'there is something I must tell you.'

They both looked up from their pudding bowls. I swallowed. My heart was pumping and I pushed my hair back from my face in a nervous gesture.

'It's something unexpected, something I have just found out.' I paused again. 'You know that while I was in France I met this man. And we fell in love.' I swallowed again. 'We would have got married! We intended to, as soon as we got to England! But then, as I told you...'

There was a pause. They had not yet grasped what I was hinting at.

'Well,' I pushed on, 'the fact is ... Oh, God.' I stopped and rested my head on my hand.

'Margaret...' my mother began.

I nodded.

'You don't mean...'

I nodded again.

My father sat back. I could not face them; I stared into my pudding bowl.

'But are you sure?' my mother said again.

'I'm sure,' I croaked.

My father stood up. 'Margaret, are you telling us you are expecting a child?'

I looked up at him. 'We would have been

married!' I repeated.

My mother burst out, 'You're *pregnant*? Why on earth didn't you agree to marry Edward? You stupid girl! If you'd married him quickly, he would never have known!'

'Mum!' I screamed. 'How can you say such a thing? You want me to lie to Edward, to let him bring up another man's child without knowing it?'

'It wouldn't be the first time,' my father muttered from the other side of the table.

A long silence.

'It's my fault,' he went on in a contained rage. 'I should never have let you go to France. I knew it at the time. I knew it.'

My mother continued to regard me with a heavy look. Finally she muttered, shaking her head, 'I cannot even begin to think of the consequences. My mind simply goes blank. How on earth will you find a husband once you have a child? Did you have no sense? What man will take you with another man's child?'

'I didn't know he was going to get shot,' I said sadly.

'That's not the point, Margaret! Oh God, that's torn it! That has really torn it. What are we going to do?'

'Mum,' I began, 'I know I've brought this on you but I want to spare you any embarrassment, really. If Dad could make me a little allowance, I could go and live with Heather—'

'In some squalid flat in Soho? Are you out of your mind?'

* * *

The atmosphere at home was at freezing point. My parents held conferences from which I was excluded. I think they canvassed various options, even wrote to an unmarried aunt who lived in Broadstairs. But nothing came of any of it. Any talk of returning to art school was squashed and for the moment I remained at home.

Then at Christmas Edward showed up again. I was astonished at his tenacity.

'Are you going to tell him?' my father asked coldly. 'Or shall I?'

'He's going to find out anyway. I'd rather tell him myself. At least it's honest. Then he really will go away.'

My pregnancy was not yet showing.

I thought, after our last meeting, that he might have changed his mind and simply want us to be friends. But his feelings were unchanged, he quickly told me. There was an awkward silence. I was very touched by his persistence. He looked so unhappy I wanted to say yes just to see the relief in his face.

'Edward, please sit down,' I began. 'There is something you have to know.' I looked down at my hands. 'Something you'd find out eventually in any case. The fact is – well, this man – I don't really want to talk about him if you don't mind. He's dead, but, well, the fact is, to be blunt, we became lovers. And the upshot of that I think you can guess.'

'You mean you're...'

I nodded.

'How long have you known?'

'Since September.'

'And the father is ... this chap?'

I nodded again. Edward got up again and walked to the window. There was a very long silence. I waited. I didn't feel anything.

The silence went on and on. I stared down at my hands, aware of Edward behind me. At last he said, in a low voice, 'I'm sorry,' he said. 'Very sorry.'

I said nothing. He was now deeply embarrassed. He glanced round at the door, as if looking for an escape. I stood up, and became almost businesslike. I held out my hand.

'Well, thank you for coming, Edward. It was kind.'

'It was brave of you to tell me, Meg,' he muttered awkwardly, then he took my hand and after another moment he left. I heard the front door behind him.

Poor Edward. I really felt so sorry for him. Now that he was gone, I could see that we might – in another life – have been quite happy together and it gave me a warm feeling, despite everything, to remember his devotion. He really had loved me. That was something to be proud of, something to remember.

I was very surprised therefore the following morning to hear a knock at the front door and, when I opened it, to see Edward again.

'May I come in?'

Once again we had the sitting room to ourselves. I was bewildered. I could not think what brought him.

Edward soon came to the point. 'I've been thinking, Meg. Didn't get much sleep last night, to tell the truth.'

'Nor me.'

He looked up, then after a moment pushed on. It was obviously difficult for him to speak.

'It was decent of you to be so straight with me. I appreciated that. You've had a hard time, it's obvious. Really hard,' he repeated, organizing his thoughts. 'As I say, I've been thinking, and the point, as I see it, is this: the other chap is dead. I don't want to know his name – or anything about him. As far as I am concerned he's dead and that's all I need to know. And you've been left – through no fault of your own – with a baby. I presume you would have married him?'

I nodded.

'Anyway, he's dead, so you can't. So that leaves you and me – and the baby. The fact is, Meg, I can't bear to think of you left with your parents and have to put up with all the looks and gossip, and your parents' humiliation. I couldn't stand that.' He drew a breath and pushed on. 'The truth is, Meg, you're the only girl I've ever wanted, and if it has to be you and the baby, so be it.' He drew a deep breath. 'So here's what I've decided. I am still willing to marry – if you are.'

I stared. 'Do you mean it?'

He nodded. 'What do you say? Shall we give it a try?'

I was so overwhelmed by his generosity that I had to say yes. He immediately became all

341

energy and organization. 'We'll get married quickly and I shall accept the child as my own. No one will ever know.' He went on with increasing enthusiasm. 'And there'll be other children of our own.' He paused. 'But, in fairness to me, Meg, there has to be one rule.'

'What?'

'There must be no talk of the past. I've told you, I don't want to know about this other chap. The baby will be our baby and we're going to make our life together and look forwards. So that's my only condition. No looking back. And I don't want to know about your art school chums either. I don't want people in the house saying, "Do you remember the time when..." It's only fair to me, Meg, do you understand? And it's not a lot to ask. I will dedicate my life to you and our children. I only ask you to do the same.'

There was an authority here that I only fully appreciated after he had gone. Putting on the uniform and committing himself fully to me gave him a gravity I had never suspected before. I was impressed, I admit it. Edward had grown into a man. The whimsical aesthete, the kite-flyer and collector of fine books was nowhere to be seen and instead I had been speaking to some-one essentially serious and committed to life. Realizing this, I realized too that by contrast I was still in France, still with Werner. This had to stop. It was up to me to make the effort and start as Edward said, looking forwards.

I need not describe my parents' reaction. There would be a quick wedding, we had decided. It was wartime, no time to delay things. So a mere two weeks later we had a quiet wedding in the parish church. Edward looked very handsome in his uniform and polished boots, and I knew the other girls thought I was very lucky.

The following April my daughter Alice was born, and two years after her, our son Nicholas. Edward has kept his side of the bargain and I have tried to keep mine.

He was at Dunkirk and returned with a medal. The unexpected thing was the effect this had on his father. Once Churchill became Prime Minister old Mr Tremayne completely changed his tune. Out went all talk of Hitler and Mosley and overnight he was an ardent admirer of the Prime Minister. We were tactful enough not to remind him of this. And there was something else: when his son returned from active service with a medal, and when Mr Tremayne heard the congratulations and respectful comments, when he was assailed by his neighbours complimenting him on his handsome son the war hero, a change came over him. And most of all when I was able to present him with first a granddaughter, then a grandson, all the good side of his nature, his essential humanity, which I had suspected even at that first meeting, came to the foreground. He mellowed. The tension between him and Edward disappeared; Edward was now in the driving seat and the old man was content to take a back seat.

I had promised to have nothing to do with my old friends. All talk of France was barred. I did once show him the painting but he was adamant:

he didn't want to see it. That was in the past and we were to look forward. I accepted that; I had agreed to it. I gave the picture to Heather and asked her to keep it for me for the time being.

I confess I did keep intermittently in touch with her through my mother. At the moment Heather is an ambulance driver and we hear hair-raising tales of her dashing through the Blitz with bombs falling all around. The bishop was, unsurprisingly, not passed fit for active service and has since joined an air-raid warning party and spends his nights on the BBC roof keeping watch. Victor Ridmore was called up and is somewhere in the ranks. He is not the sort of man to seek promotion.

But Edward is just destined to rise. He is now a Major, last time I heard, and somewhere in Italy or Sicily, I don't know where. When I do get news from him, it's months late.

I remain here with the children and we make a life together. Thank God I have them because sometimes I think I should certainly have shot myself.

Everything Edward said is right. Yes, we must make a new life together, and we do. And we must not look back. Strangely, having written this, I do feel calmer about it all. Perhaps I can see it more in perspective. Perhaps. And perhaps when Edward is back, when the war's over, we can start to build that life together that he was so confident about.

Thirty

It was three thirty when Alice laid down the last sheet. Rubbing her eyes she got rather shakily to her feet and stared about her in the night-time silence of the empty flat. Her overwhelming feeling was a terrible sympathy for her father. No wonder he had seemed brusque, no wonder he hadn't wanted to see the picture, or hear about Heather Grey.

Throughout the following days she was plagued with the question of what to say to him when he returned from America. He had grown into a hero in her eyes. It was immediately obvious from the manuscript that her mother had remained in love with the memory of Werner. Why else would she have written it? Yet Werner was dead and Edward could never take his place. It explained too the photograph she had seen in her mother's hand. But who had placed it there? It could only have been Edward; even after all these years he had undertaken this duty.

And what about her mother? Was it fair to Edward to marry him when she did not love him? Yet, looking back, thinking as hard as she could, her mother had always seemed a loving mum. All through their childhood Nick and she had loved their mother and sided with her against the distant, forbidding father. Yet it was he, all the time, who had had to carry the weight of it all, he who held them together.

She had an idea he wouldn't want to see the manuscript. How hard it must have been to go through life knowing you were second best to another man – and one you couldn't even confront, because he was dead.

She gave him a couple of days to recover after his return from America – no doubt he would have a lot to catch up on at work – then telephoned him, asked him about the trip, how he felt, and finally invited herself over to see him.

'You owe me a dinner, Dad.'

The trip had been a success and he proposed to begin a process of gradual investment in new machinery. 'Trouble is, I'm getting on a bit and I really need someone to come in with me, someone younger.'

'You mean Nick?'

He was silent. It had been a source of conflict between them.

'Can't stand it here,' Nick had said to Alice once. 'Can't stand the atmosphere at home. So I intend to put a bit of distance between me and the old man.' That was why he was living in Bristol.

Alice wondered, as her father said those words, whether there might be some room for manoeuvre here. Knowing what she now knew, wouldn't it be possible to explain things to Nick, explain the real situation, and perhaps bring him a little closer to home – perhaps even talk him into joining the family business?

Later, as they were finishing dinner, she brought up the subject she really needed to speak about.

'Dad,' she said simply, 'I owe you an apology.'

He looked up, surprised.

'Yes,' she went on. 'This may sound presumptuous, but I misjudged you.'

'What has brought this on?'

'I've found out...' she began, and then caught his eye. 'I mean – I know.'

'Know what?'

She took a deep breath. 'I know who my real father was.'

There was a moment's silence before he started up from his chair. 'I see,' he said coldly. 'It's that woman, isn't it, gossiping? Well, Alice, may I say, you know nothing. You haven't the first idea and I am very unhappy that you should go behind my back—'

She threw herself at him, snatching his hands in her own before he could go on.

'It has nothing to do with Heather! And I want to tell you, before you say anything else, that I think you were splendid, splendid, and always have been – and it doesn't matter a farthing. You're my real father! You are! And I shall never think different!'

She was so vehement that he could see the tears in her eyes and was taken aback. He looked at her in astonishment. 'But – how?'

'How did I find out? It was nothing to do with Heather – or anyone else. It was Mum herself. She wrote it all down. It was during the war, when you were away such a long time. I think she was very depressed and lonely and needed to write it all out. Then she sealed it up and put it in the bank. I honestly think she had completely forgotten about it. There was no note or message. I would never have known about it if the bank hadn't written.'

'She wrote it all down?' he repeated.

Alice nodded. 'Because it wasn't addressed to anyone, and as I was executrix of her estate, I had to open it, you see. And of course once I saw what it was, I had to read it. I mean, it wasn't private – at least not after Mum had died. It just belongs to the family. But it does mean that I know. I know everything. And as I said, I had to tell you how good you were. She didn't deserve you, Dad. And whatever is in that manuscript doesn't make any difference. You are my dad and always will be.'

He had risen from his chair and walked away, and for some time he stood with his back to her.

'Oh dear,' he muttered at last. 'I had no idea.' He was struggling to find the words. 'I loved your mother, Alice. You may not believe it, but I did.'

'I do believe you,' she whispered.

'And it was hard, very hard. It was very, very hard.' He still hadn't looked at her, and she heard the catch in his voice. 'I really did the best I could.'

'I know you did.'

He drew a shattering breath and reached a handkerchief from his pocket. She could see him wiping his eyes, though his back was still turned. 'So you see,' he went on in a shaky voice, 'if I did seem a little harsh sometimes, I hope you understand now.'

She crossed to her father and put her arms round him. Gradually he turned, and for a moment they clung to each other.

It was over a year later that Alice received a letter from Vienna. The sender's name was written on the back of the envelope and she got a shock when she saw it: Albertina Kassel. The letter was written in English.

Dear Alice Tremayne,

I am sure you are wondering who could possibly write to you from Vienna. Well, the truth is, I got your name and address from the librarian in St Tropez. You see, I believe I went there for the same reason you did. I wanted to find my father. And when the librarian gave me your name and explained that you too had been to find *Les Cigalettes*, you can imagine how my curiosity was raised. What a shame the house does not exist any longer. However I did manage to find some photographs of it and I thought you would like to see them. Where did I find these photographs, you will ask. Well, after I had spoken to the librarian, I went round the hotels and shops asking if anyone knew anything about Madame Leary, and eventually I found out that she had had a grandson and that he was still living in St Tropez, so I went to see him. He is a most strange man, a recluse, and lives alone except for a 'companion', an Arab, who is devoted to him and fusses round him all day long. I had the strangest interview with this grandson, whose name is Alcide, sitting wrapped in a shawl like an invalid while Karim – the Arab – brought us tea and little biscuits. Alcide, unless I was dreaming, was wearing make-up, and spoke in the most affected, mincing way. It was very strange indeed. But the point is that as I was leaving, Karim took me up-stairs and, after a lot of searching, found a box containing strange things, including a golden mask, though broken, some photo-graphs, and a painting of himself which he said had been painted by an English girl who came before the war. I must say, I thought it rather good. Then he took me to the cemetery. We saw the grave of Madame Leary, and then he led me to another nearby. It was my father's grave, Alice. You may understand what an effect this had on me. All my life I had wondered where my father was and whether he was even still alive. And then, to see his grave, to see his name written on it ... Karim then told me that my father had been murdered.

This is why I am writing, and also hoping that we may meet. You see, I believe we may be related. Because Karim told me – I hope you don't mind me saying this – that the English girl, who I believe is your mother, and my father had been in love and so I thought perhaps that my father might be your father too. I have to come to London within the next few months, and hope to meet you...

They met three months later in a West End hotel for tea. They recognized each other instantly. Albertina was a woman in her thirties and as they shook hands each was searching her half-sister's face intently for signs of likeness. Like Alice, Albertina was professionally, soberly dressed.

'My mother died a few months ago,' Albertina began as they settled at a table and she pulled off her gloves, 'and while she was in hospital I was going to see her every day. When she was getting very weak, she took my hand one afternoon and said there was something she had to tell me. It was about my father. Well, you can imagine how I felt, Alice. All my life I had known nothing about him. She had always told me he deserted us when I was six. But now it seems she did know where he had gone. I think she was glad to talk about it – to confess. It was just before war broke out and the secret police – the Gestapo – had asked her to write two letters. She didn't really understand what it was about but she said they wouldn't explain and if she refused she would be arrested herself. So she wrote these two letters to their dictation. Then she heard nothing more. It had lain on her conscience, she said. All my life I had had no idea where my father was or even whether he was alive or dead, then at this last minute my mother had mentioned St Tropez.' She paused. 'I couldn't go right away; I had to stay with my mother. But later, after she died, I felt I had the right at least to go and ask – just to see if I could find out anything about him. I had that right, didn't I?'

Alice nodded.

'Anyway, I thought you would like to see the photographs that Karim had kept.'

These, like the photograph Alice had seen in her mother's hand, were little two-inch-square pictures in black and white. And so Alice at last got to see what *Les Cigalettes* looked like. Then Albertina handed across another. It was a group of people clustered together, posing and smiling. 'Karim said that one was my father,' Albertina said quietly, pointing him out. Alice stared at the picture.

'Our father,' she murmured. Then she picked out her mother.

'Oh, she was beautiful!' she breathed. She handed it back, pointing out the figure. 'That is my mother.'

The other studied it. 'She was in love,' she said quietly.

'You can tell?'

Albertina shrugged. 'It's obvious, isn't it?'

Alice looked at the photograph again. 'Yes, it is obvious.'